Kay washed up on dry land. She lay on solid, gritty
earth and smelled dirt. She spent a long moment
coughing her lungs out, heaving up water until she couldn't
cough anymore. She got her first look around and realized
she'd ended up on the north side of the creek. The wrong
side of the border.

A deep, short growl echoed above her. She rolled over
and looked up. She was in shadow, and a dragon hunched
over her. A real dragon, close up. Two stories tall,
finely wrought head on a snaking neck, and a lithe
covered body. It was gray like storm clouds, shim
to ice blue or silver depending on how the sunligh
Its eyes were black, depthless black. Bony ridges made its
gaze look quizzical, curious.

Or maybe it really was curious. . . .

ALSO BY CARRIE VAUGHN

Steel

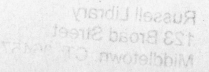

CARRIE VAUGHN

Voices
of
Dragons

HARPER TEEN
An Imprint of HarperCollinsPublishers

HarperTeen is an imprint of HarperCollins Publishers.

Voices of Dragons
Copyright © 2010 by Carrie Vaughn, LLC
All rights reserved. Printed in the United States of America.
No part of this book may be used or reproduced in any manner
whatsoever without written permission except in the case of brief
quotations embodied in critical articles and reviews. For information
address HarperCollins Children's Books, a division of HarperCollins
Publishers, 10 East 53rd Street, New York, NY 10022.
www.harperteen.com

Library of Congress Cataloging-in-Publication Data
Vaughn, Carrie.
     Voices of dragons / Carrie Vaughn. — 1st ed.
        p.   cm.
     Summary: In a parallel world where humans and dragons live in a
state of cold war, seventeen-year-old Kay and her dragon friend, Artegal,
struggle to find a way to show that dragons and humans can coexist.
     ISBN 978-0-06-154790-4
     [1. Dragons—Fiction. 2. Prejudices—Fiction. 3. Interpersonal
relations—Fiction. 4. Fantasy.] I. Title.
PZ7.V462Voi 2010   2009011604
[Fic]—dc22

Typography by Andrea Vandergrift
11 12 13 14 15   CG/BV   10 9 8 7 6 5 4 3 2 1
❖
First paperback edition, 2011

To Mom, Dad, and Rob

The dragon began to belch out flames
and burn bright homesteads; there was a hot glow
that scared everyone, for the vile sky-winger
would leave nothing alive in its wake.

—*Beowulf* (2312–2315), translated by Seamus Heaney

Facts such as these induce us to give some credit to what Democritus relates, who says that a man, called Thoas, was preserved in Arcadia by a dragon. When a boy, he had become much attached to it, and had reared it very tenderly; but his father, being alarmed at the nature and monstrous size of the reptile, had taken and left it in the desert. Thoas being here attacked by some robbers who lay in ambush, he was delivered from them by the dragon, which recognized his voice and came to his assistance.

—Pliny the Elder, *Naturalis Historia*

So if you cannot overcome this dragon, the only solution is to make a treaty of peace between you. I will find a party of wise mortal men to act as diplomats in the Earthly manner, and get them to persuade your enemy to agree.

—Rosalind Kerven, *The Slaying of the Dragon
and Other Tales of the Hindu Gods*

. . . many a pleasant night they had, sitting on the sward, while the dragon told stories of old, old times, when dragons were quite plentiful and the world was a livelier place than it is now, and life was full of thrills and jumps and surprises.

—Kenneth Grahame, *The Reluctant Dragon*

1

Her parents were going to kill her for this.

Kay Wyatt adjusted her grip, wedging her fist more firmly into the crevice. A scab on her knuckle broke and started bleeding. The pain of it wasn't worse than any of the other minor injuries she was subjecting herself to, clinging to the side of a pile of weathered boulders, slowly creeping up with only her hands and feet to support her. Free-climbing in a remote area alone? Yeah, her parents were going to kill her.

As if that wasn't dangerous enough already, she had to do it right on the border with Dragon. Not that she looked at it that way. She figured no one would notice; this really was the middle of nowhere. No Jeep trails, no hikers or campers—*no one* came here. It seemed like a good place to go when she didn't want to be found. She really didn't want to be found at the moment. She had to think of what to tell Jon about homecoming. He'd asked her out, and she should have been thrilled. Anyone else would have been. But she had to think about it.

The dragons only ever came close enough to the border to appear as specks, soaring in the distance, deep in their own territory. She'd be safe.

She'd found this place by studying topographic maps and wondering about the steep hills that lined the river. She'd climbed all the sanctioned rock faces, rafted the local rivers, hiked the trails. She'd grown up out here. But she wanted to see someplace new. She wanted to get out on her own. She wanted to *do* something.

Over the summer, she and Jon had gone kayaking on the Silver River south of town after dark. Being on the river under a full moon had been amazing, but her parents had caught her driving home with a wet kayak at midnight and chewed her out about how dangerous it was, how she could have gotten hurt, and whatever. Then there was the time she free-climbed the wall at the rec center, just to see if she could. She'd have gotten away with that one if the manager hadn't found her.

She'd stashed her gear in the Jeep the night before so her parents wouldn't ask questions, left the house after breakfast, and didn't tell them where she was going. Planned rebellion. It didn't matter that the first rule of any outdoor activity was tell someone where you were going. She'd decided she just didn't want to. And if something happened? If she managed to fall and break herself? She could imagine the brouhaha when she turned up missing—then when they figured out exactly where she'd gone. Searching the area would cause an international incident. She might actually start a war if she fell and needed to be rescued. Which was all the more incentive not to fall.

But nothing was going to happen. She'd climbed more difficult rocks than this. Free-climbed, even. She wasn't doing anything she hadn't done a thousand times before. Only the context had changed.

And nothing was going to happen to her because nothing ever *had* happened to her except getting grounded. Like she'd told her parents after the kayaking-at-night incident, at least she wasn't doing drugs. Her father, the county sheriff, hadn't been amused.

The irony of the whole thing was that both her parents were supposed to protect the border. Her dad was a cop, her mother the assistant director at the Federal Bureau of Border Enforcement. They didn't guard against the dragons—the military would be called in for that. Instead, they were supposed to keep people out, be on the lookout for curiosity seekers and die-hard romantics who wanted to see dragons and thought they could sneak over the border, and the warmongers who wanted to get close enough to go hunting for dragons. The government took protecting the border very seriously.

So, if they knew about this, her parents would kill her for more reasons than she could count.

Balancing on her toes, Kay found a grip for her left hand. Joints straining, she edged another few inches up the rock. Then a few more. Her hands were dry with chalk, cracked and bloody. Her lips were chapped. Her whole body was sweaty. The sun was baking down on an unseasonably warm day. But really, this was bliss. Just her body and the rock, with nothing but the sound of a few birds and the nearby creek tumbling down the hillside.

A few more inches, stretching spread-eagle on the rock in her quest for the next purchase. Then a few more, legs straight, hanging by her fingertips. Looking up, the rock was a solid granite wall stretching before her forever. One inch at a time, that was how her father had taught her. You can't do anything but worry about the few inches right in front of you. So she did, breathing steadily, making progress until, almost suddenly, there was no more rock, and she was at the top, looking down the hillside from her vantage. She'd done it, and she hadn't broken herself.

After resting and taking a long drink of water, Kay changed from her climbing shoes into her hiking boots and went back down the rock face the easy way, off the back side where it joined the forested mountainside, sliding down the dirt and old pine needles, bouncing from one tree to the next. It had taken her an hour to climb up and only ten minutes to fly down, to where the boulder field continued on to mark the edge of the creek. She'd follow it to where it branched south and then, before anyone noticed, cut across to the trailhead where she'd parked her Jeep.

She stopped by Border River, a couple yards wide and a few feet deep, to soak her hands in the icy water. She had new blisters and calluses to add to her collection, and the rushing water numbed the aches. For a long moment, she balanced on the rocks, letting her hands get cold, enjoying the calm.

She'd been so careful the rest of the time, she never expected her foot to slip out from under her when she moved to stand up. The rock must have had a wet spot, or she hit a crumbly piece of boulder—gravel instead of stone, it slid instead of holding her foot. Yelping, she toppled over and rolled into the creek.

The chill water shocked her sweaty, overheated body, and at first she could only freeze, numb and sputtering, hoping to keep her head above water. The current carried her. These mountain creeks were always deeper and faster moving than they looked, and she tumbled, dragged by the water, buffeted by rocks. When she finally started flailing, struggling to find something, anything, she could grab to stop her progress, she found nothing. Her hands kept slipping off mossy rocks or splashing against the current. She'd always discounted the idea of someone drowning after getting swept away in one of these creeks, when they could just put their feet down and stand up. But she couldn't seem to get her feet under her. The current kept snatching her, turning her, dunking her. She was already exhausted from her climb, and now this.

When something grabbed at her, she clung to it. A log, some kind of debris fallen into the creek. That was what she thought. But her hands didn't close on sodden bark or vegetation. The thing she'd washed up against was slick, almost like plastic, but warm and yielding. And it moved. It closed around her and pulled. Water filled her eyes; she couldn't see. The world seemed to flip.

Then she washed up on dry land. She lay on solid, gritty earth and smelled dirt. She spent a long moment coughing her lungs out, heaving up water until she couldn't cough anymore. Hunched over, learning how to breathe again, she got her first look around and realized she'd ended up on the north side of the creek. The wrong side of the border.

A deep, short growl echoed above her. She rolled over and looked up. She was in shadow, and a dragon hunched over her. A real dragon, close up. Two stories tall, a long, finely wrought head on a snaking neck, and a lithe, scale-covered body. It was gray like storm clouds, shimmering to ice blue or silver depending on how the sunlight hit it. Its eyes were black, depthless black. Bony ridges made its gaze look quizzical, curious.

Or maybe it really was curious.

It sat back on its haunches, its clawed hands resting on the ground in front of it, the wing membranes running down its arms tucked neatly back. It wasn't doing anything—not breathing fire, not tensing its muscles getting ready to attack. It wasn't even making noise anymore. That first huff of a growl had been to get her attention.

They regarded each other. Her heart was racing, getting ready to burst out her ears. The trouble she was going to get into over rock climbing by herself was nothing compared to the trouble she was going to get into over this. This . . . this was epic trouble. She waited for the thing to eat her.

But it just kept looking at her. She shivered and realized she was in its shadow. A great, huge shadow. And he wasn't even a big dragon, if she remembered her facts right. Only as big as a bus. Not, say, a house. *Adolescent*, the word crawled out of her hindbrain. It was young.

The growl came again, and with it a word. "Well?"

It sounded deep, echoey. Like the word didn't come out of its mouth, but reverberated through its entire sinus cavity. It gave the voice weight, an ancient dignity. She didn't know how to respond.

"W-well what?" Her voice was tiny and trembling.

It blinked, and the ridges above its eyes shifted. It no longer looked curious, but wry. Amused, even. "Well. Are you?"

Another word crawled out of her hindbrain. Something in the tone or in the way it arced its brow. *Male*, she thought.

It was male. He was asking if she was all right. She nodded quickly and swallowed back a scream. *Oh my God, it's talking to me. . . .*

It gave a snort and a satisfied nod.

The dragon had plucked her out of the river. Saved her life. The screaming part of her brain wanted her to get up and run, but she didn't move.

"Thank you," she said finally, "for helping me."

The dragon's neck snaked back, dipping his head in a nod. The scales flickered gray and blue in the sun. Too graceful for words. She expected him to leave. Or maybe she hoped he would. She ought to be running. Or were dragons like bears in that running only made you look like prey and encouraged them? Maybe she should wait until he was gone.

But he seemed ready to sit and watch her all day.

She was bruised, soaking wet, and starting to shiver. The sun was setting, and the shadows of the trees were growing longer. Slowly, she pushed herself to her feet, backing away from him at the same time. If she walked upstream a little, she should be able to find a narrow place to cross the creek without too much trouble. She'd look kind of stupid trying to wade in after having been plucked out on the verge of drowning.

"I should get going," she said, pointing over her shoulder. Now, the instinct to run, to get out of this situation, was almost overpowering.

A low huff from the dragon stopped her. "Wait."

He leaned forward, crouching on all fours now, bringing himself closer. She could see herself reflected in his eye. His breath was warm and smelled like a campfire. She kept herself from whimpering.

"Stay? Practice speech," he said.

"Practice—" Speech. Language. He was learning English. He wanted to practice. She almost laughed. But she shook her head. "No—no, I can't, I'm not supposed to be here, you're not supposed to be here."

"But we are."

Had he been sitting here, waiting for someone to happen along so he could practice his conversation skills? Did he come here a lot? She boggled to think that there could be some dragons as fascinated with people as some people were with dragons.

She'd just been trying to get to the one place she knew there wouldn't be any people around. She hadn't even considered that a dragon could be here. A dragon who would save her life.

"You—you sound like you speak the language pretty well. I don't think you need my help."

"Not need. Want."

"Why?" she said, but hadn't meant to. What happened to running away?

He gave a soft snort that might have been a chuckle. "Because—not supposed to."

She hadn't expected him to give her a reason at all, much

less a reason she could understand so well. The scales around his mouth and eyes shifted. Was he smiling?

"Yeah. Okay," she said, unable to stop herself. "But—"

"Yes?"

"Maybe another time. I should go home, get dried off before I freeze."

He sat back on his haunches again, curling his neck into an S. "Tomorrow?"

She had school tomorrow. What would he do if she said no? Roast her? Could he really breathe fire? "How about next week instead?"

"How many days?"

Dragons didn't have weeks. "Seven," she said.

He looked up at the sky, then back at her, and nodded. He was checking the position of the sun, she realized. "Yes," he said.

"Okay, then." Had she just agreed to come back? She didn't have to, she supposed. She'd have said anything to get away.

Again, they were back to staring at each other, not moving. It occurred to her that he'd never seen a human being up close, the way that she'd never seen a dragon.

Then he said, "Help you."

He moved, turning on his haunches to reach back into the trees. A long, undulating tail lifted and straightened as a counterbalance. Something so large should have been ponderous when it moved, clumsy, all bulk and no grace.

Instead, he gave the impression of speed contained. Of power.

He backed toward the water, pulling a fallen log with him. The claws at the very tips of his arms were prehensile. With an echoing huff, he shoved it across the creek. It didn't quite reach to the other bank, but it settled against the rocks and provided an adequate bridge. And it would still be here next week.

"Thanks."

"Seven days," he said, with a lilt that made him sound like he wasn't sure she'd really come.

"Okay."

She stepped across the bridge, happy not to have to wade and risk another fall. When she reached the other side, the dragon nodded again, then turned and crept into the woods, managing somehow to slip his bulk around the trees. He didn't fly—anyone in town would spot dragon flight this close to the border.

In seconds, he was gone. She'd been so anxious to run away a few moments ago, but now she was almost sorry to leave.

She sneaked in quietly, stowing her backpack full of gear in the garage, then ducking around to the front door, which she opened slowly, only as far as she needed to to squeeze in. She shouldn't have worried. The house was dark. No one had turned on the lights when the sun had started setting.

Dad wasn't home yet, and Kay could hear by the tapping on the computer keyboard that Mom was in her office, working. Moving quickly now, she darted to the hallway bathroom. After a hot shower, the mud, sweat, and blood would all be gone, and she wouldn't have to explain herself.

When Kay left the bathroom, wrapped in a towel and hair dripping, Mom was still in the office, in the spare bedroom in the front of the house.

"Is that you, Kay?" she called.

"Yeah." *Who else would it be?* she thought. If it had been someone else, wouldn't it be at all worrying that a stranger had come into the house and used the shower?

"I've got stuff to make mac and cheese in the fridge. Can you get it started? Dad should be home soon."

As promised, Dad came in through the garage door just as the casserole dish came out of the oven. Kay had even set the table. They usually managed to eat dinner as a family, however busy they got—that was one of Mom's rules. Conversation involved Mom and Dad trading a few words about work and the standard round of complaints about coworkers and annoyances. Kay mostly tried to stay quiet. Her mind was full of dragon, and she didn't want to let word of that slip.

Inevitably, though, her father turned to her. He was almost the stereotypical picture of an Old West sheriff: tall, broad across the shoulders, straight-backed, and confident. He had a square jaw and bright smile, and his brown hair was going gray. He even went around in a cowboy hat and boots. The tourists loved him.

"What did you do today?" he asked.

Kay's gut lurched, and she was sure her father would see the lie written on her face. "I just went hiking, out by the Bluebell trailhead." Exactly the opposite direction from where she'd been, and she could feel the depth of the lie.

"See anything interesting?"

Kay's heart skipped a beat. But she managed to keep her voice steady when she answered, "No. Nothing at all."

2

Nothing happened. No one found out. That didn't stop her from flinching every time someone talked to her.

"Hey, Kay. I said hello like three times."

Startled from her thoughts, Kay looked up to find Tam sliding into the seat across from her, lunch bag in hand. Kay's own sandwich lay uneaten before her. She'd been staring at it while her mind turned.

"Oh, sorry." Kay forced a smile.

"So, you talk to Jon yet?"

She winced, and Tam looked disapproving. Tam looked about ten years older than Kay felt most of the time: She wore makeup and did it perfectly, her silky black hair always hung gracefully around her shoulders, and even wearing a

T-shirt and jeans, she looked like she ought to be on the cover of a magazine. She made the outfit look sexy instead of just thrown together, which was how Kay felt. Kay's skimpy brown hair never seemed to stay in its ponytail; she was always pushing strands back behind her ears. Maybe she liked being outdoors so much because it didn't seem to matter if you were sweaty, grungy, and not perfect looking.

"I'll give you a hint. Say yes," Tam said.

"I'm just not sure I want to go to homecoming at all."

They'd had variations of this conversation a dozen times, and Tam always got that frustrated, motherly expression when Kay seemed to be dragging her feet.

"Come on, you know you'll have fun once you get there. Besides, *I* won't have any fun if you don't go."

Kay had to smile. Tam's enthusiasm was more than enough to pull her along, if she'd just let it. That was how it had worked since middle school—Kay made Tam go hiking, and Tam made Kay go to the mall or to the Alpine Diner to hang out, or to any of the other things that Kay wouldn't have done on her own. They lent each other confidence, and it had worked. Until Tam started dating Carson. Tam wanted Kay to have a boyfriend, too, and wouldn't listen when Kay said she wasn't sure she wanted one.

"Quiet. Here they come."

Kay craned her head around to the cafeteria doorway to see Jon and Carson approach. Kay still didn't know what to tell Jon. She tried to act normal, tried not to blush, and went back to staring at her sandwich when Jon took the seat next to her.

Carson—tall, lanky, with unruly blond hair and a handsome smile—sat next to Tam, and the two started making out. Carson put his arm around Tam's shoulders, she leaned in, and their lips were together. They didn't seem to need to come up for air. They'd been going out for six months now. Tam *loved* having a boyfriend. She thought everyone should have a boyfriend.

Kay and Jon squirmed and didn't look at each other.

When the couple finally broke apart, Tam was giggling. Her cheeks were flushed, her eyes shining. Carson looked at her with this proud, possessive expression on his face. They both seemed to be enjoying themselves.

Maybe I should just say yes, Kay thought.

"I can't *wait* until you guys get written up for that," Jon said.

"It'll be worth it," Carson said, grinning. The couple only had eyes for each other. Kay and Jon may as well have been alone.

Tam would have argued that Carson was cuter than Jon, but Kay thought Jon was more natural—more honest. He was fit and tanned from all his time outdoors, and when he listened to Kay, she was sure he was really listening. They had conversations.

At least, they didn't used to have any trouble talking. Now they avoided making eye contact, and avoided looking at Tam and Carson. There wasn't much else to look at.

Jon shook out of the funk first, focusing on her and donning a bright tone to his solid tenor voice. "How've you been?" he asked.

"Okay," she said. "You?"

He shrugged. "Okay. I tried calling you yesterday."

"I got your message. Sorry about that. I went climbing and was gone most of the day."

"Oh? Where'd you go?"

She wasn't going to be able to keep this secret if she couldn't come up with a good answer to that question. What had she told her dad? "Out by Bluebell. Mostly bouldering. Just messing around."

"By yourself? You should have called me. I'm always up for climbing."

In fact, they'd learned to climb together, back when they both ended up in a climbing safety class her dad taught at the rec center. She'd known Jon from school, but climbing gave them something in common. They discovered they had the same passion for it. He was right, she was chagrined to realize. She should have called him. Except that she'd wanted to be alone.

She didn't want to tell him he was exactly the reason she'd wanted to be by herself. "Yeah, I know. Next time."

That turned the conversation to other topics, like school and parents and next year's college applications. Tam and Carson sat hip to hip, body to body, on the bench at the cafeteria table, on the verge of kissing again, Kay was sure.

Kay finally ate, managing to finish before the bell rang, and they all had to slink back to class.

Jon touched her arm and pulled her aside before they entered the hallway to the classrooms.

"Can I talk to you for a minute?"

Her stomach knotted, because she knew what he was going to ask. "Just a minute, I guess. I don't want to be late." She bit her lip.

"I'll try not to make you late. Wouldn't want to get you in trouble." He smiled a goofy smile.

This was the problem with all this relationship stuff, this boyfriend-girlfriend thing. Why couldn't they just come out and *talk* about it? They could talk about everything else. When it came to this, he got all tongue-tied. They both did.

"You thought any more about it? The dance, I mean," he said.

She couldn't figure out what to say to one of her best friends in the world. She licked her lips and blurted out the question. "Why? I mean, why me?"

He looked at her sharply, a disbelieving expression. She flushed, her cheeks burning, because she felt like she'd missed something. Like this whole business was obvious to everyone but her.

"You're my best friend. Why would I want to go with anyone else?"

"You don't go to dances with your best friend. Do you?

You go with someone who's pretty or . . . or . . ."

"Who puts out?" he said, and she blushed again. "I don't understand why you're so down on yourself."

She took a breath and looked at him square on, meeting his gaze at last. He had green eyes, a tight smile.

"This is just really weird. I've known you since the fifth grade, and it's not that I don't want to go, or I'd just come out and say it, really I would. But I don't know. I *really* don't know what I want. Sometimes I think you're just asking me because we're supposed to have dates for the dance, and I'm the most available girl you know—"

He held his hands up in a defensive gesture. "Hey, I didn't mean to freak you out or anything. You don't have to say anything. The dance is still a month away."

She smiled gratefully and felt better, because he sounded like he meant it. No pressure. This probably wasn't the big deal she was making it out to be.

She sighed. "I've just seen what happens when people break up, and they hate each other. I don't think I could stand it if that happened to us."

"I just want to go to the dance with my friend."

That made it sound so simple. That's all it was, then. Going to the dance with her friend.

"Okay," she said.

"Okay? Okay what?"

"Okay, I'll go to the dance with you." She smiled.

His eyes lit up. He grinned and looked so pleased, she

was glad she'd said yes. He fidgeted, like he wanted to hug her. Boyfriend and girlfriend would have hugged. But they were just friends. So they didn't.

"Okay. Cool," he said. "Um . . . I guess I'll see you later then."

It didn't seem fair, that they'd made this momentous decision and then had to go off to something as mundane as class. "See you."

He had math in the next hall over and turned in that direction. She had to backtrack to English class. They were both going to be late. Kay was the last one in the room when she slipped through the door.

Before Kay even sat down, Tam leaned over and hissed, "Well? What did he say? What did *you* say?"

Surely Tam could guess what had happened, as hard as Kay was blushing. Kay wasn't sure how to say it. "I—"

Mrs. Ryan stood at the front of the class. "All right, people, we're starting Act Three of *Romeo and Juliet* today, so please open your books."

Saved by classwork. Tam managed to glare even as she retrieved her book from her pile of belongings. Mrs. Ryan was writing vocabulary words on the chalkboard. Kay hunched over her book to avoid looking at Tam.

Everyone jumped when a howling siren rang out. Dragon-raid drill. Or maybe it wasn't a drill. Someone had found out what happened, one of the dragons, and now they were coming to get back for the one little incursion over the border. One little mistake, and the decades' long peace was over.

Don't stop to look. That was the drill. Go inside if you were outside. Leave your classroom single file, go to the hallways in the center of the building—fireproofed with steel, lined with cinder blocks. Crouch on the floor, arms over your head. If you stopped to look for them, even glancing out the window for a moment, it would be too late.

They did the drill several times a year—every year since preschool—until it was routine. A few kids goofed off, elbowing each other and giggling, and the teachers yelled at them. All of it just like it always was. The only person who was nervous was Kay. She looked down the hall, trying to see where Jon was, but couldn't find him.

Dozens of kids lined the hallway, crouched on the floor, arms over their heads, waiting.

"Like this would even do any good if a dragon really wanted to set fire to the place," Tam said, leaning over to whisper at Kay. "It's not like anyone even sees them anymore."

"I saw one," said a guy named Brad, from her other side.

"Where?"

"In the air, kind of way off."

"That doesn't count."

Across the hall, Pete said, "We should just go in and bomb them all. They're just animals, it's not like they can do anything about it."

But they're not, Kay almost continued the argument. *They talk. They're intelligent. One of them saved my life.* And they could be coming right now because she'd crossed the border and broken the treaty. She gritted her teeth to keep from saying anything.

"Then why do we even do the drills, if they're not dangerous?" Tam said.

Pete answered, "I don't know—it's stupid. We've got the air force base—they could just bomb the hell out of the dragons, then we'd never have to worry again." In fact, jets from the base patrolled the border, flying over the town of Silver River a couple of times a week. It wouldn't take much for them to continue on to the mountains where the dragons lived.

"Quiet!" one of the teachers called to them.

The alarm kept going, and they huddled in rows on the floor. Kay waited for the fires, the conflagration, to sweep over the building.

Nothing happened. It was just a drill. No one had found out about what Kay had done yesterday. She tried to calm down. The alarm stopped after another minute, and everyone filed back to their classes.

The Federal Bureau of Border Enforcement organized and encouraged the dragon alarms. At home that evening, Kay tried to think of a way to ask about what was worrying her, without really asking. Dad was on duty that night, so it was just her and her mother.

"We had a drill at school today," Kay said, over a dinner of chicken casserole out of a box.

"Oh, was that today?" her mom said, still chewing. "I knew there was one scheduled, but I wasn't keeping track."

"So it was scheduled. There wasn't a particular reason for it or anything." No increased dragon activity because of a certain stupid girl getting caught on the other side of the border . . .

"Yup. It was on the schedule." Her mother was distracted by food and by the stack of reports on the table next her and didn't seem to wonder that the question was maybe a little strange.

Kay tried to make the conversation sound innocent. "So . . . why do we even have drills? There hasn't been an attack in, like, sixty years. Does the bureau really think they'd attack now?"

"It's just in case, Kay. We don't know anything about them. They did it before, they may do it again. If someone crossed the border, if they decided we were a threat—we don't even know what they'd consider to be a threat." Her mother sounded frustrated. "We just have to be ready for anything."

"Would we ever attack them instead?" Kay asked, thinking of Pete, who wanted to bomb them.

Her mother set aside the packet of papers she'd been reading and regarded Kay. "My job is to uphold the integrity of the border established by the Silver River Treaty. That's the official line, and I'm sticking to it." She quirked a lopsided smile.

"But unofficially? Do you think we'd ever attack them?"

"What brought this up?"

Kay shrugged. "Some guy at school talking."

"Repeating what his parents say at home, I'm sure," her mom said with a sigh. "Some fanatics think we gave up too much territory to the dragons and that we should take it back."

"But that wouldn't ever happen, right?" Kay asked, suddenly uneasy. They treated the drills like a joke—she didn't ever want to have to do one for real. She tried to think of what a war with the dragons would look like, but couldn't. If that ever happened, Silver River would be in the middle of it.

Her mother went back to looking at the report and said flatly, "No, I don't think so."

That didn't really convince Kay. She didn't know how many more questions she could get away with before her mother got either frustrated or suspicious. "They talk, right? Why don't we still talk to them?"

"That's the way they wanted it. They thought we'd all be safer if we stayed isolated from each other. Don't they teach you this in history class?"

"A little." They did cover dragons in history class, especially in Silver River, but mostly with broad strokes. There wasn't much detail to go on, and the dragons came across as this distant, mysterious enemy. *What else was there to know?* seemed to be the attitude. Kay wished now that she'd been paying more attention. "No one seems to know much about it. Couldn't we have, I don't know, told them we wanted to keep talking?"

Her mother said, "At the time, I don't think it occurred to anyone to argue with something that can breathe fire."

It wouldn't have occurred to Kay either, until yesterday.

3

Kay had an atlas, one of those picture-book-type deals for kids that she'd gotten one Christmas, with a world map across two pages, all the countries shown in different colors. She'd marked places all over the world she wanted to go. Climbs she wanted to conquer: Yosemite National Park; Mount Kilimanjaro in Africa; Trango Towers in Pakistan. She didn't quite know how she was going to do it, besides making a lot of money somehow. Winning the lottery, maybe. She wasn't the best student and didn't see herself in a fancy high-paying job. Never mind that many of those dots she'd marked on her map were in dangerous places. The regions of Dragon were in the north, shaded gray. Shadowy, unknown, off limits. "Here be dragons," the map may as well have said. So wasn't crossing the border another adventure? But rather than seek this one out, it had come along and plucked her out of the river.

Crossing the border by accident was one thing, and she hadn't crossed very far then. Just washed up on the riverbank. No one could blame her; no one could punish her. But crossing intentionally?

Kay stood on the human side of the creek and looked across. The other side didn't look any different. Going over there shouldn't have been such a big deal. And why did she have to be the one to cross anyway? Meeting like this was the dragon's idea. He should be the one to cross. Except she was a little easier to hide than he was, wasn't she? Her tracks would be easier to cover up on his side of the river than his would be on her side.

The log he'd dragged across for a bridge was still in place, maybe wetter than it had been. It would hold up.

She ran across it before she could second-guess herself. Her hiking boots didn't slip on the wet bank, and the log didn't budge. This could have been any makeshift bridge across any creek, and the forest on the other side was just the same: tall pines, earthy smell, calls of distant birds. The only difference was in her mind, knowing she had crossed the lines on the map. It was enough to make this another world. She stayed by the side of the creek, perching on a smooth boulder. She pulled her knees up and waited. No dragon appeared.

Half an hour, she told herself. That was how long she'd give him. If he didn't appear by then, she'd run back home and pretend that none of this had happened. Then again, maybe it hadn't happened. Maybe she'd been knocked on the head and imagined the whole thing. But she wanted to know. She hadn't thought about how the dragons had their own side to the story; now that she had, she wanted to know what that side was. And she would never, ever get another chance at this. This was another impossible rock face, and her uncertainty was the usual fear vying with exhilaration. Sure, she might fall. But she'd rather reach the top.

She heard the dragon's breathing first. A short gust of wind rustled nearby trees, then another, and the gusts, like those that sometimes came suddenly from the mountaintops before letting the forest fall still again, were too regular. These gusts didn't rustle, murmur, and startle. They breathed.

How could something so large move so quietly? Trees creaked all the time, branches rustled, so when he wound his way around the trunks, the sounds were no different. His steps were silent on the soft earth.

Her heart pounded hard, and she almost ran back across the log. She didn't remember standing, but there she was, ready to take off like a rocket.

And there was the dragon's head, right in front of her, his neck lowered almost to the ground so it was at eye level—with his eye nearly as big as a car window. The large, black, glistening surface showed her stricken face back to her. His body stretched out behind him, nestled among the trees.

"You came," he said softly.

She nodded quickly, feeling like a mouse—a mere bite of food—caught in his gaze.

"Wondered," he said. "Thought you might not."

"I almost didn't," she said, backing away a couple of steps. Every time he spoke, warm, smoky breath brushed by her.

He gave a small growl, and her heartbeat sped up to a jackhammer rhythm. Was he angry? Maybe he was angry. She glanced over her shoulder, but didn't think she could run fast enough to escape that long neck and lithe body.

Or maybe he was chuckling.

"Not hurt you," he said softly, like a roll of distant thunder.

"Won't. Won't hurt you." She winced at her own tone of voice. She sounded like an English teacher.

The dragon flexed his neck in an expression she couldn't read. "See? Practice."

Almost, it was too much. "But *why*?" she said, her arms spread, pleading. "You're not even supposed to be here. *I'm* not supposed to be here. We're not supposed to be talking to each other. If anybody finds out about this, they're going to be so pissed off, it might start a war like the last one. So why do you even need to learn to talk to people? Why?"

"Too fast," he said. "Again. Slow." His expression shifted,

the scales around his mouth turning downward. A frown, she realized. She'd been talking too fast, and she'd confused him.

She took a deep breath and started over. Slower, this time. Simple.

"Why do you want to talk to people, when there was a war between dragons and people? When dragons haven't talked to people for sixty years?"

He sat still as a rock, the bulk of his body resting motionless. He could fall asleep and be mistaken for a pile of boulders—shimmering, silvery boulders, but still boulders. However, tiny flickers of expression—a twitch around his eye, a stretching of scales around his mouth, a tension in his neck—revealed that he was alive, that he was thinking. Considering how to answer.

"To understand," he said finally. "Both sides."

He gazed at her. Kay tried not to think of how neatly she would fit into his mouth. Two bites, at most.

She said, "We have stories. Thousands of years of stories about dragons. They're always evil. They always destroy."

Until sixty years ago, the stories were only stories. Over the previous centuries, the dragons withdrew to strongholds underground, beneath mountains and in unexplored caves, until people forgot they'd ever been real. Then the atomic blasts at the end of World War II brought the dragons out of hiding. When the shockwaves from the bombs in New Mexico and Japan reached them, they clawed their way back to the surface, and humanity's nightmares came to life. The old stories—tales of Leviathan, of serpents and the evil they brought, of virgin sacrifices, warriors slain, and miles of land burned to nothing—had been history. Even recent sightings of sea monsters and lake monsters that had been discounted as legend may have been lone dragons, briefly reemerging into the world.

This time, though, unlike in the days of swords and armor, human technology very nearly matched the dragons' power. They'd gone to war, fire-breathing dragons against fighter planes and tanks. Both sides feared such a war would destroy them all, and the land they lived on, so they called a truce, made a treaty, and the dragons retreated to a territory carved out for them in the northern Rockies, Siberia, and the Arctic Circle. Each side promised to leave the other alone, so they could all live in peace. That taut, anxious, so-called peace had lasted since. People lived with the images lurking in the backs of their minds, of fire blasting from the sky, melting ships, tanks, and cities. Silver River, Montana, where Kay lived, was the closest American town to one of the dragon territories and home to the U.S. branch of the international coalition that monitored the borders of Dragon. Fighter planes from Malmstrom Air Force Base patrolled the border, the schools ran dragon-raid drills, and you lived with it because that was just the way things were.

"We have stories," the dragon said. "Of people with

swords. They hunt us down. Seek us out. Wicked deeds."

Kay wondered what stories the dragons told about human beings. Saint George—Silver River High's mascot was Saint George—must be like the devil to them.

"Foolish, maybe," he said. "But I want to see for myself. To understand. We used to talk to people. Maybe we should again."

How unlikely was it that they even met at all? People and dragons weren't supposed to meet. They weren't supposed to walk around on the same planet. Except for old stories from China where dragons represented good fortune and luck, there'd been only conflict between them.

But there were those stories of Chinese luck. Somewhere back in history, maybe something like this had happened before. Pure chance had brought them both here: her to climb rocks and him to fish her out of the river. *That* was luck. And it gave them something to talk about.

"If I hadn't fallen into the river, what would you have done?" she said. "I had to talk to you because you saved my life. But if you had tried to talk to someone who was just walking along, and they saw you and ran screaming, what would you have done?" Kay could see it: That someone, seeing a dragon so close to the border, would have fled, reported to the Federal Bureau of Border Enforcement, maybe even her mother, and there would have been evacuations, more jet patrols, maybe even bombing—everyone would have assumed the dragons planned an attack. But that wasn't why he was here.

"Thought, the stories about humans are true. But you didn't scream. Didn't run."

In spite of herself, unconsciously almost, Kay smiled. No, she hadn't run away. And the dragon hadn't tried to eat her, and she had to rethink a lot of the old stories. She liked the idea that everyone had been wrong all this time. This wasn't just an adventure—it was an adventure no one else had even thought of before.

The dragon tilted his head, peering more closely at her. Like a bird might.

"That—smile? Why?"

"Because this is good," she said.

4

They met again the week after that.

The dragon, it turned out, knew how to read. Dragons had scholars and writing. Using soot on stone, working with their claws, they made marks and symbols. They had also collected human books, and some of them, peering very closely to make out the tiny (to them) letters, could read human words. So at the dragon's request, Kay brought him books, and they read them together.

"How can you read?" she asked him early on. "You're huge. The print's so small."

"Very good eyes. Like hunting prey. We see rabbits while flying."

She wasn't sure what to make of the image, of reading being like hunting.

During that same meeting she asked him his name. He tilted his head, a quizzical, curious movement. It meant he was thinking. When he spoke, he made a trill and click, dragon noises, deep in his throat.

"That's your name?" she said, and he nodded. "I can't say that. What's it mean in English?"

He paused again, still bemused, and she wondered what dragons called themselves, what their names meant. But she thought about what her name meant and what she'd say if she had to translate it, and how she would have been just as perplexed.

"I can choose a name." He looked at the book they'd been reading, *The Faerie Queene*, a thick edition with clear print she'd found in the library. She'd brought it because the picture on the cover showed a knight battling a dragon. "Artegal. Call me that. Your name?"

"Me?" It seemed surreal, trading names with a dragon. "Kay."

"The letter?"

She knew she wouldn't be able to explain it. "Kind of." He simply huffed in response.

He wanted to talk about the books with dragons in them, to see the human stories of dragons and people fighting. To try to understand why they fought. She figured her just standing in front of him would explain it.

"You could swallow me whole. That scares people."

"People fight when scared?" he said.

"Of course they do." He still seemed confused by the

whole idea. His gaze narrowed. She was learning to read his expressions: the arc of scales above his shining dark eye, the curve of his lip. The way his head tilted when she spoke too quickly, and he didn't understand.

She asked him, "What scares dragons?"

He cocked his head. "Nothing."

The answer didn't surprise her. But after a moment he added, "Each other." That did surprise her.

"Dragons fight with each other?"

"Rare. We fight to defend. But there has been no fighting in my lifetime."

At first she was shy about asking questions. One of them might make him angry and finally inspire him to eat her. But he was more interested in the books, in the stories, and in asking questions himself. He really was interested in talking. She grew braver.

"Where do you live?"

"North," he said.

"No, I mean, do you live in caves? Like in the stories? Do you make them, or do you find them?"

"Caves. There are always caves to find. But we make them larger. We carve. Decorate."

"How?"

"Stones. Ones that shine in the light. Gold. That story is true—dragons love gold."

"How many of you are there where you live?"

"You'll tell this to your army?"

36

Stricken, she shook her head, denying it. But then she recognized the curl to his lip, a rumble that was a chuckle. He'd been joking. He understood: She couldn't take this information to anyone without admitting that she'd crossed the border and spoken to a dragon.

He asked her many of the same questions. Where do you live? What do you do? The dragon understood school— they had something like it. Each dragon was taught by a mentor, an elder in the family.

He said, "My mentor was a . . . speaker. After the last battle. The one who spoke to make the treaty."

She remembered seeing pictures, old black-and-white photos of a trio of dragons crouched in an open field, surrounded by tanks and soldiers with guns, and a handful of unarmed, tiny-looking people standing before them.

"Like an ambassador," she said.

He tilted his head and ducked his chin, something like a nod. "Yes. Ambassador. Then he taught me. I learned language from him. But had no one to speak to after he left. Many years ago now."

"Where did he go?"

Artegal settled, a shiver passing along his neck that made his scales ripple. "East. Not sure where. But . . . he did not like that we kept silent."

"And so you came looking for someone. Won't your people get mad if they find out about this?"

He snorted at this. A hint of steam curled from his

nostrils. "An acceptable risk."

The same acceptable risk she was taking, for the sake of adventure. She understood.

She turned her phone off during these Sunday afternoons with the dragon. Reception was spotty out here anyway, but she didn't want to have to explain it to him if it happened to ring. And she certainly wasn't going to talk to someone in the dragon's presence.

Usually, she had missed calls when she reemerged into what passed for civilization in Silver River. This time, a text message from Tam screamed at her: *Where RU?*

Kay called her back. Tam didn't even say hello.

"Kay, where are you? We're supposed to go looking for dresses, what's up?"

Kay winced. She'd forgotten. "I just went out for a little while. I'm driving into town right now. I'll pick you up at your house."

She didn't go straight to Tam's house, because she had to change out of her hiking clothes and take a shower to get the dirt and sweat off. How could being out in the woods for an hour get her so grubby? By the time she got to Tam's, she was an hour late, and Tam wasn't happy.

"This is the most important dance of our lives. Shopping for a dress—you have to take it seriously."

"Sorry," Kay said, as Tam slid into the passenger seat of the car. "So what happens when junior prom comes along?

Then senior prom? Isn't that supposed to be the most important dance of our lives?"

That got a smile out of Tam. "What have you been doing all day?"

Kay shrugged. "It wasn't all day. Just a couple of hours. I was just out hiking."

"You're always hiking."

"I like hiking."

"If I didn't know better, I'd say you had a secret boyfriend stashed somewhere."

Kay stiffened and couldn't think of what to say, so she glared at Tam as if to say, *Don't be ridiculous*. But maybe Tam kept thinking it, and maybe that was okay, if it meant Kay didn't have to explain what was really going on.

The closest mall was fifty miles away and wasn't much of a mall. Only one department store, which made shopping for a dress either really easy or really hard, depending on your perspective.

"Maybe we should have stayed home and looked for dresses online," Kay said.

Tam gave her a look. "That's not as fun."

Easy for her to say. All the dresses Tam tried on looked great on her. Kay could barely bring herself to try on any. They looked so glamorous, shimmering with beads and glitter, tight and clingy. She didn't feel very glamorous.

She was glad Tam was there. Tam made her try on dresses

she never would have thought of wearing herself.

"Don't slouch," Tam said, tugging at Kay's shoulders as they stood before a three-way mirror.

It was hard not to. The black, form-fitted dress had spaghetti straps, leaving Kay's shoulders and a big part of her chest bare. The tan on her arms ended where her T-shirt sleeves did. She felt self-conscious, and she slouched. Turning one way and the other, she studied the dress and herself. The minute she leaned over or tilted the wrong way, the front hung open, revealing way too much for all the world to see.

"I'm not big enough for this dress," she said, grimacing at her small chest and the excess fabric. Tam, however, would fill it out nicely.

Tam grimaced right along with her, which meant she couldn't try to deny it. "Okay. We'll try something else then."

Tam was still wearing the dress she'd tried on and was in the process of falling in love with. Royal purple, shot through with silver, it was a skintight sheath that showed off every inch of her curvy body. It had off-the-shoulder straps and a rhinestone broach between her breasts. Nobody else at school would have the guts to wear a dress like that; Tam looked amazing.

Shuffling through the hangers of the dozen or so gowns they'd picked, Tam pulled out the next one: spaghetti straps, snow white and silver, sparkling with beads, with a gather in front that would make Kay look like she had more rather than less.

"That's too fancy," Kay said, shaking her head.

"It won't hurt anything to try it on."

Kay peeled out of one dress and squirmed into the other.

It was beautiful. It made Kay beautiful. Experimenting, she scrunched up her hair and held it on top of her head, letting a few strands fall loose around her face.

"Wow," Tam said.

"I look like I'm getting married," Kay pouted. This was too much. She didn't want a dress like this.

"No, you don't. You look like you're going to the Oscars."

Tam may have been right, but Kay didn't recognize the svelte young woman in the mirror. Wearing a dress like this was . . . crazy. Like free-climbing a rock face or crossing the creek into Dragon. She wasn't hot enough for it, and she'd look like an idiot walking into the dance. Then again—maybe Tam was right. Maybe she really could be glamorous—and maybe she ought to try. An acceptable risk, as Artegal had said.

Kay didn't dare look at the price tag. She'd pulled a hundred dollars out of her savings from her summer job working for a river rafting company. Her mother had been adamant: "It's just a dance. It's not even prom. Don't break the bank on a dress." Try explaining that to Tam.

"So what's the damage?" Kay asked, turning so she could reach the mess of tags hanging out the back. She braced. It was going to be too much. She couldn't afford it.

In the mirror, she could see Tam smile. "Eighty-nine ninety-nine."

5

Kay didn't know why she should be so nervous. She was going to the dance with a friend. That was all.

When Jon came to pick her up, her parents insisted on making them pose for pictures. Like that wasn't embarrassing. She couldn't complain—most of the time, they let her alone, didn't pry too much, didn't harass her. She could sneak out without drawing too much attention. Not this time.

But she had to admit, Jon looked good. She'd never seen him in a suit and tie before. He looked slick. Very Hollywood, Tam would say. Or Secret Service. Kay thought it was mostly because he managed not to slouch. She still had to think about it.

"Why don't you two stand over here, under the tree?"

Dad said, camera in one hand, gesturing them over with the other.

"It's getting too dark out," Mom argued. "I think we should do this inside. Or at least on the porch, where there's more light."

Dad smirked. "We can do both. You two mind?"

Kay mostly wanted to hurry up and leave. But she wasn't going to ruin her parents' fun by arguing. They seemed happy. They beamed at her, eyes shining. Tearing up? Her tough cop parents tearing up? All she'd done was put on a nice dress.

Jon was smiling; he didn't seem to mind. Finally, Kay realized she'd have to put her foot down or her parents would take pictures all night.

"We really need to get going. We're supposed to be meeting Tam and Carson," she said hopefully.

"Oh, gosh, I didn't realize how late it is," Mom said, glancing at her watch. "Of course you should get going. Have fun." Kay hugged her mother, then her father.

He said, "Kay, back by midnight, right?"

"Right."

Then she and Jon piled into his car. Jon was chuckling.

"What?" she asked.

"When your dad's the sheriff and he says be home by midnight, you don't have a choice, do you? He could send the cops after you." His expression turned thoughtful. "Do you think he'd really do that?"

Kay's father had pulled her over for speeding once. That was all it had taken.

She said, "I think we'd better plan on being back by midnight."

If you wanted to go to a dance with a friend, there had to be an easier way.

The gym had been done up with a ton of streamers and balloons. A disco ball had been temporarily suspended from the ceiling. It still looked—and smelled—like the gym. The football team had won the game earlier that day and were acting rowdy, screaming at one another, mostly incomprehensible phrases, except for an occasional "Saints!" Now that Kay thought about it, calling the closest high school to Dragon the Saint Georges struck her as being kind of rude. The football players' girlfriends stood to the side, pouting and looking embarrassed at the team's rowdiness, a few people danced to recorded music, and lots of others stood to the sides, sipping fruit punch from paper cups and nibbling on cookies. Like any other school dance. While lots of people managed to look nice in their new dresses and suits, many others looked exactly what they were: uncomfortable.

On the other hand, this was about as fancy as Silver River ever got.

Kay and Jon leaned against a wall and watched the drama.

Jon pointed to where Principal Reid, who always wore

pressed dress suits in dark, respectable colors, even while chaperoning a dance, was tapping Carson on the shoulder. Carson and Tam stopped making out on the dance floor. It was the third time Reid had split them up. They returned to dancing in the acceptable manner: her arms across his shoulders, his hands on her hips, six inches between them. Reid had been known to measure with a ruler.

They'd been making out during one of the *fast* songs.

"I give them ten more minutes before they get stopped again," Jon said. "Or before Reid kicks them out."

Kay grinned. "If she hasn't yet, she's not going to."

"They'll just find some place where no one'll bother them," Jon said.

When a group of them went out for a movie or a game or to hang out, that's how a lot of the evenings ended up: with Tam and Carson going someplace where no one would bother them. They were kind of famous for it.

Jon called it exactly. Ten minutes later, when the next slow song came up, Tam and Carson were at it again. Reid marched toward them, but before she reached them, Carson took Tam's hand, and they ran off the dance floor and out the door together.

"They didn't even say good-bye," Kay said. Never mind. Kay would hear all about it tomorrow or Monday, how they'd parked at a trailhead outside of town or sneaked into Carson's attic. The attic actually stored an old bed that they used, but then they had to be quiet, and how hard was that when Carson was just *so hot*.

Reid had other targets by this time. Chaperones watched the dancing couples like hawks during the slow songs. The scene made Kay nervous. She didn't know whether she was relieved to be outside that whole game or sad that she was missing out on something. Jon hadn't asked her to dance a slow song yet. She half hoped that he would, but was glad that he hadn't. The whole evening was confusing her.

By ten o'clock it was clear one of the football players had smuggled in some kind of alcohol and was passing a flask among his friends, because the team got more rowdy, the girlfriends got giggly, and the smell of it was starting to seep in among the smells of sugar from punch and cake and sweat from the gym. More people were dancing, the talking got louder, the music got louder, and the faculty chaperones were looking resigned. At least the punch hadn't been spiked. Her parents would just love her coming home drunk and wouldn't take "It's not my fault" as an excuse.

About that time Jon rested a hand on her shoulder. "You want to go outside and get some air?"

She nodded, and they slipped through the gym door to the parking lot, after retrieving their coats from the coatrack.

They just walked, following the sidewalk around the school, even though Kay's strappy high heels weren't great for walking, and her feet were cold. As long as she kept moving, she'd be okay. They walked shoulder to shoulder, looking up at the sky, the stars. The air was cold enough that their breath fogged. Kay's ears tingled with cold. She hugged her coat tightly around her.

"Are you okay?" he said, after they'd walked the length of the sidewalk in silence.

"Yeah, I'm fine. It's so beautiful out." On clear nights like this, the sky was black, rich and depthless, and millions of stars sparkled.

They turned the next corner; she couldn't help but look out past the football field and highway to the forest beyond, and to the mountains in the distance that marked dragon territory. She thought of Artegal, wondered where he was and how hard he had to work to keep from telling anyone about them. She wondered if any of his people suspected.

There seemed to be a glow among those far mountains, almost like a touch of sunset, but it was north instead of west. It seemed to flicker, orange and yellow, like a distant campfire.

Jon looked to where she stared. "Is it the northern lights?"

On clear nights, or when the aurora was particularly strong, the northern lights were visible in Silver River. But she shook her head. The glow was too red and too close to the horizon to be the aurora. Visible among the hills, shadows moved, dipping in and out of the light in graceful figures, visible in brief flashes.

"It's them," she said.

A few times a year, the dragons grew active, and their

skies lit up. People assumed it was their fires reflecting off the mountains. No one knew for sure, and no one knew why. Nothing ever came of the nights of fire. No attacks, no demands, nothing to tell if the dragons were angry. Maybe they had their own festivals, their own holidays. Like Christmas. Because no one had a good explanation for it, it was probably one of the reasons people had stayed jumpy about dragons, even after all this time.

The activity was well within dragon territory, so the human authorities couldn't do anything about it. Kay imagined how many dragons were needed to make the mountains glow like that.

Shivering suddenly, she wrapped her arm around Jon's for warmth. He didn't pull away. They walked on.

It felt almost like dancing, this walking arm in arm. She felt warmer. Wasn't sure it was all from him.

After a dozen steps, he looked at her and said, "Does this mean you want to be more than just friends?"

A few more steps. She had to think. This was Jon, her climbing buddy, her friend. It was hard thinking of him outside of that. She wasn't sure she wanted to be one of those figures Principal Reid accosted on the dance floor. She wasn't sure if that was really what being boyfriend and girlfriend meant. This was all way too much to explain to Jon right now.

"I don't know. Is it okay if I don't know?"

"Yeah," he said after a moment. "I think I know how you

feel." He gave her arm a squeeze.

Arm in arm, they went back to his car.

Kay groaned when she saw the light on in the living room. Mom or Dad or both were waiting up for her.

"It's not midnight yet, I know it isn't," Jon said, looking at the clock in the dash in a panic. It read 11:30.

"No, it's not. They're just being uptight."

"You're sure it's okay? You're not going to get in trouble?"

"No. They said midnight, they meant it." She gathered her coat around her and paused before she opened the door. "Thanks, Jon. Thanks for bugging me until I said yes. I had a good time." She did have a good time; maybe the best part was just walking with Jon outside, watching the stars.

"Good. I'm glad." His smile glowed. He really was glad. "Maybe we should do it again sometime."

"Maybe we should." This sounded serious. She considered: Was she reluctant to say yes because she was scared? Was that all?

Maybe that was what made her lean forward and kiss him, just a light press on the side of his lips, before she could scare herself out of it. He blinked at her, mouth open, startled. His hand touched hers.

"Bye," she said, and scrambled out of the car before he could say anything. She ran to the front door, but looked back once. He was watching her through the windshield. Quickly, she went inside and closed the door. She stood there, listening, until she heard his car start and drive away.

Behind her, a newspaper rustled. Her father, sitting on the sofa in the living room, set aside his reading.

"Hi," he said.

She smoothed out her coat, trying not to be self-conscious, and wondered if she was in trouble after all. Maybe her father had set his clock fifteen minutes ahead, just to be sneaky. "You didn't have to wait up for me."

He shrugged. "I know. I just wanted to make sure you had a good time. Did you?"

"Yeah, I did." She shoved her hands in the pockets of the coat and sat on the edge of the armchair across from him. "We saw lights. It looked like fires in the mountains over the border."

"Hmm. That's the third time this year."

"You keep track?"

He smiled. "It's hard not to. We get probably a hundred 911 calls about it the nights it happens."

"But there's nothing you can do about it," she said.

"We tell people we're monitoring the situation. If telling us about it makes them feel better, well, I can't argue, can I?"

"It's weird. It feels like they're watching us."

"I'm sure they are watching us," he said. "They'd be stupid not to. And I don't think they're stupid."

They're not, she almost said. They read. They make art.

They could talk to us, if they wanted to. She pursed her lips, trying to find the right way to ask—without letting on about her secret.

"We do the drills, the jets patrol—is it because we really think they're going to attack?" If most of the dragons were like Artegal, she didn't believe they would.

"It's hard to say. We just don't know enough about them."

"Do you think there'll ever be another war with them?" What had been banter in the hall at school had become an appalling idea.

"I hope not. The way I see it, my job's keeping the peace. The more peaceful it is, the better I look." He grinned.

She must have been staring off into space, frowning and thoughtful, because her father said, "You're not worried about the dragons, are you?"

Yes. At least, she worried about one dragon. . . . "No," she said quickly. "Not any more than usual." She tried to figure out how to change the subject. Her father did it for her.

"You're sure you had a good time? You seem a little down."

"Oh no, I was just thinking." He gave her a questioning look, prompting more detail. She'd be better off calling it a night and running away to her room. She took a deep breath and said, "How did you know? You and Mom, I mean. How did you know you wanted to be together?"

He leaned back against the sofa, glancing at the ceiling. Avoiding the question, she thought. He'd say something trite and tell her to go to bed.

She was surprised when he shook his head. "I don't know. It's not something I can put into words. We just knew. Well, *I* knew. She took a little persuading." His smile turned wry.

Kay wondered what her mother would say if she asked her the same question. His answer didn't help much. It was the same thing Tam always said: It just felt right.

Kay just felt confused.

Her father said, "I like Jon. He's a good kid."

She'd have to tell Jon that, so he could stop worrying about Sheriff Wyatt coming after him. Kay smirked and said, "So you want me to go out with him, too."

"If you're ready. I don't want you to get involved if you don't want to."

She sighed. "But how do I know if I'm ready?"

"Sorry, kid. Can't help you with that one."

He seemed smug. He had that look that adults got when they thought their kids were being cute. She sighed again.

He came over and kissed the top of her head. "I'm going to hit the sack. Don't forget to turn the lights out."

"Night, Dad."

She followed suit a few minutes later, carefully hanging her dress in the closet before going to bed.

6

The weather turned cold. Snow fell, and the edges of the creek at the border froze, forming a crystalline skin that crept out over the running water. Kay went to their meeting spot bundled up in her parka, with scarf, hat, gloves, and thermals under her clothes.

Artegal didn't seem bothered by the cold at all. His breath blew out through his nose in billowing clouds of fog.

"So I guess dragons are warm-blooded," she said to him by way of greeting.

He tilted his head, curious. "Warm-blooded? Of course, blood is warm."

"Well, yeah. But it means you're not really reptiles." She tried to remember all those science class notes and wished she'd paid more attention. "Reptiles are cold-blooded. They can't keep warm by themselves, so they have to sit out in the sun. Warm-blooded animals maintain their own body temperature, so they can be out in the cold. People have always wondered about dragons. No one's been able to get a blood sample or take their temperature or anything to find out." Imagine getting a dragon to sit still for that.

"Reptiles. Small, scaled creatures. Snakes, lizards."

"Yes."

They sometimes still had trouble with vocabulary. But the more they talked, the more he learned. She could tell he was getting better. She wondered sometimes if she wasn't the best person in the world to be helping him—plenty of people were smarter. He could be learning so much more from them. Then again, the really smart people didn't do things like go climbing on the border of Dragon. Maybe she was exactly the right person to be here. She'd earned this chance.

"We are to them as you are to mice. Like them, but far removed. We have scales like them, but we have more."

Like speech, for example, though only some dragons learned to speak human languages—like Artegal and his mentor. Kay was getting answers to questions her mother faced in her work monitoring the border, and the scientists would love this. As if she could tell anyone. She didn't even dare make notes, in case someone found them.

She said, "We see a glow sometimes, to the north toward

the mountains. Like something's on fire. It was there last week. I could almost see dragons flying around it."

He rested, his wings folded to his side, propped up on his elbows, back legs tucked under him, and tail curled around his body. He nodded thoughtfully, but said nothing.

"Nobody knows what it is," she said, hinting. "We know it has something to do with dragons, but we don't know what."

"We see a glow all the time from your town. Lit up, all night long."

"Streetlights. We can't see in the dark, like dragons can," she said.

"Used to be humans didn't go out at night at all."

"Well, now we do. Now we can."

Artegal resettled himself, flexing his tail and shifting his forelimbs. He seemed to be considering how to answer.

Kay sat on her usual rock nearby, so they could look at each other at almost the same level. His expression seemed uncertain, though she could have been wrong. He couldn't think that she'd been sent to spy on him, any more than she thought he was sent to spy on her and learn more about people—right? They'd found each other by accident.

"You don't have to tell me if it's a secret," she said.

"It's like singing," he said finally. "Like a choir."

She tried to imagine a dozen dragons like him, raising their necks, tilting back their heads, flames pouring from their open mouths along with music. Music that sounded like roaring. It was an odd image.

"Is it like a celebration? It must be special. It only happens a couple of times a year."

"Yes. A ritual. Births. Deaths."

"What was last week?"

Again, he hesitated. This was one of the questions the scientists—and the military—kept asking: How many of them were there? How often were they born—or hatched? How much did we have to worry about them building up numbers and overwhelming us?

"A birth," he said after a long moment.

She felt an odd thrill that he trusted her with the information.

"Congratulations," she said.

He tilted his head in the way that made her think of a smile. "Thank you."

"Have you done it yet?" Tam asked.

It was the first day back at school after winter break. Kay was reacquainting herself with her locker, wincing because she'd forgotten to bring home a baggie of cookies that someone had given her for Christmas. They were probably stale. Tam was leaning on the locker next to her, making demands.

Kay and Jon had gone out a couple of times during the break. They went to a movie and grabbed dinner at the Alpine Diner. They'd gone cross-country skiing the day after a big snowfall on New Year's. They hadn't done anything they wouldn't have done when they were "just friends." The presents they'd given each other were the same kind of thing they'd always given each other. She gave him a CD; he gave her a box of chemical hand-warmers, perfect for days of winter hiking or cross-country skiing. She hadn't expected anything like flowers or jewelry—she wouldn't have wanted anything like that, not from Jon.

It didn't really feel different. They hadn't done any more than kiss good night.

Kay decided to pretend that she didn't know what Tam was talking about. "Done what?"

Tam rolled her eyes in disgust. "Come on, you know. You've been going out with Jon for like a month. Have you slept with him yet?"

"Oh, I thought maybe you were talking about math homework," Kay said, grinning because she knew that would infuriate Tam.

Tam huffed and stomped her foot. "I've been dying to talk to you about it."

"Ah, so that's why you've been so anxious for me to get a boyfriend."

"Kay, come on. It's not normal. You're supposed to, you know . . . *want* to."

Was she? She supposed so. "Can't you find someone else to talk to about sex?"

"Sure. Like, *everybody*. Everybody except you."

It was true. Out of the corner of her eye Kay spotted three couples walking hand in hand. One of those stopped to kiss. She never knew whether to believe all the rumors about how far who had gotten with whom. Tam was right, though. Sometimes it seemed like it was everyone but her.

"You're a junior in high school. You're way too old to be a virgin," Tam said.

Kay stared. "Seventeen is not too old to be a virgin."

"Whatever."

"We're taking it slow," Kay said. Tam just huffed in irritation again. That made Kay frustrated. This was supposed to be about her, not what Tam or anyone else thought. "What's the big deal? Why do you even care whether or not we've slept together? It's none of your business."

Tam looked hurt, and Kay realized she'd spoken more harshly than she'd meant to. But she didn't apologize. She bit her lip and wouldn't look at Tam.

"Don't get angry," Tam said, shrugging, brushing it off. "You can do whatever you want to."

"Then why do you keep asking me about it?" Kay said under her breath.

"Because I'm worried about you."

"Well, don't be," Kay said. "I'm normal. I'm perfectly normal." She didn't sound all that convinced.

"Are you sure about that?" Tam shot back.

Kay wasn't sure—because she wasn't normal. Normal people weren't friends with dragons—and were she and Artegal really friends?

"I'm a little stressed out right now," Kay said, sighing. "That's all."

"Why? What's up?"

The whole story ran to the tip of her tongue. She'd say, *Can you keep a secret?* Then everything would come out. Tam had never blown a secret Kay had told her. And Tam must have known something was up, the way Kay looked at her, her lips parted, her gaze pleading. Kay almost told her everything.

Then she shook her head and looked away, because this was way too big. Kay breaking the law by crossing the border was one thing, but asking Tam to break the law by keeping a secret? She'd keep the secret, Kay believed. But Kay didn't want to get her in that much trouble. "Never mind. It's nothing."

Tam lowered her voice to a sly whisper. "You're stressed out because you're not sleeping with Jon. That'll clear it right up, I bet."

"Jeez, Tam, give it a rest!" Kay slammed shut her locker door.

"I'm just trying to help!"

Thankfully, the bell rang, and they couldn't argue anymore. They walked side by side to first-period chemistry and pretended the conversation never happened.

As usual, Kay sat at lunch with Tam, Carson, and Jon. As usual, Tam and Carson greeted each other with a long, enthusiastic kiss. These moments, which had been merely annoying before, had become uncomfortable with Jon sitting next her, and she and Jon sort of being together. She could only glance surreptitiously at Jon and wonder if he wanted her to kiss him like that, out here in front of everyone. She felt his warmth next to her. She'd have to move only half an inch to be touching him. Out of the corner of her eye she could see him glance at her, then look away, blushing.

"Hey, get a room," he finally said, turning a lopsided grin. Tam and Carson gave each other one of those sly looks that suggested they were way ahead of Jon and thinking hard about that room. Or maybe they'd already been there. Kay had heard stories about the janitor's closet.

After lunch, Kay and Jon left the cafeteria together.

"You okay?" Jon said. "You're kind of quiet."

She shrugged, not sure how much she wanted to say. Here she was, not able to talk to Tam *or* Jon. "Tam and I kind of had an argument. She seems to think that two people who are going out should carry on just like them. She can't understand why we don't."

"I guess you guys talk about everything," he said.

She thought of everything they *didn't* talk about. They never talked about Tam's mother's boyfriends. Tam would just give her trademark huff and shake her head whenever

61

Kay asked. Until last year, when Tam starting dating Carson, they'd talked about boys all the time—who liked who and what they were going to do about it. But now, they never really *talked*. Once, she'd asked Tam what sex was like, *really*. Tam had said, with a sly grin, "You'll just have to find out."

She said to Jon, "Not really."

They slowly walked a few more steps down the hall, putting off when they'd have to arrive at class.

"Sometimes I wonder if they get tired of it. Seems like all they ever do is make out," Jon said.

"According to Tam it's the best thing in the world and everybody should do it. All the time."

"I think I'd rather go out with someone who likes to ski every now and then."

"Really?"

Maybe, Kay thought, *there is something to this relationship stuff*. On a whim—no, not really on a whim, because she wanted to try it, to see what it was like—she let her arm brush his and let their hands meet, then close together. Just like that, they were walking hand in hand down the hall at school. His hand was warm, dry. He didn't squeeze. Just let their fingers lace together. She didn't want to cling to him, and maybe he felt the same way. He was a few inches taller, but she had to bend her elbow only a little. They'd held hands before, helping each other up a rock face or across a creek on a hike. But nothing like this. Kay found herself worried that she was doing it wrong.

But Jon smiled a kind of thin, distracted smile. He glanced at her for a second and didn't say anything. Just kept walking with his hand in hers. And it felt good.

7

On clear days in January, Kay continued hiking out to see Artegal. It didn't occur to her not to. Snow and cold were tiny obstacles, when she could bundle up. Because of the cold, she couldn't stay long, but the dragon would have lingered all day, nestled in the snow, his tail sweeping back and forth through drifts.

The creek was frozen now. Kay could walk across it if she was careful. Instead of sitting while she waited for him, she paced to keep warm. This day was one of the sunny ones, and the light gleamed, sparkling like crystals off snow-covered ground, and snow-dusted branches.

The distant peaks in the interior of Dragon never had snow on them. Warmed from the fires of dragon lairs within, the snow melted.

She hadn't been waiting long when he arrived. She recognized the sound of trees creaking, as if in a wind. Especially today, when no breeze blew. He came into view, gunmetal gray against the snowy world, and settled on his forelimbs, bringing himself closer to her. The light in his onyx eyes blazed.

"Hi," she said.

His lip curled. "Wanted to show you this," he said, and opened a foreclaw, offering her an object. She hadn't noticed that he'd held his claws tightly shut. "Belonged to my mentor. It's human." He sounded excited.

It was a book, and for a moment she was horrified. It looked ancient, bound in brown leather, worn and stained, with tarnished metal fixtures on the spine and corners, and here it was in the outdoors, in cold and snow. It was maybe the size of one of her schoolbooks, and she wondered how a large dragon could handle something so small. Artegal's claws worked like pincers, setting it in her hands. Once she had it, he tucked his arm back to his side. She hardly noticed how comfortable she'd become around him; she hardly noticed his size and no longer thought of his claws and teeth as weapons that could tear into her. He was just Artegal, who liked to talk about books.

The book was heavy and seemed fragile. Somehow, it had survived time and being carried in the claws of a dragon.

"How old is it?" she said.

"Centuries."

That didn't sound ridiculous spoken in the growling voice of a dragon.

"It should be in a museum," she murmured, running skittering fingers over the cover. Tiny dimples from the animal's hair were still visible in the leather. She'd seen pictures of books like this in history class.

"Has been safe, dry, and cool, in dragon caves," he said. "I brought it when I was sure you would understand. Look inside."

His trust in her made her pause a moment, overcome. This was an honor, and she was flattered. After the lump in her throat faded, she opened the book to the middle.

Dense, black writing covered thick parchment pages. Vivid drawings looped around the borders of each page. Vines, multicolored flowers, large letters touched with gold. Figures stood here and there among the foliage: dragons—silver, red, mottled green and brown, black—their tails looping and tangling around themselves and other tails in knots, long necks stretching over letters, around corners, fire twining from pointed mouths. And with them, people. Women in tight-fitting gowns, men in brightly colored tunics. Sheltered by the bodies of those huge beasts, resting their hands on lowered snouts, touching the tip of a raised wing. Perched on their backs, even. People, riding dragons.

She couldn't read the text. The writing was strange; so

was the language. But she could make out the first word on the first page, an obvious title written large: *Dracopolis.*

She looked at Artegal and would have sworn he was smiling.

"People and dragons used to be friends," she said. "Is that what this is saying?"

"Seems so," he said smugly.

"Is this real?" she said. "This isn't just made up?"

Artegal nodded. "My mentor told me stories, told to him by his mentor. He kept the book. Not many have seen it, he said. Not many want to believe it. Most have forgotten."

"But I've never heard of any stories—the human side doesn't tell stories." Except for stories of Chinese luck . . .

"The tales faded in the time of hiding. Except for this."

This showed a secret history that no one knew anything about. How could people have forgotten this? Why did only the stories of war get passed down?

"I can't read it."

"Latin," he said. "I can read, a little. *Dracopolis*: City of dragons."

"We can show this to people," she said. "Then maybe we won't have to sneak around. People won't be afraid of dragons anymore." She thought about the dragon-raid drills, and how wonderful it would be never to have another one.

He snorted. "Not so simple. The conflict is older than we are. Not as easily forgotten."

"But we can try," she said.

"Will they listen?"

Silent, she turned the pages, studying the haunting images. The drawings were stylized, flat, the poses awkward. But she could almost see emotion, the expressions on their faces, faint smiles, as the people and dragons looked at each other. It would be easy for someone to say it was all made up, to call it fiction. She had only Artegal's word for it, that this was history. And the example of the two of them, talking together week after week. That made the book feel true. But it also felt a little like fighting a war of their own, against all the more familiar stories of people and dragons as enemies. Artegal was right—would anyone listen to a couple of kids?

She frowned. "Is this worth it?"

"This what?"

Hugging the book to her, she paced, wondering if he would even understand her explanation. "I'm keeping these meetings secret from everyone I know. My parents, my best friends—though there are actually a lot of reasons I can't talk to Tam and Jon right now." She sat on the rock and sighed.

"Tam and Jon—friends?"

"Yeah. It's complicated. Ever since Tam started going out with Carson she's been obsessed with him, and now Jon and I are sort of going out, and it doesn't matter how much we say that it won't change anything, it *does* change things. Half the time I don't even know what to say to him. Never mind keeping *this* secret from him."

"Confusing," Artegal said, tilting his head. "Don't understand."

"Neither do I." She smiled weakly.

"Can I help?"

"I don't know. I guess just talking about it helps."

"Then you should talk. That's why I came—talking is always good."

"Even if I am breaking who knows how many laws—"

"Me as well," he said, huffing through his nostrils. "Breaking dragon law."

"What'll they do to you if they find out?"

"Grounded."

She almost said, *Hey, me too,* then realized he was talking about something different. "They'll keep you from flying?"

"Yes," he said.

Pursing her lips, she turned back to the illuminated page. Across the top of a page, a dragon soared, its wings spread over the upper third of the parchment. Straps looped across its chest, around its wings, over its back. They formed a kind of harness, and clinging to the dragon's back, hands gripping the harness, was another of the tiny medieval people, a man with wide eyes and curling hair.

"Did you see this?" She held the book up over her head, tilting it so he could peer at it with his shining eye. He snorted an assent. In the cold air, the breath from his nostrils billowed.

"Did this really happen?" she asked. "Did people really

fly with dragons? Or is this just a story? Imaginary." She tried to remember the terms from English class. "Like some kind of symbolism?"

"My mentor had a harness," he said, nodding at the book. "Broken, though. Very old. Like the straps there, see?" His predator eyes hadn't missed a detail. Of course they'd have harnesses, so the riders wouldn't fall. If this had been fiction or symbolism, would the artists have bothered showing that detail?

"So people really did this. Dragons carried them. They flew." She was starting to get a really bad idea.

Artegal must have had the same really bad idea. He had that lilt to his brow, the same one he'd had the first time they met, when he'd said, "Because—not supposed to."

She shook her head, even though she could feel the smile creeping on her own lips. "Maybe we could make one like it, if you wanted to."

She climbed smooth rock faces with ropes and harness and didn't fall. Already she was thinking of how to loop the ropes, how to knot them together to secure them and hook herself to his back.

"Am curious," he said, his lips curving in a wry dragon smile.

This was like free-climbing a forbidden slope of granite. She wanted to see if she could. She just wanted to *see*.

"I think I have an idea," she said.

Artegal gave her the book to take home and study. Opening it on her bed, she crouched over it and turned the pages, from beginning to end. Each page seemed fragile, like if she turned it too quickly it would disintegrate. Yet the parchment was soft. Pettable, almost, like a very fine leather. She resisted an urge to stroke the edges, because that kind of treatment couldn't be good for it. Toward the end of the book, the images changed. They no longer showed the two species smiling at each other, working to move boulders from a field or build city walls. Instead, there was fire. Dragons sailed across the sky, raining down fire, and lines of human warriors carrying spears and swords approached dragons whose necks twisted back in anger. Something had happened, and a war had started.

Tucked between the last couple of pages of the book was a piece of paper—actual paper, not the thin parchment that made up the rest of the book. It was old, yellow, brittle—but not as old as the rest of the book. She was afraid to unfold it; it felt like it would crumble in her hands. She partially unfolded it, just enough to see. It was a map. It looked like an ocean, with large islands around the edges. A black dot on one of the spots of land was labeled Dracopolis, with numbers after it—latitude and longitude, maybe? The handwriting was different from the writing in the book, flowing and precise. The ink had turned to a pale brown. After copying the numbers—she was sure they were coordinates—she folded the page and returned it to the book.

She checked the coordinates on the map in her atlas, tracing latitude and longitude to a place near the northern edge of Greenland. But that couldn't have been right, because there was nothing there, just the Arctic Ocean and a bunch of ice. She drew a circle around the general area and put an X roughly at the intersection of the coordinates. Not exactly a point on the map to chase down, but she was still curious. She'd ask Artegal about it.

Kay took a spiral notebook from her pile of schoolwork and turned to a blank page. Back at the beginning of the medieval book, she started copying letters, trying to make out the words. Artegal had said this was Latin. She ought to be able to find some kind of translation site online to tell her what this all meant, if she could just make out the letters. Unfortunately, whoever had written this had decided to leave out all the spaces between words. She could put the letters down, but didn't know where anything started or ended. When she put the lines of gibberish into the translator, she got back . . . gibberish. Despairing, she wondered if she was going to have to learn a whole new language.

When she finished, she carefully wrapped the book in a clean towel and hid it in a drawer.

Looking at local topographical maps, she found a valley—barely a valley, more like a forgotten space between a set of hills close to the dragon side of the border. It was too close to the border to be frequented by dragons, but hidden from surveillance on the human side. It may give them enough space to experiment.

She told Artegal about the place, describing it in terms of compass readings based on the map, so many degrees from north. He better understood when she marked it in relation to the setting sun.

"I know this place," he said. "It is good."

"I found something else in the book," she said, after they'd agreed on their plan. "It's newer, I think. Someone wrote down coordinates on a piece of paper and slipped it between the pages. It's for a place way north and east—near Greenland, do you know where that is?"

"The Arctic islands?" he questioned.

"I think so."

He purred thoughtfully. "East, where my mentor vanished."

Someone had copied down latitude and longitude, believed they were important enough to write down. But they didn't label the coordinates—to keep them secret? "You think he went there?" Kay said. "Who wrote the note?"

"I do not know," Artegal said.

A week later, they met somewhere other than their secret glade by the creek. Knowing her parents, knowing the patrol schedules and where she could go and have it be unlikely she'd be found helped her hide. It also helped that she'd grown up in these woods and knew the landmarks. She could leave the trails and not get lost.

She parked her Jeep at a trailhead where it wouldn't be

out of place. This required a couple of extra miles of hiking to reach their meeting spot, which meant starting out stupidly early. She brought along with her yards of rope and her rock-climbing harness. She kept thinking, *This is crazy. Completely insane.*

"You've been doing a lot of hiking. Especially for this time of year," her mother had observed when Kay left the house.

"It's been helping with all the stress at school," Kay had explained. Her mother seemed pleased with the explanation, as if proud that Kay was handling the stress on her own.

She wore her warmest layers of clothing and brought along chemical warmers for her boots and gloves. She didn't need them at first, hiking hard with her climbing gear in a backpack. She was sweating.

Artegal had already arrived and was waiting. He tilted his head to study the equipment slung over her shoulders. "Make harness. With this?"

"I'm not sure it'll even work. It may not work." She kept saying that, and yet she wanted to try it. How different could it be? You secured your line. You clipped in. You didn't fall. End of story.

"We'll try," he said, and that was that.

First, she arranged the line on the ground in front of Artegal, eyeing the dragon and trying to estimate how much it would take to circle that giant frame. A figure eight would work best, she decided, looped over his chest in front of and behind his wings and meeting in the back. "Will this hurt you if it goes over your wings?"

He snorted a puff of steam out his nose. "As you say, I'm not sure."

Leaning forward, he lowered himself to the ground, on top of where Kay had spread the lines out. Taking one end of the line, she touched Artegal's shoulder. The scales were smooth, cool. She imagined that if she knocked her knuckles on them, they'd ring out. She lay her hand flat. A jump and a couple of steps would carry her up to his back. They'd been meeting each other for weeks, but they'd only talked. This was the first time she'd touched him since the day he fished her out of the river. It seemed awkward.

Artegal, his head turned to watch her, nodded once.

Pulling with her hands, pushing with her feet, she scrambled up the slope of his shoulder and found herself kneeling on his back. She had to think to keep her balance. She could feel his body shift as he breathed, the rhythmic movement of lungs, in and out.

He seemed huge from this angle. She could stand on his back, and it would be like standing on a smooth, flat floor.

She did this three more times, to bring the other ends of the rope up. She looped them together and knotted them securely as if she were tying a rope to someone else's harness. She left herself a loop and a carabiner—a steel oval with a hinged closure—to secure her harness to.

He didn't seem to mind her clambering all over him. She thought she would have felt it if he flinched or winced. Leaning on his back, she called to him, "Tell me if I'm hurting you."

His lip curled. "Would take much more to hurt me."

She checked every line, knot, and carabiner three times. Finally, she put on her climbing harness, secured around her waist and legs. She'd left her helmet at home—if she fell from the air, a helmet wouldn't do much good. She thought she was ready. Standing on the ground by his shoulder, she looked at Artegal, into his shining eye.

"Are we sure about this?" she said.

"We can prove the book is not false," he said. "And—is exciting. An adventure."

That, she understood. "It sure is."

"If something goes wrong, call to me," he said.

Once again she climbed up his shoulder, to the middle of his back, between his forelimbs. She snapped the carabiner on her harness onto the loop on Artegal's harness. She stretched out, lying facedown, bracing with her legs.

"Ready?" he said. Even with his head turned, she could just see the corner of his eye at the end of his long stretch of silvery neck.

Not really. But she never would be until she did it. She held onto the ropes as tightly as she could. "Yeah."

He walked, carrying her on foot for a quarter of a mile, to the line of forest that marked the valley. The motion felt lurching, shoulders bunching and lifting as he moved his arms and wings, his hind legs causing his whole body to roll like a boat as he pushed himself forward. If she were prone to motion sickness, she would be sick from this. But she crouched, sitting up slightly on her hands and knees, letting her body shift and rock with the motion. She could even start to look around her and marvel at the world from fifteen feet off the ground. High branches passed by at eye level; birds flew below her.

The path he took crested, then started downhill. He didn't warn her when he launched straight up, fast as a rocket.

She fell and slammed against his scaly back, grunting as the harness took all of her weight. The breath was knocked out of her. Dangling, she rolled over until she was looking up at bright blue sky. She grabbed the rope and pulled herself back to stability, digging her toes in, bracing. Artegal flinched a little—no more than the shiver of muscle she'd have when shrugging off a fly. If he was going to do things like that without telling her, then he'd just have to put up with her scrambling on his back.

The muscles under her bunched as he stretched his forelimbs and raised his wings. They became gleaming sails on either side of her. At the same time, he tipped up, almost vertical, and she gasped as her legs swung free. But her knots held, her harness gripped her comfortably just as it was supposed to. She'd secured the lines well enough that they slipped only a few inches, shifting along his back. They didn't seem to interfere with his wings. It was just like climbing. She wasn't going to fall.

Almost immediately he flattened, skimming along the treetops where he was less likely to be seen. Lying on her stomach, she mostly saw him, his neck stretched forward, the wedge of his head cutting a path through the air, the thick muscles of his back bunching, relaxing, bunching again as his wings dipped like oars. When the wings swept back, she could see past his shoulder to a carpet of treetops, the tips of conifers speeding past in a blur. In the distance, mountains surrounded them. Above her, nothing but sky. It was a big world.

The scales were slippery, and when he made a sudden banking movement, she lost her grip again, letting out a yelp as she fell. Scrabbling for purchase, she rammed an elbow into the base of a wing. He grunted, and the rhythm of his wing strokes faltered. He swerved and flapped harder to keep upright.

"Sorry," she called, wondering if he could hear her over the wind.

He leveled off again, and she regained her balance in the center of his back. Her muscles were already stiff from bracing, but she thought she'd found the best position: lying flat, propped on her elbows, holding the rope across his shoulders, using her feet to keep her steady, shifting with his movements instead of against them. Struggling against his rapid turns had caused her to fall.

Wind howled around her. Gripping the ropes tightly, she huddled as if in a storm. But she was flying with a dragon. Flying. She grinned, laughter bubbling up, but the wind kept her gasping for air, and the sound never quite burst forth.

He sailed around the valley, dipping his wings to turn one way or another, soaring just above the treetops. No fancy tricks—they were both getting used to this. But she grew comfortable enough with the harness, the movement, the view, and the feeling of being at the mercy of a large, living creature. No, not at the mercy of—they were partners in this. She started to enjoy herself enough that she was disappointed when the dragon tipped his nose down and dipped into an open space among the trees.

He tucked himself, pulling up his neck and body, stretching his hind legs forward to take the landing, and sweeping his wings back like a hawk to control his descent. She was practically dangling off his nearly vertical back as they passed by the top of the trees.

She'd have expected them to crash into the trees, ripping through branches. A total mess. But for all his size, Artegal was agile. He hit the ground without a stumble, while inertia slammed her into his back, causing her to lose her breath again. Just as carefully as he'd unfurled them, he tucked his wings in and settled, leaning forward on the tips of his fingers and shifting on his hind legs.

Her hands were cramped from holding a death grip on the ropes. She almost couldn't open them. She shivered because even her coat and winter clothes hadn't been enough to protect her from the blast of wind. If they did this again, she'd have to wear warmer clothes. And learn to trust the harness and rigging. If she could learn to use it to balance, she wouldn't have to hold on so tightly, and she might be able to look around more.

If they did this again—she couldn't wait to do this again, even though they weren't supposed to be doing this at all.

She hung there, unable to move for a moment, trying to catch her breath and unclench her body. Artegal curled his neck around, trying to see her. Over his shoulder, she caught the corner of his gaze.

Then she laughed. "Oh my God!"

"Well?" he rumbled.

"That was amazing!" Fumbling, she unclipped her harness and fell, sliding down his shoulder to sprawl on the ground. "What about you? Are you okay?"

"Your weight is little. Easy to carry. But we could adjust the ropes."

With his clawed forelimbs, he showed her where the ropes had slipped and pinched under his wings, where they could be tighter across his back and looser across his chest to allow easier movement while remaining secure. She did the best she could with cold, stiff fingers. As she stepped back, Artegal rolled his shoulders and stretched his wings, flexing

80

against the harness. He seemed to nod in satisfaction.

"Better," he said. "It will need testing to be sure."

Half hopefully, half fearfully, she asked, "So this means you want to do this again?"

Instead of speaking down to her, he lowered his head, almost to the ground, so they were on a level. "Don't you?"

She nodded as enthusiastically as she could, hoping he'd understand. "Of course! I mean, I've flown before, in airplanes, but this—this was so different, so amazing. I could see everything, everywhere. I felt like I could touch clouds— I mean, the air even smelled better."

He purred, as if in agreement, and seemed pleased.

"Is it always like that?" she said. "Do you ever get tired of it?"

"No," he said. "Never. We are made for flight."

He'd made her a part of that. It was better than conquering a rock face. And they would fly again.

8

Kay started doodling dragon wings in the margins of her notes in class. Then, drawing in harnesses around the wings, in different patterns, thinking of different ways to arrange the ropes. Then she'd scribble it all out, glancing around nervously, hoping no one saw what she was doing and got suspicious. At night, she dreamed of falling and of stopping abruptly, pulled up short by the ropes and harness, then soaring. She lost sleep, thinking of and waiting for the next time she and Artegal would go flying.

It came two weeks later.

They experimented to find the best way of fitting the ropes into a harness. He crouched low so she could reach the knots and make adjustments. Kay added a knot in front so she could adjust the lines from both sides, and not just at his back, and that seemed to help. She learned to make the knots lay flat so they didn't irritate Artegal's skin. His scales looked hard, and they seemed like armor—they could act like armor, too, the dragon said. At least in the old stories, against weapons like swords and arrows. But the skin underneath was sensitive and would chafe and itch if pressed wrong, like an awkward wrinkle in a piece of clothing.

Never mind what the military wanted to know about the dragons. The biologists would kill for a chance like this.

Finally, they had a harness that looked a little more solid and functional than the first one. She couldn't believe they'd managed to get away with it at all last time. Not only had the flimsy set of ropes she'd rigged up as a harness worked, hadn't fallen apart and sent her plummeting—but she and Artegal hadn't been discovered flying. So, why not try it again?

She cracked open a pack of hand warmers and put them in her gloves, hoping they would keep her from getting stiff with cold like last time. Her own climbing harness was on and secure. Once again, Artegal crouched and flattened his wing to let her climb up his side.

Settling on his back felt familiar. His back was broad enough for her to lie flat on, but not so large that she couldn't see over his shoulders to the world around them.

She snapped in, told him she was secure, and braced as he lurched into motion, walking to the launch point. This time, she was ready for it. When he bunched his muscles, so did she, bracing. This time, she didn't slip or lose her breath when he launched straight up, leaping into the air.

The valley fell away below them. Wings stretched to their fullest, Artegal started a wide, lazy circle across the width of it. A carpet of evergreens lay below, climbing both sides of the U-shaped valley. Swaths of snow were visible on bare rock outcroppings. High overhead, the sun painted the whole scene gold and silver. Except for the wind whipping around her head, all was silent. Artegal didn't make a sound, except for a faint rippling in his wings, like sails.

At this height, nothing mattered. Not school, not dating, not arguments with Tam, not laws about the border that weren't fair. Her smile grew wide.

Artegal stretched out like an arrow, streamlined, cutting effortlessly through the air. He changed direction, tilting his wings, and she held on, adjusting her weight to keep her balance. He could see her if he lifted his head and turned slightly, but that broke his aerodynamic shape, so he didn't do it often. They'd have to work out a way to communicate. He could feel her, so maybe they could work out a system of signals. As it was, she hoped he could see her smile and know that everything was okay.

He turned the valley into a track, flapping a swooping oval up one side and down the other, tipped almost on his side as he passed along the hills. The force of his flight pulled Kay down, but her harness held her, and as Artegal increased speed, she stayed anchored to him.

He huffed—she felt the sudden expansion of his lungs—and she took that as a sign he was about to do something. She gripped the ropes and anchored herself by lying flatter against his scaled back.

Then, he swung around. Instead of the gentle, lazy tilting of wings and gliding in a wide arc, he lurched, and dived. Wings swept back now, he turned a sharp angle and plummeted, racing faster and faster to the ground. He spun until Kay thought he was out of control, and she shut her eyes to keep vertigo from overwhelming her. Surely they'd hit the trees soon, they were going so fast. She opened her eyes, just a slit, in time to see his wings reach out at the last moment, fill with air, and swing his body upward again. If she hadn't already been lying flat, she would have slammed into him and lost her lunch. They were definitely going to have to work out some kind of communication.

She laughed, screaming.

This was what maintained the balance of power between the dragons and human aircraft over the last sixty years. Human forces may have had bombs and missiles, but their planes could never maneuver like this, turn on a dime in midair, brake and hover without stalling out. The dragons needed so little effort to outfly artificial human wings.

Artegal climbed and dived again. Kay was a little more ready for it this time. The dragon's body was definitely better designed than the human body for this sort of thing.

She gasped for air every time he made a sudden turn.

But when he caught an updraft and simply glided—a ship of the air sailing in the breeze as if he'd been born there—she felt as if she herself were flying.

An explosion echoed, too sharp and vicious to be thunder. Kay flinched and felt Artegal's back muscles shiver with the same surprise. He turned, swooping around and gaining altitude to look. She sat up to try to see over his shoulder.

Past the ridge, over the forest north of the border, a black smudge drifted at the end of a trail of dark smoke. Something had caught fire and fallen out of the sky. A short distance away from what must have been a plane crash, a white parachute drifted down, a pilot dangling at the end.

For a moment, both dragon and pilot seemed to hover in midair, the pilot slowly falling, twisting back and forth at the end of his lines, looking straight across at the dragon with the girl on his back. He couldn't possibly miss them.

Artegal folded his wings and plunged straight down, into the trees.

Amazingly enough, the dragon found space in the forest and came to a rough landing, slamming into the ground, taking the impact on his hind legs and chest. Kay swung over his shoulder and jerked against the harness.

Air force jets had patrolled along the border her whole life, but nothing like this had ever happened. She couldn't tell: Had the plane been across the border when it crashed?

Was the pilot going to land across the border, in Dragon? What would happen then? This wasn't exactly secret, not like her and Artegal.

"Did he see us?" she called to Artegal. The pilot had seen them, she was sure of it, and he would take the news back to the military, the police—she was going to get in so much trouble.

"He will land on this side of the border," Artegal said. "The elders will know of this. They will find him."

Black smoke from the plane crash formed a tower. Everyone would see it.

"What'll they do to him? What if he's hurt? What if—"

"We are ambassadors. We'll find him first."

When he launched again, she was ready for him, gripping the ropes, watching earnestly. The tower of smoke formed a beacon, which they aimed toward. Growing more confident and feeling secure, Kay looked around, above them and over her shoulder, for aircraft. She assumed the military would send rescue helicopters or maybe even other jets. She didn't see any, but that didn't mean anything. They were flying too low for her to see the main road across the river.

But everyone must have been looking this way. Someone was going to see them. This was going to end it all for them, but they couldn't turn back. If the pilot was hurt, they had to help.

Artegal began circling. She didn't feel it at first, it was so subtle. His right wing dipped slightly, and the sun changed angle. She could look across his right side and see the forest spread out below them, the sky wheeling above them. His wing dipped again and the circle tightened. She recognized a search pattern. He was skimming over the large swath of trees where they'd seen the parachute come down, circling until he found the spot. She knew she wouldn't be much help searching, not compared to his hunter's vision. But she tried, and on the third loop around she saw a spot of white among green branches.

"Artegal, there!" she called, but didn't know if he heard her, since her voice was probably lost in the wind. She slapped his shoulder to get his attention. He was already dipping his wing and banking in that direction.

He approached the white spot—the nylon of a parachute—and chose his landing site. She was getting better at this, and so expected the lurch to the ground when it came and was able to brace. This time, the whole landing procedure almost felt elegant.

Once on the ground, Artegal moved forward, striding by using his wingtips to balance, weaving through the spaces between trees. When he stopped and settled back, Kay held the ropes so she wouldn't fall. She felt the dragon's lungs breathe under her.

"Oh, *shit*," she heard a man say.

Artegal's neck curled into an S, and he cocked his head. This let Kay see over his shoulder, where she saw a man in an olive green jumpsuit running away. Behind him, he'd left his parachute and helmet.

Before Kay could react or think of an alternative, Artegal followed, stretching forward and low to the ground—as low as he could—and balancing on his forelimbs. He took large strides, covering ground quickly. Kay lost sight of the fleeing pilot until Artegal shifted his path and hesitated.

The pilot was still fleeing, looking over his shoulder, stumbling through underbrush and around branches, and heading into a dense section of forest where the dragon couldn't follow. Artegal huffed and changed his path to skirt around and intercept him. In that moment, when he must have seen the dragon wasn't following, the pilot hesitated and looked right at Kay, braced in her harness on the dragon's back. He was maybe in his thirties and had dark, close-cropped hair and a tanned, rugged face. She may have seen amazement in his gaze as they looked at each other. Then Artegal moved on, and the pilot went back to running south, toward the border.

That was it. He'd seen her, and he'd tell the air force. Somehow, they'd figure out who she was, and she'd end up in jail.

"Artegal, stop. Wait a minute." She thumped him on the shoulder.

Artegal sat back and tilted his head toward her. "Not hurt," he said, almost wryly.

"But he's seen us. He'll tell everyone about us," Kay said.

"We should catch him. Talk. Convince him not to."

Talking was his solution to everything.

"No," she said. "Let him go. We need to get out of here before more planes get here."

"And dragons will come as well," he said.

She didn't even want to think about what would happen if other dragons found them.

He didn't fly this time. People on both sides of the border were looking this way and would see them, even close to the treetops. She could already hear engines of aircraft approaching. Artegal was awkward on foot, but still faster than she would have been, as he strode through the trees, balancing on his wingtips. She stayed clipped onto his harness, because it was still a long way down.

When they reached their morning's meeting spot, she slid to the ground, almost reluctantly because she didn't know what was going to happen. She released the ropes and carefully coiled them, as if they would get to do this again. The crisis would blow over, she told herself. Nothing bad would come of the crash. Patiently, Artegal watched her. They'd barely spoken.

Finally, she stood, gear over her shoulder, ready to leave. "When can we meet next?" she asked.

"Don't know. We should take care."

"Maybe lay low for a couple of weeks," she said. "Wait to see if anything happens."

"Three weeks from today. At the highest sun—noon," he said. "We meet at the old spot and assess."

"Assuming we haven't been thrown in jail."

He grumbled. It sounded like a distant tree falling. She could almost feel it through her feet, through the ground. He said, "I'd never know. You'd just not be there."

"Maybe he won't tell anyone."

His responding growl sounded doubtful.

"It'll be fine," she said, resolved, for both their benefits. "This'll all blow over. Just watch."

"Take care, Kay," he said.

She tried to smile. "You too."

They both turned and set off through the trees, in opposite directions.

9

The sun was low, marking afternoon. It was much, much later than Kay had thought. She expected, or rather hoped, that her parents were so busy with the plane crash that they wouldn't have made it home yet to notice she wasn't there. She didn't want to look at her cell phone for missed calls, but she did and found a dozen, with messages from just about everyone: Mom, Dad, Tam. Three from Jon. Helicopters circled overhead. She wondered if the pilot had made it to the river okay.

The tower of smoke was still visible, though thin now, an echo of what had burned earlier. To the north, within Dragon, a dozen bodies swooped and circled in the sky, closer than usual. Maybe they were too far away to see that the smoke was on their side of the border. Then she remembered what Artegal said about their eyesight. They'd see it, and they'd know.

Maybe they'd understand. Maybe they wouldn't think the humans had broken the treaty intentionally, but realize that the crash had been an accident. She didn't want to think about what they'd do if they decided the treaty had been broken and decided to attack. They'd come to Silver River before anywhere else.

She was driving too fast because she needed to get home. With the plane crash and all the chaos around it, she didn't think any cops would be out looking for speeders. But when she passed an SUV mounted with police lights, it did a U-turn, flashed its lights, and turned on its siren. Busted. Groaning, she pulled over.

Glancing in the rearview mirror as the police car pulled to the shoulder behind her, she felt nauseous. It wasn't just any cop car. It was her father's, and sure enough, he climbed out and strolled on over, looking smug. If it had been one of his deputies, she may have been able to talk her way out of it. She didn't know what she was going to say now. She slumped in her seat, as if she could shrink down and disappear through the floorboards.

When her father—Sheriff Wyatt, now—stood by her window, looking down at her under the brim of his cowboy hat, she considered not opening the window. She could just sit here looking at him. The thing was, her father could wait her out. He wouldn't even say anything or knock on the window. He'd just wait until she couldn't stand it anymore.

She rolled down the window. "Hi." If she acted innocent enough, maybe he wouldn't suspect her of anything.

Her father wore a crooked "gotcha" smile. Kay's hopes sank.

"You were going pretty fast there," he said, like it was a joke.

He'd caught her. Okay. She could deal. Just get it over with as quickly as possible. Surely he had better things to do than go after her. "I guess. Sorry."

He didn't say anything. The first—and only, until now—time he had pulled her over, he had written out the entire ticket, showed her how fast she'd been going and how big the fine was. Then he'd torn it up. A warning, he'd said, with the clear indication that next time it would be for real.

But he didn't have his ticket book with him. He just stood there, not saying anything, not doing anything. Dad was the strong and silent type. Kay wanted to scream.

"What are you going to do?" she asked.

"You know this road's been closed?" he said.

He hadn't pulled her over because she was speeding. He'd pulled her over because she wasn't supposed to be here at all. She hadn't even thought about that, that they would quarantine this whole area until they found the pilot and figured out what the dragons were going to do. She had no possible excuse to get out of this.

She shook her head and hoped she looked innocent. "No, I didn't know."

"That means you were out here before the roadblock went up."

"I was hiking," she said, playing as dumb as she could. She'd almost said she was hiking with Jon, but her father would have no problem calling Jon to check on her. Jon could only cover for her if he knew he was supposed to. She hadn't returned his calls yet, and if he heard from Dad first, he might assume the worst.

She could feel her father studying her, and she wondered what she looked like. Her hair was windblown, tangled, even though it had been in a ponytail. A sunburn was prickling on her nose, but that only backed up the hiking story.

"Did you see the crash?" her father said. Fishing for some kind of answer. If only she knew what he was looking for so she could avoid it.

"Yeah, I did. Mostly the smoke afterward. Is everything okay? Did anyone get hurt?" Maybe he'd let drop whether the pilot had made it.

"You saw it and didn't think to call anyone?"

"I couldn't get reception." She winced, because that really was lame. It was getting pretty hard to find anyplace that didn't have coverage. On the main road there was no excuse.

"Kay, what are you doing out here?"

Her parents—especially her mother and the bureau—were not primarily concerned with protecting the border from the dragons. If the dragons decided to cross, the local law enforcement agencies couldn't do much about it. That would be classified as an invasion, and Malmstrom Air Force Base, with its missiles and fighters, would take over.

Mostly, local law enforcement worked to keep people—the overly curious on the one hand, and the malicious on the other—from crossing into Dragon. Just last year, before she got her driver's license, her father had been driving her home from school when one of his deputies called him out to an arrest. Kay had lingered by the car, watching while Dad and two deputies struggled to put handcuffs on a hysterical young couple. They'd looked like hippies, a white guy and girl with long hair partly done in tangled dreadlocks. She wore a peasant skirt, combat boots, and a torn sweater. He wore what looked like army surplus fatigues. They both had huge frame backpacks with sleeping bags and mess kits slung on them. They'd hitchhiked from Ohio and had planned on sneaking across the border. They wanted to find a dragon and "partake of its ancient wisdom." They screamed at the sheriff and deputies about how they didn't have the right to keep people from crossing the border, calling them fascists.

Her father had joked that at least they could prosecute them for resisting arrest, if nothing else. Kay had thought they were weird and maybe a little crazy. They obviously didn't come from a place where you could sometimes see dragons flying on the northern horizon and where they practiced dragon-raid drills more than once a year.

People like that would be insanely jealous of Kay and her conversations with Artegal.

But more, her parents would be mortified if they knew what she'd been doing. If her parents found out, they'd report it. They would have to. She knew that. She just hadn't realized how that would feel. They'd never look at her the same way again. They'd never trust her again. She couldn't ever get caught—and there was no way the pilot would keep his mouth shut.

She waited too long to answer. Nothing was going to sound reasonable now. "Really, Dad, I was just hiking. I didn't know there was a roadblock or I would have called. I'm sorry."

They'd had enough arguments to recognize the standoff. She wasn't going to say anything else, and nothing he said would change that.

"You know the plane crashed on the other side of the border? In Dragon?" he said finally.

The tower of smoke was close enough to the river; from a different angle it may have looked like it hadn't invaded Dragon. She let him think the hesitation was shocked silence.

"What's going to happen? Do you think there'll be a fight?"

Her father leaned on the car, looked north, and shook his head. "We're doing everything we can to prevent that.

We have to assume they're doing to the same on their side."
She pressed her lips and nodded. He sounded sure, and that
was encouraging. "Now, Kay, I want you to get home. And
call your mother."

"Okay, I will." She didn't have to fake sounding nervous
and scared. Her stomach was knotted.

"I love you," he said, pursing his lips in a thin smile.

"I love you, too." She watched him return to his SUV in
her rearview mirror. He didn't drive away until she did.

She spent the rest of the way home sitting at the edge of
her seat, gripping the steering wheel hard.

As soon as she got home, she called Jon.

"Kay," he answered. "Oh my God, are you okay? Where
are you? Do you know what's happening? Do your folks
have any idea?"

She knew way more about the situation than she wanted
to. Trouble was, she couldn't tell anyone. "I just talked to
my dad. He didn't say much. Everyone's worked up."

"Where have you been? I've been trying to call you." He
sounded tense, like he'd been really worried about her.

She winced, guilty. "I'm sorry. I had my phone off."

"At a time like this? FOX News is talking invasion,
Kay."

She sat on the couch in the living room and rubbed her
hair. She was exhausted and was starting to feel the aches
and bruises where she'd been knocked around on Artegal's

back. Even with gloves, she had blisters on both hands. She needed a shower.

"Who's invading?" she said tiredly. "Them or us?"

Jon was silent for a long moment. She was about to apologize again because she knew she was sounding irrational. Then he said, "The plane crash was an accident, wasn't it?"

That made her straighten. "What do you mean?"

"It was a malfunction. The plane crashed; the pilot bailed out. It just happened to be on the wrong side of the border. The air force didn't do it on purpose, did they?"

For a moment, just a moment, it made sense. If you *wanted* to start a fight, you'd provoke the other side somehow. Just to see what they'd do. But she was tired and not thinking clearly, so she shook her head. "Is that what the conspiracy websites are saying?" She tried to make it sound like a joke.

"I guess that's crazy, isn't it?"

"Yeah."

"But no one knows what the dragons are going to do," he said.

"No." She wondered what Artegal was telling his people right now, if anything. If he were having to lie like she was. "The police have the highway closed down. They're worried."

"Can I come over?"

It would take him a little longer, but he could get here via back roads. She almost said no. The more time she spent around people, the more likely she would be to finally let it all out and tell someone about Artegal, especially with all this going on. Anything she said would be talking around the dragon. Her secret was starting to eat at her.

At the same time, the idea of hugging Jon as hard as she could made her feel warm, made her finally start to relax. "Yeah, okay. My parents are out working. It'll be good to have company."

"Okay. I'll be right over." He clicked off.

She'd have to hurry if she wanted to take that shower.

As soon as she hung up, her phone beeped another missed call from her mother. Kay didn't want to talk to her, afraid of what she would ask about the crash and how much Kay would have to lie about it, but the calls would keep coming until they connected. She called back.

"Kay, are you home now? Please tell me you're home."

Mom and Dad had probably been conferring back and forth about what she was really doing. She couldn't change her story.

"I'm home, Mom." Her mother sighed with obvious relief. Before her mother could ask more questions that she'd have to dodge, Kay launched in with her own. "Is everything okay? Do you know what's happening?"

"Oh, it's a mad house here." She must have been at the FBBE main office. Kay could hear voices, telephones, and activity in the background. "I think every newspaper and

TV station in the country has been calling us for a statement. We don't have enough people to take care of the PR and assess the situation at the same time. They've got me handling the press, and I can't keep up with it."

"What is the situation?"

Her mother sighed again, and Kay imagined her—brown hair with its scattering of gray strands coming loose from its ponytail, suit jacket looking rumpled, face lined with stress as she dashed around the office from one phone, desk, or computer to another.

"Waiting, unfortunately. We can't do much until we see what they're going to do. The biggest problem is we have no way to get in touch with the dragons to try to prevent a misunderstanding."

Kay could say, *But Mom, Artegal will talk to them. They'll know what happened because of him.* But then she'd have to explain Artegal, and she couldn't do that. She was hoping the pilot wouldn't tell anyone—or maybe no one would believe him. Maybe they'd think he hit his head on the way down or something.

Mom said, "Kay, I'm probably going to be here all night. Can you get yourself dinner? Will you be okay?"

"Yeah, Mom. Don't worry. I'll be fine." Now that she wasn't flying around on the back of a dragon. . . .

"Stay inside. I'll call you if anything else happens. Or Dad will, but he's going to be working all night, too."

"Okay."

"I love you."

Again, like she had with her father, Kay said, "I love you, too."

If nothing else, all that love told her how worried her parents were.

Jon arrived ten minutes after she finished her shower. She baked a frozen pizza for dinner, and they camped out in front of the TV watching news channels, even though no one had any new information. The pundits spouted predictions over video footage of the territory north of Silver River, the endless forest, distant peaks, and dragons wheeling above them. This far away, they were like insects fluttering, like dragonflies—maybe that was how the insect got that name. It was almost as if the cameras were waiting for the dragons to get closer. Wouldn't the networks love it if there were an attack?

Her mother was interviewed at one point. She looked harried, no makeup, her hair quickly pulled back. Even on TV, Kay could see the shadows under her eyes. The caption under her image read, ALICE WYATT, ASSISTANT DIRECTOR FOR THE FBBE IN SILVER RIVER. She gave the camera a thin-lipped frown and said, "Other than some increased flight activity, we haven't detected anything suspicious on the dragon side of the border, but we're going to continue to monitor the situation closely."

That was it, her mother's fifteen minutes of worldwide

fame, looking like she needed to sleep for twelve hours.

A little later, CNN showed a video of a group of military guys leaving a helicopter parked on the black tarmac of a runway. The camera focused in on one of them; he looked pale, tired, and the worse for wear. She recognized the pilot from the crash. They'd found him. He'd crossed the border okay and was safe.

A caption at the bottom of the screen labeled him Captain Will Conner.

Everything the news anchor said about him had to do with the "downed pilot not talking to reporters" and various "statements issued by the air force." No one said anything detailed about what had happened to him on his adventure. And no one said anything about him encountering a girl riding a dragon. Maybe he would keep silent about them.

"Hey, you okay?" Jon asked.

They were sitting on the sofa, plates with pizza crusts and empty soda cans to the side. She held the blanket draped over their laps in a death grip. Consciously trying to relax, she smoothed the blanket and rubbed her hands together. "Yeah. I guess this is stressing me out more than I thought."

"If they thought there was going to be trouble, they'd evacuate, wouldn't they? If they knew something—"

"No, I think it's okay. I think everything's going to be okay."

He took her hands in his and squeezed. She gave him

a tight-lipped smile. His hands were warm; she hadn't noticed that hers weren't until he touched her. It had gotten dark outside, and they hadn't turned on any lights. They just had the glow from the TV.

She felt suddenly nervous, her skin prickling all over, and it had nothing to do with the uncertain situation outside.

Jon leaned forward, very slowly, and kissed her. She didn't move away. If she was really that nervous, she would have turned her head, stopped him. She wasn't scared of Jon, because she trusted that he would always listen when she said no. Of course, if she kept saying no, he may not stick around. At least that was what Tam kept saying. But her heart was racing, and her hands were trembling a little. She didn't want Jon to think she was scared. She squeezed his hands back, and he kissed her again, longer this time, his mouth opening, hers opening with his.

Her hands weren't cold anymore.

She broke away to take a breath and smiled. "It almost looks like you set up this whole thing."

He looked around at the dark room, at them lounging together on the sofa. Even in the near dark she could tell he was blushing. She was close enough to feel the warmth. He shook his head.

"No, not like that. I mean, it wasn't on purpose, it just happened—"

"I'm teasing you." She gave his arm a light punch.

"If you're uncomfortable—"

"No. No, I'm not." She wasn't, she realized. Not uncomfortable, even if it was strange. *If I wanted to,* she thought. *If we wanted to go all the way, we could, right now.* But this was good, just the way it was. So she leaned against him, nestled her head on his shoulder, as he put his arm around her. They rested, just like that, and she finally relaxed. She settled into his embrace, tipping her head back to look at him. "But you'll probably want to get home before my dad gets back," she said.

Jon tensed at that, looking nervous. Kay reflected that it took some bravery to date the sheriff's daughter. Grinning, she said, "I'm teasing again."

"You sure about that? Your dad's scary."

"Not that scary." Although when he'd pulled her over this afternoon, he'd been pretty scary. He didn't look all that terrifying, but he projected attitude without ever saying a word. She'd love to learn how to do that.

A cell phone rang—Jon's, by the ringtone. His mother this time, calling to find out where he was. Kay could hear the strain in her voice over the phone. Everyone in town was probably worried.

"I have to go," he said, folding his phone shut and putting it back in his pocket.

"Yeah, she sounded worried."

"You'd think if something was going to happen, it would have happened by now," he said.

"Nobody knows what to expect. That's the problem."

He pulled his coat on, and she saw him to the door and lingered. "Thanks for coming over," she said. "It was good to see you." She took his hand, and he kissed her. That warm flush ran through her again. She could get used to this.

After he'd gone, Kay cleaned up the remains of dinner and returned to the sofa, curling up in the blanket and watching more news. Nothing changed, but she felt like she ought to be keeping vigil. Her parents were out there working. She wanted to be doing something, too.

Something besides worrying about Artegal and wondering if their secret would be discovered.

10

"Kay, honey. Wake up."

Someone shook her shoulder.

Kay sat up, bleary eyed, and brushed hair out of her face. Her mother kneeled beside the sofa. The TV was still humming with the same footage and text scrolls as earlier in the evening.

"What's wrong?" Kay said. Suddenly anxious, she knew that something had to be wrong.

"Nothing, everything's okay. I just thought you'd be more comfortable in your bed."

"Yeah, I guess. Is Dad okay?"

Mom actually smiled. "He's fine. He's on his way home. Everything's fine. Nothing's happened so far."

"I saw you on the news."

She rolled her eyes. "They didn't even let me run a brush through my hair."

"You looked fine. You sounded good."

"You, on the other hand, look beat. Did you eat something?"

"Yeah, some pizza," Kay mumbled. She didn't say anything about Jon coming over.

"Good. Get to bed, all right?"

Kay must have looked exhausted for her mother to comment. But she couldn't exactly say, *Well, of course I'm tired—I rode a dragon and dodged the air force today.*

Strangely enough, once she'd made it to bed and under the covers, she couldn't sleep at all. Her father arrived home shortly after, and sounds of conversation from the kitchen distracted her. She couldn't make out what her parents were saying, but their tones were serious. There were pots and pans and kitchen noises, probably them eating something, then footsteps down the hall, their bedroom door closing, then silence. Kay rolled over and looked at her clock. Two A.M.

She stared at the ceiling. Wondered if dragons slept.

Over the next few days, statements from the air force confirmed that the fighter was on a routine patrol when an electrical malfunction caused the pilot to veer off course and lose control completely. All planes of that type, the F-16, were now being examined to ensure that the malfunction didn't repeat. The pilot was praised for doing everything he could to keep the plane out of Dragon and for minimizing his own presence in dragon territory. Incursions by firefighting helicopters had been necessary to douse flames started by jet fuel, but once again it was hoped the dragons would understand and not take offense. The president even made a speech about peaceful coexistence and understanding and all the same lines that presidents had always gone on about. It sounded rote. How could there be peaceful coexistence when everyone was so scared? When the two sides never even talked?

They had a drill at school that week. When the alarm went off, a couple of people screamed—short, shrill, panicked—because it could have been real. Nobody joked, nobody talked as they found their places in the hall and huddled, waiting for an attack. Even the teachers, most of whom usually looked bored or annoyed during drills, seemed pale, nervous. The vice principal kept glancing out the front-door windows—against the rules, but Kay couldn't blame him. The front doors looked north.

After that night of eating pizza, watching the news, and kissing Jon, something felt different to Kay. She felt closer to him, but more uncertain, too. They never talked about it directly. Kay couldn't be sure how close they'd really come to going further, physically. "We're taking it slow. It's okay. It's totally okay," Jon kept saying, as if he had to emphasize it, afraid that she was actually nervous—when he was the one who sounded more nervous, like he was trying to convince himself. She used to be able to tell what he was trying to say. But now, was he trying to say it was okay that they were going slow, or did he really did want to go further?

On the other hand, Tam didn't have any doubt. They were in the bathroom when Kay told her what had happened. She hadn't meant to. She started by talking about the day of the plane crash.

"What were you doing out driving around?" Tam asked. Just like Kay's Dad.

"I just was. I'd been hiking."

"And your dad caught you? Oh my God, how pissed off was he?"

She shrugged. "I think he was too busy. He just sent me home. He and my mom didn't get home 'til like midnight."

"So you had all night to think of an excuse."

"Sort of. I mainly just watched the news with Jon."

A pause. Kay wished she could see Tam, but Tam was still in the stall. "Jon came over?"

Kay hesitated, because she knew she'd walked into a trap and Tam was about to pounce on her. "Yeah—"

"Wait a minute," Tam said, throwing the door to the stall open as the toilet flushed behind her. "You and Jon were home alone, your parents were gone, you were together on the sofa, and you *didn't* do it?"

"No." Kay pouted, defensive. "It was kind of in the

middle of an international crisis. Not exactly the right kind of mood." Except for all that kissing they'd done . . .

"What better time?" Tam glared while she washed her hands. "I swear, there's going to be a big war and you're going to die a virgin. Then how will you feel?"

"A lot like I do now, I bet," Kay said.

"Which is?"

"Annoyed."

"There, you see?"

Kay let the subject drop by not commenting. Jon didn't seem to mind, and that was the important thing. This was about the two of them and no one else. At least, she didn't think Jon minded. He'd have said something, wouldn't he? Wasn't it normal for guys to want to sleep with their girl-friends? She was the crazy one, according to Tam.

Arguing with Tam over whether or not to have sex was bad enough. If she and Jon started arguing about it . . . Maybe it would be just as well if the situation never changed at all.

That Saturday, Jon called Kay in the morning and asked if she wanted to go climbing. "I have to get out of the house," he said. "Away from all this news."

She knew the feeling. Her mother had been interviewed again about Dragon and the border, along with historians discussing old newsreel footage and commentators agitating either for peace or for an invasion to take back the territory with all its valuable oil reserves and mines. "How danger-ous can the dragons be?" reporters kept asking, referring to the old films from when the Silver River Treaty was nego-tiated. They could fly; they could burn entire towns with their fire. But they'd taken people by surprise last time. This time, we knew what they could do, we'd be ready for them. That's what people were saying, and the talk made Kay nervous. She didn't want to find out how dangerous the dragons could be.

Jon picked her up, and they went to a favorite spot south of town, an established sport climbing rock with perma-nent anchors—and well away from the border, thankfully. Driving, they talked about nothing in particular. School gossip, summer job prospects—both of them had worked for a rafting company the summer before and were debat-ing about returning. College, the future. It seemed so vague, especially when all Kay could really think about was whether Artegal was okay. Whether Captain Conner had told anyone about them.

Then, fortunately, there was the climb, and that took all of her focus. Other problems slipped away.

It seemed strange to be using her climbing gear for actual climbing. In fact, she was seriously out of practice. Her hands cramped, and her calluses had faded. It was like learning to do this all over again. Jon had to talk her through tough spots once or twice. In terms of excitement, rock climbing left something to be desired after you'd flown on the back of a dragon. Maybe her mind wasn't on the climb after all.

It was nice to be outside: The day was unusually warm, with a blazing sun heating the crisp winter air and making the snow on the trees sparkle. She wore sweats and a T-shirt, and was sweating from exertion. The warmth felt good.

When a jet raced overhead, roaring and leaving a contrail behind it, they paused, watching it. It moved parallel to the border—just a patrol. Nothing unusual.

Kay still had to swallow her heart out of her throat.

Jon was on the ground below her, holding her belay line while she clung to the craggy rock face, resting a moment. Finally, looking at him, she called, "I'm coming down," because her limbs were shaking and she didn't want to keep going. Kay braced on her feet and sat in her harness while rappelling down with Jon's help. On the ground, she absently brushed chalk off her hands. Jon was still looking up, where the jet's contrail was dissipating.

"Have your parents heard anything?" he asked.

"No," she said. "It's all just wait and see."

"Even if they did attack the town," Jon said, "it's not like we're all going to die. We can run. We can hide out, fight back. That's what people did in the Middle Ages before the dragons disappeared, right?"

So, neither of them was really thinking about climbing. She'd gone almost a half an hour without thinking about the dragons and what could happen, and in a moment Jon had come up with the worst case scenario.

"Can we talk about something else?" She untied the rope from her harness and handed it to Jon for his turn up the rock face.

"Sorry. It's just kind of hard not thinking about it, you know?"

Kay didn't want to fight the dragons. She didn't want to see those old films come to life, with the fires, bombs, and crowds of people running in fear. It would mean never talking with Artegal again, never flying again. She didn't want to have to be afraid of him. But it was like her mother kept saying—they didn't really know anything about the dragons. Could Kay say she knew anything about dragons, or just Artegal?

"What if we could talk to them? I keep thinking we ought to find a way to talk to them." She was blushing. Talking around the issue, so close to blurting out what she'd been doing.

"But how?" he said.

"I don't know. Maybe someone should just . . . walk across the border." She'd never been so close to telling anyone.

Jon shook his head. "Somebody would shoot you. Or eat you."

If she could trust anyone with the secret, it would be Jon. He wouldn't tell anyone, she was sure. But she wasn't sure how he would react. He certainly wouldn't be happy. But he might not be curious, either. He might freak out, and he might tell someone—for Kay's own good, to protect her. He'd tell someone for all the right reasons.

"I don't think there's going to be a war," she said.

"Why not? Does your mom know something?"

"No, I just think it would be too weird."

"Yeah, it would," he said. "Hey, can you hand me a little chalk? I think I'm out."

She scooped a handful and handed it to him. She rubbed the chalk on his hand, and he squeezed her fingers before pulling away.

Hooking the belay to her harness, she anchored for him, studying him as he knotted the other end of the rope to his harness and started his climb. The muscles of his arms flexed under his T-shirt, his strong fingers keeping a sure grip on the rock. His skin shone with sweat, and his face flushed with the effort. His smile was wry. He looked really good. She was lucky, dating one of the best-looking guys at school. Lucky to be dating someone who thought it was cool to go rock climbing on a warm winter day.

Silver River settled back to normal, mostly. Most of the news vans and crews that had arrived to cover the situation packed up and left. The sense of relief was plain—people tended to smile a little too big, laugh a little too hard, for the next week or so. A few more cynical people said that the dragons were just biding their time, lulling the town into a false sense of security, and that the air force ought to bomb them first, before it was too late. Everyone else felt like they'd avoided a disaster. They could still see dragons flying around the mountaintops, far to the north.

She counted down the days to the next meeting with Artegal. She was grateful that she hadn't been grounded or had her driver's license confiscated after her run-in with her father. This time, she carefully constructed her story of going hiking. Asked permission in advance. Promised not to shut off her cell phone. Promised to keep an eye skyward and come home at the first sign of trouble. That said something, if her mother was still worried about trouble.

Alibi in place, she raced to the trailhead and the usual meeting place.

There was a chance he wouldn't be there. She had no idea how the crash and its aftermath had played out on his side of the border. That was part of why she was so anxious to talk to him. What had the dragons really thought of it all? The pundits on the news shows could only speculate.

The creek was mostly frozen. Icicles, lattices, and sprays lined the bottom of the log bridge. On this sunny day, the whole scene sparkled like diamonds. Kay crossed the bridge, then paced to keep warm, bundled up in her parka, hands in her pockets.

If he didn't show, she couldn't even leave him a note, on the chance someone might find it. If he didn't meet her, maybe that would be for the best. Maybe they'd both be safer if he stayed away and they never met again. But then she'd always wonder. She'd always worry that he'd been grounded, whatever dragons did to ground someone. But her heart ached at the thought of never flying again, of feeling the high wind scouring her face, and of looking down on the world as if it were a map.

She heard a brushing sound, like a branch dragged across soft earth. The creak of trees, like in a wind—but there wasn't any wind. It was a dragon moving on foot through a forest.

Then Artegal appeared, his head leading, snaking forward on his long neck, arms and wings pulling him along. She had almost forgotten how bright his scales were, the way the mottled sunlight played off them, the way they shimmered in light and shadow, like sunlight on the ice. Her heart raced in fear at the sight of him all over again.

He saw her, blinked, and sighed, a noise like a growl. "You came."

Her smile was thin. "So did you. I guess that means things aren't so bad?"

"Elders understand. An accident, not an invasion." He rumbled a growl, qualifying the statement. "Was a long argument, though."

"Did you tell them? Did you talk to them about what happened?"

He settled on his haunches, pulling his wings close, and his lids grew heavy. Almost like a wince, Kay thought. Like he was trying to decide what to say. "I wasn't there. Not old enough."

"So you couldn't—" She stopped herself. She couldn't expect Artegal to have an influence on the dragon elders any more than she could influence her own government.

"I did what I could," he said, fog curling from his nostrils as he sighed. "And you? Did the pilot tell?"

"No," she said. "No one's said anything about it."

He grumbled, in either agreement or relief, or was simply sighing again. He looked at her, looked at the sky. "What now?"

She knew what was probably the safest thing to do— stop doing this. Stop meeting at all. Hope nothing more happened. But that didn't feel like the right thing to do. "My mom works for border enforcement, and the thing that frustrated her most is that we didn't have a way to talk to you guys, to explain what happened. She thought if we could just explain, everything would be all right. Instead, we sat around waiting for something bad to happen, for you to attack. If something like this happens again, we can keep talking. You and me. We have to."

The lip curled, scales flashing. "Agreed." Then he purred. "And the flying?"

She'd been thinking about that far too much. Because she was pretty sure she had the same gleam in her eyes that he had in his. "I don't see how we can get away with that again. I don't know how we got away with it before."

"You don't want to," he said.

"No, I do," she said quickly. But the consequences. It wasn't the falling off, the getting in trouble, the lying she was having to do to keep this secret. This was so much more than staying out after curfew or getting pulled over by her sheriff father. This involved the rest of the world. "But if we got caught . . . I'm not sure people would understand. That we're—"

"That we're friends?"

She scuffed her feet in the dirt and looked up to the bright blue sky, wanting to go back there. There was still so much she hadn't seen. But she didn't know what she was getting into.

"My mentor would understand," Artegal said. "Others will, too. So we should practice. In case."

"In case?"

"In case we're needed."

She couldn't imagine when that would be or what it would entail. But she remembered the first few times she went climbing, how she didn't make any progress at all, and how her hands and arms hurt so much, she cried. But she'd practiced, until it came naturally. Artegal was right. They had to practice, if for no other reason than they may need this someday.

That was a good excuse, anyway. Really, she just couldn't wait to fly with the dragon again.

11

Kay returned to the book, *Dracopolis*, continuing to try to ferret out some kind of translation. She had decided, mostly by looking at the pictures and the kind way the dragons and people regarded each other, and the angry way the men who carried the swords and spears appeared toward the end of the book, that the person who had written and drawn this had loved dragons, and hated when people fought with them. Maybe the author had some advice for a person who lived in a world where humans and dragons feared each other.

Copying out the Latin from a page that seemed to recount when the fires and wars started, she found a word she recognized: *virgo*. And variations: *virginem*, *virgine*. From the pictures surrounding the text, she could work out a meaning before she found a translation.

There was a sacrifice. A woman in a white gown—one of those characteristic medieval figures, flattened, with large, oval eyes, a tilted head, thin curving limbs—stood on a platform raised up in a clearing at the edge of a forest. Iron shackles, painted black, bound her to the platform. Her brown hair flowed loose down her back. She was neither smiling nor frowning, and it was hard to tell if she was really so calm or if she was simply a flat medieval drawing incapable of showing emotion.

Amid the trees, the dragon came for her. His mouth was open and filled with sharp teeth.

The virgin sacrifice. They really did it. So, according to this scene, Artegal was supposed to be *eating* her, not flying with her. But Kay looked, double-checked words in the online Latin dictionary, and didn't find anything on the page that meant "eating."

It was all so vague.

She studied the pages with references to flying. If she ever were caught and needed to defend herself, maybe she could bring the book. Work up some story about doing a history project. *That* would go over well.

In the meantime, they flew again. It was an all-day activity, because of how far into the hills Kay had to hike in order to reach their valley. After flying for an hour, Artegal walked back to the border as close as he could, and Kay hiked the rest of the way to her Jeep, which was hidden on a turn-off near a little-used dirt road—with all the ropes and gear slung over her shoulders. Exhausted, she then had to call Jon and tell him she was too tired to go out on a Saturday night. He'd sounded hurt and asked questions about what she'd been doing, why she was tired. She couldn't answer, of course, and she couldn't blame him for being grouchy. She kept assuring him that she really wanted to see him, but she wouldn't be good company. The excuses sounded lame, but what could she tell him? The other alternative was to stop going to see Artegal, which she wasn't going to do.

Two weeks later, she and Artegal flew again. Kay felt she was starting to get good. Or at least better. She didn't scramble every time he swooped or dived. He started to be able to do corkscrews and loops without her yelping and wrapping the ropes around her hands in a death grip. She learned to let the force of movement keep her steady. By balancing and steadying herself instead of gripping as hard as she could, the flights were much easier on her hands. She stopped getting blisters.

Part of it was Artegal simply loved flying, and so was willing to be very patient with her, was willing to fly and circle as she grew more confident and secure. He said that not all dragons loved to fly. Some of the older ones stopped being able to. They tended to stay underground, guarding hordes, raising the young. Kay realized that the human military could never be sure of the number of dragons by counting the ones that flew. They based their estimates of dragon population on this. She wondered how far off those estimates were.

The *Dracopolis* manuscript described a system of communication used by dragons and their human riders. Kay had worked out some of it, a few phrases, including a section admonishing the reader that riding dragons was not like riding horses and you couldn't use bits or bridles. That seemed clear to Kay. Why would you need a bridle when you could just talk? Who could even contemplate putting a bridle on a head that large, and how did you talk a dragon into putting a bit in its gigantic mouth without it eating you? But in the air, dragons couldn't always hear, so in ancient times riders would use a rope with knots tied in it and stretched across the dragon's back. By pressing the knots into the scales, a rider could get the dragon's attention and communicate simple ideas: *Look left, turn right, I'm in trouble.* Kay made up a rope like this for her and Artegal—it had three knots, one for left, one for right, and one in the middle to get his attention. They tested it and found their own code to use.

In mid March, they made their third flight after the jet crash. Life had gotten back to normal, everyone breathing sighs of relief because it seemed the dragons understood what had happened and didn't hold it against the humans. It made everyone feel better because it meant that maybe the dragons weren't so alien after all, and maybe the humans didn't have to be afraid so much.

Kay could have told them that.

But the jets came again.

Kay and Artegal were in their valley, circling, enjoying the first day in weeks that was warm enough to melt snow. Flying, Kay felt so much closer to the sun, so much warmer. They'd had a lazy practice, and Artegal dipped lower, preparing to land.

Far overhead, far distant, a mechanical roar echoed. She could feel Artegal snort more than she could hear him, a vibration deep in his lungs. A questioning sound, confused. But Kay recognized the noise—the roar of a jet engine. She looked up, scanning the sky, searching for the plane. Hard to tell how close it was or where it was going, because sound was unreliable when it came from something moving that fast. It seemed far away. She hoped it was far away.

Artegal climbed, swooping upward in a wide loop, craning his neck, looking for the intruder along with Kay. She grew worried—the engine sounded loud. Probably just a trick of the air. No plane would cross the border into Dragon air space, especially after the crash. They needed to hide, just in case.

"Artegal, we should get out of here!" she cupped her hand and yelled. She pressed the left and right knots in the rope across his shoulders, which meant, *We need to land*. He cocked his head; she couldn't tell if he'd heard her.

Then, the plane sped overhead. A narrow triangle, sharp nose, angled wings, engines in back—a jet fighter shaped like an arrowhead. It didn't make a sound; the roar followed a moment later, which meant it was traveling very, very fast—faster than its own sound.

Artegal roared. Kay had never heard him make a sound like that. It surged through his whole body; the vibrations rattled her teeth. His lungs worked like bellows under her, and the sound echoed through the valley, like thunder, like a mountain falling. The appearance of the plane had startled him. It may even have scared him. She could only tuck her head in and hold on as he dived, flattening his wings to streamline his body and increase his speed.

He pulled up as he reached the treetops and skimmed along the tops of them, up the side of the hill, over and out of the valley. He kept going, beating his wings hard to speed up. Level now, somewhat stable, Kay had a chance to see where the plane had gone. The plane was on the wrong side of the border, and this time it looked to be on purpose. But that was crazy.

The jet had looped around and was following them.

It had seen her. That was the only reason why it had turned. The pilot had seen her and Artegal together and had to investigate. The dragon was growling with every breath; he'd seen the jet following them. They both knew he couldn't outrun it.

But she didn't expect Artegal to slow down.

The whole sky seemed to be filled with the mechanical roar of the jet. It echoed and thundered like Artegal's roar had, but felt different. It had no breath of living air behind it.

The dragon's flight had become almost lazy. He barely moved his wings, and the trees passing below them slowed to a crawl. Kay wanted to scream at him—why wasn't he doing something? Why wasn't he doing more? But his strategy became clear when the jet roared past and raced far beyond them.

Artegal wheeled, changing direction and flapping back the way they'd come, back to the valley where maybe they could hide before the jet had time to loop back around and find them.

But the jet did a flip in midair. Artegal stopped and hovered. The plane overshot them—then it pivoted, starting another long loop and simply flipping until it faced backward and shot ahead, barely losing momentum. Kay had been watching jets patrol her whole life, and she'd never seen one do that. They weren't supposed to be able to do that. The dragons had always been more maneuverable.

Artegal panicked. He twisted in midair, wings flapping, shifting, until he launched in yet another direction. Then he flew, straight and fast, not wavering—away from the border, to what he thought of as home and safety. He roared again, and for the first time Kay saw the beast of legend, the dragon that had haunted human tales for thousands of years. No wonder people had been surprised that dragons could speak. A dragon flying over a medieval village, roaring like this, maybe breathing fire, wouldn't notice people scattering like ants before him. She was just a piece of fluff clinging to his scaled hide, helpless. The direction that meant safety to Artegal meant a greater danger to her.

The jet, for whatever reason, did not follow them any farther into dragon territory. Again, it did its strange midair flip to match Artegal's direction, but after following a mile or two, it looped back and rocketed away, south and across the border to human territory.

Kay was relieved. But she couldn't get Artegal to slow down, to consider landing. He wouldn't look at her no matter how hard she leaned on the knots in the ropes.

He just kept going, as if terrified of the monster that had chased him.

She huddled on his back and tried to figure out what to do. Really, though, she wouldn't be able to stop him no matter what he did. She was so small and weak.

Maybe this was why people had started killing dragons. People didn't like being helpless, and some people weren't very good at being friends. So people and dragons fought. Now, both sides were too scared to even look at each other. Artegal seemed like he was going to fly all the way to the distant mountains before stopping. If that happened, she was pretty much screwed.

Her parents would never know what happened to her. She'd never see Tam again. She'd never see Jon.

She got up on her hands and knees and pounded her fist on Artegal's shoulder, putting her whole body into it. He had to feel that—scales flinched under her hand. Then she screamed, "Stop!"

He snorted, shuddered, as if waking up from a nightmare. He spread his wings, which caught the air like sails, and braked, dropping straight down to a clearing below. Kay closed her eyes and sighed, breathing out thanks. Once she was on the ground, she could run. On the ground she could do anything. It was only a hundred feet up that she was helpless.

Hind legs forward, he slammed to the earth, and she slid across his back, yanking hard against her harness. Instead of folding his wings back, he rested them on the ground. His neck slouched, and he was breathing heavily. Exhausted, maybe. Still frightened.

Hands shaking, she unhooked herself and slid down his shoulder. The ground rocked under her. Her legs wobbled, and she sank. It was as if she'd ridden a roller coaster times a million. She sat there, trying to breathe, reminding herself that she was supposed to be running away. She was facing a wall of silvery scales, and a great gray wing was tented almost directly above her.

He raised his head on its long, snakelike neck. She looked back into those onyx eyes. She scrambled backward through dirt and pine needles. She didn't mean to, but she saw those eyes, that mouth that could close over her in one bite, remembered how scared she was and wanted to get away.

Artegal lowered his neck and head, pressed his body to the ground. Pulled his tail tight around him, making himself smaller. He looked like a rock now, instead of a monster. This was a different kind of frightened.

He said, voice low, "Panicked. Didn't think of you."

He was apologizing. This was dragon body language she'd never seen before. Almost like a dog with its tail between its legs.

Kay stopped. Her heart was still racing; she was still having trouble catching her breath. But she didn't want to run away anymore. This wasn't his fault. He'd been frightened—of course he had, they both had. Like he'd said, no one had ever done this before. They were still learning.

"Are you okay?" she asked, her voice shaking.

He drew a couple of deep, steadying breaths. Then he said, "That plane. Flew like a dragon." And that was what terrified him. "What is it?"

"I don't know. I've never seen anything like it. I could ask—my mom might know something. The bureau must be *freaking*." She stood, brushed dirt off her hands, looked around. She had no idea where she was. North of home. That was all. "I have to get back. I have to get back right now." She was *miles* from the border. This was completely different from being able to hop over the creek to get back home.

"The plane. Saw us. Yes?"

It hadn't just seen them, it had followed them. "Yeah."

"What will they do?" he said.

"I don't know. It depends on if they figure out who I am. I have to go back and find out." She was going to get in so much trouble. She could just feel it.

"We should stay away from the border," he said. "For a little while."

And how long was a little while? A lump stuck in her throat, because this felt so final. A real good-bye this time. She didn't want to go, not knowing when she'd be able to come back. "Then . . . then I guess I'd better get going. Let's get that stuff off you—"

He sat up, his neck curled, his usual pose. "Will carry you. As far as I can."

After his panicking and flying blind, she may have hesitated ever riding him again. But she didn't. It wasn't his fault—they'd both been scared. Besides, she could either ride him or hike for hours with climbing gear slung on her back.

They didn't fly again; Artegal carried her on foot. Compared to the headlong flight, it was slow going. The motion wasn't a smooth glide, but rocking that almost made her sick. It took a lot more effort for him, and he was getting tired. She was going to be much later than expected getting home. If there was any kind of an uproar going on about the jet, her parents would be livid.

As soon as she recognized the lay of the land, the slope of hills, she tapped Artegal's shoulder. "I can walk from here, I think," she called.

But he went on farther, until she could hear the rushing water of the creek at the border. "Here," he said.

The care he'd taken made her life a little easier and his harder. She smiled grimly. "Thanks."

Quickly, because the sun was now fading into afternoon, she undid the knots of his harness and coiled the rope.

"You'll walk back?"

"For a time," he said. "Until I won't be seen."

"Be careful."

"You too."

He had turned to go when she said, "Artegal? What happens if we don't see each other again?" For whatever reason, whatever the fallout after this new plane, and whatever its pilot said about seeing a girl riding a dragon.

Artegal thought for a moment. She might have expected denials, assurances that surely that wouldn't happen, that this would blow over and they would see each other again. But he didn't do that. That's what a human being would have done.

"Then we will remember. Tell stories, so others know it's possible for us to be friends. Keep the book safe. Pass it on, if it will help."

She nodded, trying to convince herself that nothing would change. "Okay."

Once again, they hiked away from each other. In moments, he was gone. She couldn't even hear him anymore.

She focused on her own journey.

Even though she wasn't across the border yet, she was close enough that she thought she was safe. She let her guard down, just a little.

Then she heard voices.

12

Human voices echoed through the trees ahead. Kay couldn't make out what they were saying nor could she tell exactly where they were, but they were definitely looking for something. She dropped to a crouch at the base of a tree, hiding as well as she could, just in case.

She took a chance and found her cell phone. Muffling the sound, she checked for messages. One, from her mom, an hour ago.

"Kay, something's happened, there might be trouble at the border, so I need you to get home right away. Call me as soon as you get this."

She wouldn't call until she was back in her Jeep and driving away from here. But she couldn't do that until those people left. For whatever reason, it seemed the pilot who'd crashed hadn't told anyone that he'd seen Kay and Artegal, but the pilot of this new plane must have reported it. And now, people were looking for her. Kay wasn't used to hearing people this far out—no one came here, that was the point. Who were they? Military, police maybe? Her dad? She really didn't want to see him right now. She didn't want to have to explain all this. She hiked along the border until she couldn't hear them anymore.

She found a narrow place with stepping stones where she could cross. Once she was on the right side of the border, nobody could say anything, even if someone caught her. But if she showed up with wet boots, people would ask questions.

Safely away from Dragon, she ran straight through the woods, back to the trailhead where she'd parked her car before the searchers could find her and ask what she was doing out here by herself.

She threw her car into gear and drove. A few miles away, about halfway to home, she pulled over, gripped the wheel, and caught her breath. Her heart was racing as if she'd been running. But she was safe. Nobody was looking for her.

When she was breathing a little more normally, she found her phone and called her mother. It rang once and went to voice mail.

"Hi, Mom. Sorry I didn't get your call, but I'm on

the way home right now. I'm okay." She hoped that was good enough.

Back home, she left the climbing gear in the car. She didn't want anyone asking about it.

Her mom was at the dining room table. Her laptop, papers, books—work—were spread all over it, and she was talking on her cell phone.

"Yes, of course I've seen the photos. They're supposed to be classified, but I think everyone and their goddamn dog has seen them. CNN'll probably have them next." A pause. "No, I can't explain them. If I could, I would. Clearly." Another pause. She seemed to be arguing with someone. "I'm home because I'm sick of talking to the press. Look, in this day and age you can't hide something like this. That jet crossed the border, and everyone knows it."

She hung up without saying good-bye.

"Mom?"

"Oh, Kay, thank God." Her mother looked exhausted. She ran a hand through her hair, which was loose, limp, in need of washing. "Are you okay? Deputy Kalbach saw your Jeep way north. Were you hiking? What were you doing? Are you okay?"

"Yeah, I went hiking. I'm fine. I saw the jet." It wasn't exactly a lie. Kay sighed a little because her mother seemed more concerned with the jet crossing than with what her daughter had been doing.

135

"Everybody saw the jet," she said. "The last one may have been an accident, but this one was a blatant border violation. The air force should know better; they ought to know better."

"Then why'd they do it?"

She smiled a thin, ironic smile. "I have some ideas, but they're not politically correct and I'm not allowed to say them to the media."

"That jet—it's new, isn't it? I haven't seen anything like it before."

"That's right. I think since the dragons didn't react to the crash last month, they're testing the border. They've got this fancy new plane, and they think maybe the dragons won't do anything about it. But I can't say that, because that means, or at least it suggests . . . never mind." She shook her head, shrugging the subject away.

"That maybe the first crash wasn't an accident," Kay said softly. It made sense. Of course the press would figure it out. The military and government could deny it all they wanted. The pundits would still talk, and people would still make assumptions.

"Don't go repeating that to anyone with a camera," Mom said. "The official line they're trying to feed people is 'A navigation error caused the pilot to drift temporarily off course.'"

There was nothing drifting about that jet. Kay had been there; she'd seen it up close. But she couldn't tell her mother that.

Kay sat at the table and looked over the mass of paperwork.

When her mom didn't send her away—Kay assumed this was all classified—she looked more closely. Emails showed on the laptop screen. The folders looked like case files, some of them old. Records of military patrols from the last sixty years. And photos, eight-by-ten, black-and-white printouts. Kind of blurry, as if they were taken from a distance at high speed. As if they were taken by a jet's surveillance camera.

They showed a silvery-gray dragon and a tiny human perched on its back. Blurry, unidentifiable. Kay felt herself flush, skin burning to her ears. She shook the feeling away and tried to keep her heart from racing. Tried to act surprised.

"What's this?" She showed the picture to her mother.

Her mom took the picture away from her, put it with the others, and gathered them into a folder. "That's even bigger news than the jet. Looks like someone's been having a little fun across the border. Don't tell *anyone* you saw these, okay?"

"Oh my gosh," Kay said, and hoped it sounded convincing. "Who?"

"If I knew that, I'd send the FBI, the National Guard, and your father to arrest his ass. Unfortunately, we don't have any way of identifying him. I don't suppose you saw anything while you were out?"

Him. So they thought it was a guy. Kay almost sighed with relief. Instead, she had to lie fast. "No, I didn't see anything."

Brow furrowed, her mother studied the folder. "I just want to know how someone walks across the border and talks a dragon into letting him ride around on its back. Or maybe it was the dragon's idea."

"Maybe it was both," Kay said, and flinched when her mother looked sharply at her. Blushing, she continued, hoping it sounded like innocent speculation. "Maybe they talked about it. Maybe they're, you know, friends."

After a pause, Mom said, her tone sardonic, "I suppose that would explain it." She set the folder aside.

Kay felt as if she'd escaped a trap. "What are you going to do about it?"

"Until we figure out who it is, there's not a whole lot we can do. Except keep better watch on the border. Obviously."

Kay realized her mother probably had not had the best day ever. "I can cook dinner. Do you want me to make something?"

The look of relief and gratitude on her mom's face startled her. Making dinner was such a little thing in the end.

"That'd be great," she said. "God, I don't even know if we have anything to cook, I haven't been to the store in weeks."

"There's always pasta."

Her mother smiled. Then her phone rang again. She took a deep breath and answered it. Kay could tell from the tension in her mom's voice that she was barely keeping her temper in check.

"Yes, sir. No, we don't have any more leads on who the

trespasser is. Yes, I've considered that the suspect isn't crossing the border, but is living over there. Well, sir, how do you propose investigating that possibility without violating the border?" Her voice had become shrill, and she took a breath before continuing. "I'm sorry, sir."

Making dinner wasn't enough, Kay thought, pouring a jar of pasta sauce into a pot to simmer on the stove. If she really wanted to help her mother, she'd tell. She'd tell her everything.

Then what would happen? Kay couldn't imagine. And that was why, in the end, she kept quiet.

13

The next day at dawn, three dragons perched on a cliff ledge less than a mile from the border. The sentinels stood upright, wings tucked close, faces turned toward human lands, barely moving. One of them would shift a hind claw or stretch its neck for a moment. One was a deep ocean blue, shimmering to black and gray as the light shifted. One was green, the color of a cartoon dragon, like you'd expect a dragon to be, except the green turned lighter and lighter, almost becoming a creamy yellow on its legs and belly. The third was mottled brown, camouflaged like a lizard. CNN kept a box in the upper right corner of its broadcast showing the scene, just in case they did something. News crews returned and took over Silver River.

Network commentators couldn't say enough.

Kay kept watching the dragons, noticing how they were different from Artegal—this one a little stouter, this one's tail a little shorter, this one larger. She wondered at how many different colors there were. In *Dracopolis*, the dragons had been drawn in at least a dozen colors, every pigment the artist had. Did a dragon inherit its color from its parents? Was it random? What did a dragon's color say about it, if anything?

Jon called her early. "I'm not going to school. Mom and Dad want me to stay home. Just in case."

"Just in case of what?" Kay said.

"I don't know." He sounded frustrated, not actually excited about getting a day off school. "It's like they think it's the end of the world or something."

Maybe it was. But the dragons were just sitting there, watching. "Maybe the dragons just want to remind us they're out there."

"What do your parents say?"

"Mom's pretty stressed out. She left really early. She started getting calls as soon as the dragons showed up."

"I'm sorry I won't be there. I really wanted to see you."

In case it was the end of the world, she thought. So they could be together. But surely things couldn't be that bad.

"If they were going to do something, they'd have done it already," she said, trying to convince herself.

"Maybe we can get together this evening, assuming my

parents let me out of the house."

Kay's father hadn't left yet. They had breakfast together—juice, toast, cereal—and she told him about Jon's call.

"So, you going to let me stay home?" she finished.

Grinning, her father explained. "If the sheriff's daughter doesn't go to school, people will think the worst. It'll be mass hysteria."

She hadn't looked at it like that. It was a little unfair, in her opinion. She pouted. "I'm not that important."

Jack Wyatt got a funny look on his face, a kind of half smile, furrowed brow, and sad gaze. It lasted only a moment. It was gone before Kay could ask what was wrong.

Then he looked into his cereal bowl with his usual amused expression. "I guess you lost the parent lottery. Sorry, kiddo."

"It shouldn't matter that I'm your daughter. I should be able to do what I want to. Right?" Like speed on the highway, like stay out late with her boyfriend . . .

"Kay, after high school you can move away to where nobody knows you're the sheriff's daughter. Until then, you're stuck with it. And if being the sheriff's daughter means that maybe you can make a difference, like showing people there's nothing to get in a panic over, don't you think you ought to do it?"

This was a long-running argument, the unfairness of being Jack Wyatt's daughter. If she really hated it that much, she supposed she could have run away from home.

But she didn't hate it that much.

She sighed. "I'll just have to go out and be a role model then, won't I?"

"That's the spirit," he said, smiling.

A lot of kids weren't at school. Their parents apparently thought it was the end of the world. In first period, a third of the seats were empty, but class went on as usual.

Tam showed up.

Kay said, "You couldn't convince your mom it was the end of the world?"

"I didn't think of it," she grumbled. "I bet I could have. And you?"

Kay took on a fake-official tone of voice. "As the sheriff's daughter, I'm a role model to the community." She rolled her eyes.

"Wow. Sorry. So that's why you never speed."

In the cafeteria at lunchtime, the librarian had brought in a TV on a cart and turned it to the news. The room was quieter than usual, and not just because so many people were gone. Conversation was subdued.

The three dragons hadn't moved.

Someone in a uniform came on the TV. Labeled General somebody-or-other, he'd just arrived at Malmstrom Air Force Base from the Pentagon to deal with the crisis. Kay couldn't hear what he said.

The news didn't say anything about photographs showing someone riding a dragon. Despite her mother's fears, the pictures hadn't leaked yet.

"All those drills we do," Tam said, watching Kay watch the TV, "I never thought we might actually have to do it for real."

Kay shook her head, tried to think positive. "We're not there yet."

For days, the dragon sentinels didn't move. They might have been statues perched on the mountainside. Some people wondered if they were really the same dragons, if maybe new ones arrived to stand watch while no one was looking. But someone was looking at them constantly, and they didn't move, didn't eat. Dragons, somebody on one of the news shows said, were timeless. They'd reappeared after World War II, just as they'd always been, unchanging. They could sit on that mountain forever, looking down on Silver River. Kay noticed that much of what people said about dragons on TV wasn't based on reality, but on old stories, half-baked legends, and old cultural memories rather than real knowledge. She kept wanting to argue with people.

The military issued a statement supposedly explaining the new jet and why it had crossed the border, and the international coalition issued a statement advising caution regarding the border, without outright condemning what had happened. The dragon territory border on the Taymyr Peninsula in Siberia had remained quiet. There was a press conference, which Kay watched live on TV because her mother was there and called, telling her to watch. Her mom sounded agitated on the phone—more so than usual—but she wouldn't tell Kay what was wrong and hung up quickly.

The guy behind the microphone was almost a stereotype: broad shoulders, square jaw, balding, with a hawkish, hooded gaze. He wore a blue air force uniform decked out with insignia. GENERAL MORGAN H. BRANIGAN, the TV caption said. The Pentagon guy who'd arrived a few days ago to make everything better.

For the first five minutes, he read from a written statement explaining the new jet: an experimental fighter called the F-22, designed for maneuverability and speed, exceeding all expectations, and so on. What he didn't say, but what was clear, was that this was a jet sixty years in the making, a plane specifically designed to be able to hold its own in flight against dragons. His staff presented visuals: drawings, a poster showing simple schematics, a video.

Then, with the might of the air force's new tool displayed behind him, the general announced, "An aircraft this unique requires special consideration. We would hope to negotiate with our neighbors about the use of portions of this territory—portions they are not using—in order to fully test our new aircraft."

So, the plane accidentally crossed the border because it needed more room to practice? Kay might have bought it if the guy didn't look like he *wanted* a war.

The general stopped talking, and the reporters shouted questions that he didn't answer. Kay spotted her mother off to the side, arms crossed, looking surly. Her pantsuit was rumpled, and Kay wondered when was the last time anyone had done laundry. The stress must have been just killing her.

Everyone made it home for dinner that night. Kay's mother was furious. She went through the motions of making food—pasta again—but slammed the fridge door, cupboard doors, and pots on the stove. Kay made a salad—poured it out of the bag and into a bowl, really—and tried to stay out of the way.

"They're not telling us everything," her mother said.

"It looks to me like they're poking a wasp nest to see what comes out," said Dad, as he sat at the table and skimmed the newspaper.

Mom dropped the bag of pasta on the counter and put her hands on her hips. "That's the problem. The military doesn't think they're going to respond. They don't think the dragons are actually going to do anything, no matter what the coalition says about it."

"And what do you think?" Dad said.

"I'm not paid to think, apparently," Mom said, and slammed an empty jar of sauce into the trash.

When they were all finally sitting around the table with food on their plates, Dad asked Kay how school was, and for once she rambled on about classes and grades, eager to change the subject until her mother calmed down.

Kay knew she was getting only half the story. She knew the dragons were talking about this as well, and she was desperate to talk to Artegal about it, call him up on the cell phone, tell him what was going on here. Although, it occurred to her that someone like General Branigan would call that spying.

She and her father cleaned up while her mom went to take a shower and lie down. She hadn't gotten much sleep over the last couple of days, and Jack quietly urged her out of the kitchen. She touched Kay's shoulder as she passed, as if needing the contact for reassurance or for balance.

The only useful thing Kay could do was load the dishwasher, so she did.

Her father was usually laid-back. It was hard to read him. But there was a tension in the room, as if he were worried. Kay wondered what he was thinking and didn't know how to ask. By way of observation, she said, "She's really upset."

He was sealing leftovers into plastic tubs. He didn't look up but smiled his wry, thin-lipped smile. The small-town sheriff smile, as she thought of it. Like he'd give the richest guy in town—maybe the Hollywood star who owned a ranch twenty miles south—just before writing him a speeding ticket.

"She's upset because the military is kind of telling her

that her job doesn't matter anymore," he said. "The military's snubbing the bureau and the coalition."

It made sense, because her mom's whole job was to protect the border, and this jet had crossed it as if it weren't there, and wanted to keep crossing it.

"She's just tired," Dad added, and he patted Kay's shoulder, too. Rather than comforting her, the gestures made her more worried. This wasn't normal, and nothing was the way it should be.

The news channels got tired of showing the same footage of the dragons not doing anything, though the image still enthralled Kay. She found herself staring at it, moving closer to the TV to see it better, waiting, hoping the reptilian statues would do something. She wondered what they were thinking, what they felt about the human town they gazed over.

But the channels cut away to do what they called in-depth reporting. Instant history they used to fill time, showing mini documentaries and historical film clips, reviewing the background that had led to this moment. Kay had seen a lot of this in school, in history class. History classes at Silver River High maybe spent a little more time on the subject than schools in other places. It was history that lived within view, every day.

Kay remembered one of the old film clips from a documentary—the first footage of the dragons' return, after they'd faded into myth hundreds of years before.

Black-and-white, scratchy, shaky, the footage hardly seemed real. It showed dragons in Anchorage, Alaska, right after the war. Two of them, as large as airplanes, flew back and forth over the city, mouths open, heads up. The film didn't have sound, but clearly, they were screaming. No one had known where they came from. Later, people speculated that they must have been hibernating in the far north for hundreds of years. Anchorage was just the first place with any kind of population they arrived at. No one believed it at first. The war had just finished, so when civil air defense spotted large figures swooping in, dark shapes against the sky, they thought of Japanese fighters. But as they came closer, it was clear the figures had long tails that curled and waved, and translucent wings that stretched behind long, slender fingers. The two of them landed on the mucky coast that lined the city, roared in what had to be anger, and spat flames from gaping, fang-filled mouths. They set fire to a section of the city. The weathered wood buildings burned quickly. No one was killed.

Then they flew away before the army could respond. The planes tried to follow them, but the dragons flew faster.

No one believed the reports until more dragons were spotted, flying down the Pacific coast to Vancouver, Seattle, San Francisco, and west to the Soviet Union, Korea, Japan. They were seen in Siberia, Norway, Iceland. Dozens of them.

All the aircraft involved in World War II were still on

alert, and they confronted what was seen as a new threat. There were battles, violent skirmishes over London, Tokyo, Seattle. Then after a week, the dragons stopped attacking and fled the aircraft instead. Some so-called experts speculated that the dragons were surprised to find that people could now fly, and that the two sides were now evenly matched.

The so-called experts were often medieval scholars and mythology experts who had studied the stories and lore of dragons, most of it so old it was assumed to be fiction. People had forgotten.

The Silver River Treaty came about when three dragons landed in Washington, D.C., London, and Moscow, asking to negotiate a peace. That was another shock, learning that dragons could speak English, Russian, and even Icelandic. They asked to have their own territories, and to be left alone. They were even willing to take uninhabited regions, far to the north, if it included a portion of the mountains in North America. They loved the mountains.

The human governments appointed delegates. It took a year of negotiations and serious economic incentives to the Soviet Union, Canada, and the United States, who were being asked to cede most of the territories. The treaty was established and was named for the town where the U.S. bureau was formed to enforce the human side of the treaty in the Rockies. A Soviet version of the bureau existed on the Taymyr Peninsula in Siberia. Humans and dragons had been at peace for over sixty years.

Now the talking-head commentators on TV were saying it could never have lasted more than that.

Newsreel footage and a few recordings of the Silver River negotiations made up most of what modern agencies knew about dragon diplomacy. Only a few of the people who had been at those negotiations were still alive. While people like Kay's mother had been trained to deal with dragons, none of them had any experience. No one knew how to negotiate with the dragons further, because, after the Silver River Treaty, the monsters retreated and never spoke to anyone again.

Still licking its wounds from World War II, humanity had been unprepared. The creatures were supposed to be myths, legends, something invented by the unenlightened to explain the odd dinosaur fossil. Even after the horrors of the war, of the Holocaust, of atomic weapons, no one had been prepared for the dragons that rose from a long sleep in the earth.

It had been clear that the two sides could annihilate each other. The new weapons, machine guns, and high explosives could kill dragons when little else in human history had succeeded. But the dragons still had their fire and their sheer size, speed, agility. Kill one, and another would burn a city to the ground in revenge. A continuing war between the two species meant destruction for both, so they'd reached the compromise.

People asked: Dragons lived long lives, so were any of the ones involved in the original treaty negotiation still alive? Why didn't they try to talk as they had before? Didn't they remember? Or did they not care? Did they want to fight as well?

The pundits kept saying that no one knew how to talk to the dragons; most of the people who'd been alive then were now dead. If the dragons didn't want to talk, they said, the humans had no choice but to defend themselves. But Kay knew they were wrong.

She knew how to talk to at least one of them, if only she dared tell anyone. And if only she could be sure she and Artegal would see each other again.

It was early when the jet, the F-22, flew out again. Kay was in the parking lot at school locking up her Jeep when a roar boomed over the town. She couldn't see the border or the dragon sentinels from where she was, but she followed the jet's sound to that direction. She spotted a contrail, but the jet was already gone, headed toward the border.

Everyone outside the school had stopped to stare at the northern sky, knowing what was happening.

Kay heard the first-period warning bell ring, but she didn't care. She ran to the cafeteria, hoping the librarian still had the TV out and still had it turned to the news. She wanted to yell, *What's happening? Is anything happening?* There was already a crowd of teachers and students gathered around the TV at the front of the big room.

Kay peered over a dozen heads to see the screen. The sound was turned up loud enough that she could hear easily. A reporter was talking over video footage of the three dragons across the border, the same scene they'd been watching for days now. The man sounded excited and spoke too quickly.

". . . ten minutes ago. It's presumed to be the F-22 jet fighter described at yesterday's press conference. It was traveling very fast, and it passed, I don't know, it must have passed within a mile of the dragons that have been stationed within view of Silver River for several days now. It continued on and is now out of sight. We're still waiting for some reaction from them. And—what's happening? I'm trying to talk to someone at the location. . . ."

But those watching the live video could see what was happening without the chatty commentary. The dragons—the mottled one first, then the green, then the blue—roused themselves. They shook their heads, stretched their necks as if waking from a sleep—had they really been asleep all that time? Turning their pointed snouts to the sky, they spread their wings wide and launched. They seemed to fall off the rock gracefully, like divers. Then their wide wings caught the air, and they sailed, one after the other, spinning into the sky. They were big, bigger than the jet, even. But their flight seemed to take little effort. Air bladders, biologists said. Maybe even filled with helium, the only way to keep such bulk aloft. They flew after the jet. Sunlight shimmered off their scales.

They were so beautiful.

She felt a hand on her back and turned, startled. Jon was at school today. He glanced at her then returned to watching the TV.

They were all thinking, *What will happen now?*

"You okay?" Jon asked.

"Yeah, just a second." Kay pulled out her cell phone and called her mother. They weren't supposed to use their phones during class hours, but none of the adults stopped her. In fact, a few of the teachers and kids watched her anxiously. Small town—they knew who her parents were.

She wandered a few paces and turned her back to them to try to get some privacy.

Her mother didn't even say hello. "Kay, are you okay, is everything okay?"

"I was going to ask you that," she said. "I've been watching the news at school."

"I don't know anything. Malmstrom Air Force Base isn't returning calls. Honey, I have a call waiting on the other line. I only took this call because it was you. If I find out anything I can tell you, I'll call, I promise."

"Okay, Mom. Thanks. Be careful, okay?" That was a stupid thing to say—her mother wasn't actually doing anything dangerous except talking to bureaucrats.

"I love you," her mother said, and clicked off the line.

She turned to the eager faces looking back at her and shook her head. "My mom doesn't know anything. Sorry."

Now, the scene on the TV screen was empty. No jet, no dragons, nothing happening. The news repeated video of the jet speeding past, the diamond-shaped craft flying at low level, close to the mountain where the dragons sat, wagging back and forth as if to tease them. Then the reporter came on-screen, his face a determined blank, and started talking, saying little in particular.

Students and teachers drifted away. Kay didn't know what to think. If anything was going to happen, it would happen soon. Maybe they'd hear the alarm, and maybe it would be for real this time.

Then again, maybe the military was right. Maybe the dragons wouldn't do anything. Nobody had any way of knowing. Kay just about decided then and there to go over the border that afternoon, on the chance that Artegal may be there.

She sneaked into first period late. The teacher gave her a look, but didn't say anything. Kay pretended to pay attention and not worry.

But that afternoon, Kay's mother called her. Kay had left her phone on and took the call in class. Math this time, and Mr. Kelly gave her a dirty look, but Kay said, "It's my mom," and ducked into the hall.

"Hi, Mom?" she said, leaning against the wall in the hallway.

"Kay? Kay, I want you to go home right now. Go home and stay there. I need to know where you are."

Somehow this was worse than the siren, worse than the drills, worse than thinking about the worst that could happen. Kay had never heard such concern, almost panic, in her mother's voice.

"What happened? What's going on?"

She took a deep breath, a tense pause, and said, "Three more jets crossed the border."

"Why?" Kay said, confused. It was the first thing she thought. It made no sense. Not unless they really were trying to start a war.

Mom didn't bother answering. "Until we know what's happening, I want you to go home."

"School's not out for another hour."

"I know, but I need you at home. If anyone tries to stop you, have them call me."

"But what about Dad? Dad said that if I stayed home people would panic—"

"I've talked to him, and he agrees with me."

Kay hadn't really been scared until then. "Okay. Okay, I'm going right now." They hung up.

She went back to class. Her face burned, because she felt like everyone was watching her. She stepped carefully, as if the floor were made of glass. Tam looked at her, brows raised, questioning. Kay shook her head and gathered up her books and things.

Her voice seemed small when she turned to Mr. Kelly. "I have to go."

The teacher called after her, but she ducked out before anyone could ask any questions and ran out to the parking lot.

The skies above Silver River were clear.

14

At home, she tried to call Jon, but his phone was off. She left a message. He called her back twenty minutes later.

"What do you mean you went home?" he said.

"I mean my parents are freaking out and made me go home."

"That doesn't make any sense."

But it did, because she was watching TV—had been for the last hour—and this time the news shows were saying things like "bombing."

"I've got the TV on right now, and it looks bad," she said.

"You've been watching way too much news."

She couldn't argue. The TV just kept saying the same

things over and over. It all sounded awful. "It'll be okay," she murmured. "It has to."

"Do you want me to come over? I can ditch school."

Even though seeing him would make her feel better, she wasn't sure even he could distract her from the TV, make the news stories go away, and make her worry less. He'd only worry more, when he saw how bad she felt. "That's okay. Your folks are probably worried."

"Naw," he said. "My mom's only called four times in the last hour."

She chuckled. "Sounds like she wants you to go home."

"I'll stop by on my way," he said, and that sounded like a good compromise.

Both her parents called to check in. Her father was first.

"When are you coming home?" she asked him. If she needed to stay home, where she'd be safe and where everyone would know where she was, why didn't they?

"I may be out all night," he said, not sounding concerned or annoyed. He sounded like it was just part of the job. "There's got to be a thousand reporters in town, and they're getting unruly. We've called everyone in to keep an eye on things."

"Can you come home for dinner?"

"I'll probably grab something on the go. I may meet Mom if she isn't swamped. We'll call to check in later."

"Dad—" She didn't like the way her voice whined,

making her sound like a little kid. "What's going to happen? I've been watching the news. Everyone says it's bad. How bad is it?"

"I don't know. All this press is making it worse, making people panic. I'm hoping it'll blow over. If we don't panic, it'll blow over. How does that sound?"

"Okay, I guess." But he hadn't sounded confident. He was just saying it to make her feel better.

"Kay, I have to get going. Be good, all right?"

Not "be careful." That was something. It had to mean things weren't so bad.

Then Mom called. "I just talked to Dad," Kay said.

"Me too." She sounded better, as if as long as they were all still in contact, all was well with the world. "We're going to grab dinner at the Alpine before he goes back to work. Will you be okay? Can you find something to eat?"

"I'll be fine."

Jon stopped by for a hug and kiss and asked for news.

"My parents are doing okay. If they don't sound worried, things are okay, right?"

"Yeah. Probably." Then his phone rang. It was his mom, wanting to know where he was. "I guess I need to get going. Call me if anything happens, okay?"

"Assuming I can get my mom off the phone." They smiled, and even Kay started feeling better. They kissed again, and she almost asked Jon to stay. He lingered, as if he were going to ask if he could. But he squeezed her hand and left, to go home and reassure his mother, and it was too late for Kay to change her mind.

She wanted to ease into a relationship, not plunge in like Tam wanted her to. They should be together because they wanted to, not because they thought they were supposed to. But did she and Jon want two different things? If they did, then what?

Kay watched the news all evening, trying to do homework and failing. It was hard to keep her mind on algebra when an endless parade of politicians and commentators on TV went back and forth between predicting disaster and reassuring that everything was fine. That was stupid, because nothing was fine. She could feel the balance of the world changing around her. Maybe because she was part of it. The person who rode the dragon. She kept expecting to see pictures of her and Artegal flashing on the screen. So far, that hadn't been made public.

But she and Artegal were safe for now, and as long as nothing else happened, they'd stay safe.

Around ten, her mother called her and told her to get to bed. Or at least think about going to bed and getting some sleep. Kay was long past the age of being told to go to bed. But since things were quiet for the moment, she agreed. The morning would come more quickly if she slept through it all. Assuming she could get to sleep.

Sirens woke Kay. Lots of them: fire engines, police cars, ambulances. It sounded like every emergency vehicle in the county was on the road and speeding toward a disaster.

The air-raid sirens were also howling.

She sat up in bed enough to push aside the curtain over the window. She didn't see anything, except a passing blue-and-red flashing light, quickly vanishing down the road. Her window faced away from downtown Silver River, where the police car was headed. She couldn't see anything else.

She padded into the living room and turned on the TV. Two in the morning, and the Great Falls, Montana news was broadcasting. Letters in the corner announced LIVE.

A pretty but flustered woman reporter was glaring at the camera and delivering her line: ". . . fire department primarily concerned with containing the blaze so it doesn't spread to other buildings . . ."

The camera shifted to a taped segment. She recognized the fire chief, his middle-aged face red with exertion, shining with sweat and smudged with soot. He was wearing a helmet and his big coat. Fire trucks made up the backdrop of the scene. Except for flashing emergency lights, the street was dark and nothing else was visible. Nothing gave a clue as to his location.

Where are they? Kay's heart pounded. What was in the process of burning to the ground?

The fire chief said, "We're just lucky we don't have strong winds tonight. We could have lost the whole town in minutes. Right now we have a good chance of containing the fire by morning."

Back to the reporter: "Chief Perez would not give details, but he said there have been several serious injuries, and people have been transported to area hospitals. Once again, I'm in downtown Silver River, where several government administration offices are burning . . ."

Her heart nearly gave out. At least it was night. The buildings would have been empty. Her parents wouldn't have been working—except, because of the trouble on the border, they hadn't stopped working.

She retrieved her cell phone from her bedroom and dialed her mother. The call rolled to voice mail.

"Crap," she muttered. Everyone in town who had any vaguely official position was probably either at the scene or on the phone. She'd have to keep watching the news and get the one-sided filtered version of what was happening. Or not.

She changed quickly, pulling on jeans, a sweatshirt, and her hiking boots. She called her mother again, then her father. Neither was picking up, which shouldn't have surprised her. No doubt they were way too busy to talk to her. And she knew better than to head down there and get in the way.

But she wouldn't get close enough to get in the way. Just close enough to flag down someone who could tell her what was going on. May as well—she certainly wasn't going to get any more sleep tonight, and she didn't want to wait until morning to get more news. Mom and Dad may yell at her for leaving the house, but that was all they could do. She'd take it as a fair trade for finding out what was happening. She got in her Jeep and set off.

An orange glow sat over the entire town, flames reflected into the night sky, billowing and flickering. Kay had seen wildfires in the distance that looked and sounded like this, a constant crackling of wood. The air smelled of heavy soot and ash. But this wasn't a distant wildfire; this was right in the middle of Silver River. She had to squint into the light.

Six blocks away, the streets were barricaded, police cars blocking access. The flashing blue-and-red lights hurt her eyes. She felt only half awake, muzzy-headed, as if maybe she were still in bed dreaming. Kay pulled over and left the car, moving closer to the disaster on foot. She wasn't the only one. A crowd had gathered outside the police barricade, people huddled together, murmuring questions: *What was going on?*

"Kay! Hold up!" someone called out to stop her. She recognized the voice—one of her father's deputies, at the open door of his car across the street. It shook her awake. Someone to answer questions, that was all she wanted. Deputy Kalbach could answer her questions.

"What's going on? What's burning? I can't get ahold of my folks. Have you seen them? Are they around anywhere?

Where's my dad?" She hadn't thought she'd have sounded so panicked. This must have been what it felt like to be in an earthquake, when all the phone lines went down and you didn't know if anyone was alive or dead.

When he crossed over to her and took hold of her arm, she saw it as a bad sign. There was too much tension in the grip. She didn't think her stomach could drop any farther.

He touched the radio at his shoulder. "Yeah, I got Kay Wyatt here. What should I do?" She couldn't make out the reply that scratched back at him, but he didn't look happy about it. "Okay, got it." He turned off the receiver and pulled her toward the car. "Come on."

She dug in her heels. "Wait a minute, where are we going? What's happening?"

"Your folks are at the hospital. I'm taking you there now."

At that, her mind stopped working. She let the deputy push her into the passenger seat of his patrol car. They drove, lights flashing and siren blaring. People got out of the way instantly. It was eerie.

"What happened?" she finally managed to ask, when her mouth started working again. "Are they hurt?"

"It's your dad," he said, his face a grim mask. "He got to the scene first. The night dispatcher was on duty, and he went in to make sure she got out. It was pretty bad."

Kay leaned her head on her hand and tried not to

imagine what "pretty bad" meant. *Wait 'til you see before you start crying.*

"Alice—your mom—rode in the ambulance with them."

"Why didn't anyone call me?" Her voice was hoarse and unreliable.

"This happened twenty minutes ago! We've barely been able to think!" His expression twisted, and Kay realized with a shock that he was holding back tears, too. "I'm sorry," he said softly. "I don't mean to yell. It's just we're all shaken."

Her father's deputies were honorary uncles and aunts to her. They looked after her. They were anchors. Seeing Deputy Kalbach like this—face twisted, shoulders slouching—Kay almost burst into tears right there.

Instead, she hugged herself and stared ahead, trying to be numb.

The hospital wasn't in town, but a few miles out on the highway. It wasn't big, just an emergency room and a few clinics to serve the outlying areas. For anything serious, people went to Great Falls.

She tried to reassure herself that if this were serious, they'd have airlifted him to Great Falls. So he had to be okay.

With the police siren heralding them, Kalbach brought them right to the emergency room doors. Kay rushed inside before the deputy had climbed out of the car.

The place was crowded. There'd obviously been more

people injured than her father. A couple of men wearing blackened firefighter's coats lay on beds sucking oxygen through masks. Walking wounded were being led to backrooms by orderlies. A reporter with a cameraman was being herded out none too politely. Panicked, Kay looked around for a familiar figure on a bed, for her mother standing watch, and couldn't find them.

The deputy pushed past her and tapped a white-jacketed nurse on the shoulder. "Sheriff Wyatt, where is he?"

The woman pointed to a corridor. Kay rushed past them both.

Two steps into the hallway, she stopped, froze. Her mother sat in a plastic chair, part of a row of them lining the wall. Her elbows rested on her knees; her hands covered her face.

A doctor, a woman in a white coat, closed the door of a room a few paces down. She kneeled by Kay's mother, touched her shoulder, and said a few words. Mom didn't respond. When the doctor stood to return to the emergency room, she spotted Kay, and her lips pressed in a line.

Kay wanted the world to stop right there, she wanted to run away, and she wanted not to have to live the next five minutes of her life. The universe could end and she wouldn't care, as long as it prevented the next five minutes.

The doctor approached her. "Can I help you?"

"I'm Kay Wyatt. My dad—"

The doctor looked back at Mom, seemed to debate with

herself. Then she lowered her head. Her smile was probably meant to be comforting, sympathetic. But it was just sad.

"I'm very sorry. We did everything we could."

Just make everything stop, Kay begged. She was still asleep. Her brain couldn't hear the words.

The doctor touched her arm, then walked away. Kay managed to sit next to her mother, though her limbs tingled when she moved. Like her body wasn't hers, or she was leaving it. Still, her mother didn't react.

Kay eyed the door that the doctor had closed. A door to a room where a body lay on a bed. She said, "Can I see him?"

Her mother looked up at that. Her face was red; her eyes were red, swollen. Her hair was mussed. A streak of black soot smudged her cheek, and she smelled like smoke. She didn't look at all like Mom. She only stared at Kay, expressionless.

Kay started again, pointing at the door. "Can I—"

"Oh, baby, you don't want to see him, not like that, you don't—" She broke down, folding against Kay like her bones had disappeared, pressing her face to her shoulder. Numb, startled, Kay held her while she cried wrenching sobs.

If Kay had been about to cry herself, she was now shocked to stillness.

After a long while, her mother stilled, but Kay suspected it was exhaustion and lack of oxygen rather than spent grief that made her stop crying. She remained curled up in Kay's arms like a child, sniffing and clinging desperately to Kay's shirt. *Don't go,* the gesture said.

At one point, she noticed Deputy Kalbach looking at them. Then he bowed his head and walked away.

Kay didn't know how long the two of them stayed frozen in that tableau. She was aware of Kalbach blocking the end of the corridor and of a reporter shouting at him. Then the doctor, the same who had told her about Dad, sat by her and whispered close to her ear—so her mother wouldn't hear.

"Kay, I know this is very difficult. But can you take her home? We're going to have to move him soon." She nodded to Mom. Translation: *Get her out of here before they pull the body out of the room.*

Kay almost shook her head. No, of course she couldn't take Mom home. Mom was the grown-up, Kay was the kid—she wasn't expected to do anything. But Mom wasn't doing anything right now. Her eyes weren't even seeing.

So Kay nodded, taking her mother's arm. "Mom, we have to go. Come on."

Mom had aged years in moments. She walked hunched and wouldn't let go of Kay, who kept her own mind numb and focused on the task at hand.

With one arm around Mom's shoulder, she approached Deputy Kalbach and touched his shoulder. "Can you take us home?"

The young deputy nodded quickly.

Then came the gauntlet.

More reporters had arrived. More injured had been brought in, and their families and colleagues filled the emergency room. Word spread. It couldn't help but spread in a town like this when something terrible happened. People would have to take only one look at them, Kay with her face a rock and Mom huddled in her arms, to guess what had happened. She recognized faces, heard her mother's name called out, but she didn't react, didn't respond. A flash went off, someone taking a picture. Deputy Kalbach was their shield. Kay felt his arm across her back, pulling them both into the sphere of his protection. His other arm stretched out before them, cutting across her vision. It deflected all comers. Reporters shouted at her. She didn't hear a word of what they said. Only Kalbach's voice saying, "Move aside. Please, get out of the way. Clear the way."

The journey to the door outside was chaos. A blur. Kay kept her gaze forward and absorbed none of it.

She sat with her mother in the back of the patrol car. Mom still leaned on her, still seeming unable to hold herself up.

Kalbach kept looking at them in the rearview mirror. He started, "Kay, I—"

"Don't say anything," she said, closing her eyes. If he said anything, she'd break, and she couldn't break. She had to take Mom home.

The air still smelled like smoke, and the sky over Silver

River still glowed orange, fires still burning. She remembered the news report: The fire could have swallowed the town in seconds.

She asked the deputy, "Do they know how the fire started?"

Her mother stirred in her arms, straightening, turning her tear-and-soot-streaked face to the window.

"It was them," Mom said, nodding in the direction of the border.

_15_

The dragons circled. The next morning, three of them flew just over the river, banking sharply when it looked like they might pass into human territory. The sight of them made people cringe, as if they wanted nothing more than to run and hide. Lock themselves behind castle walls. Like mice in view of soaring hawks.

Kay watched the news on TV. Several people, mostly firefighters, had been injured in the blaze that destroyed two of the four buildings in the administration complex. Only one was killed. Sheriff Jack Wyatt's face appeared in newspapers and on TV screens all over the world, and the eulogies poured forth from people who never even knew him. It was because he was a cop. They could use words like *hero* without knowing anything about him.

The president went on TV to declare the attack an act of aggression. Several of the more shrill pundits called it war. These were the same ones who questioned why humanity had ever agreed to the Silver River Treaty in the first place, and argued that an international coalition should launch an assault to reclaim the vast territories so blithely handed over all those years ago. We could have wiped the dragons out then, they said, and we can do it now. The time of the dragons is over, was over millennia ago. This is the age of humans.

Kay watched the dragons from the living room window. She felt like her brain hadn't turned back on yet. She couldn't think of Artegal at all. She kept wondering what happened next, and her mind kept going blank.

Mom had taken sleeping pills. She was still asleep, curled up on her bed in her clothes. Kay had taken her shoes off, put a quilt over her. She didn't know what else to do. The phone had been ringing all morning. She finally turned it off. And her cell phone and her mother's.

A trio of news vans were parked on the street outside, and a crowd of reporters milled around them, everyone wanting interviews with the family of the first person killed by dragons since the treaty. Sixty years of tension stretched to the breaking point.

She scrolled through the missed calls on her cell phone and on the house phone, wondering who she should talk to and what she would say. She didn't know how long her mother was going to be out of it, and she didn't want to be in charge. She wanted to talk to her dad. Her parents may have been workaholics, both of them, always out doing their jobs. But they always answered their phones when she called. Her father had always taken her calls. She almost called him now, just to see. Maybe it had all been a mistake.

Kalbach had set up a rotation of deputies to stand guard outside the house and keep the reporters at bay. She could tell him if she needed anything. She could call any of the deputies. Some of them had already stopped by to deliver food, casseroles and salads, dishes covered in tin foil with instructions for heating. Kay wondered why. She wasn't hungry. Kalbach said that was just what people did when something like this happened. When she was hungry, she wouldn't have to think about what to eat, the food would be right there. It didn't make sense to her.

Jon and Tam had called. She didn't call back because she didn't know what she'd say to them.

She finally lay on the sofa, wrapped herself in a blanket, watched the news, and waited for her mother to wake up. The world would start moving again when her mother woke up and told Kay what happened next.

Her father hadn't hurt anyone. He hadn't bothered anyone. He'd worked to keep the border safe. The dragons should have burned the air force base. They should have talked to people. They should have been talking all along, like her and Artegal, and none of this would have happened.

Now, none of them would talk with each other ever again.

That afternoon, the air force started bombing, almost as if they'd planned it and had been waiting for the opportunity. The excuse.

Kay could hear it. If she hadn't known the cause, she might have thought it was thunder—a distant, roiling storm, part of dark clouds lurking on the horizon. But this was too steady to be thunder. She could almost time it. Jets flew overhead from Malmstrom, and thirty minutes later, rhythmic thunder echoed from the mountains. At night, the glow of fires burned on the distant, mountainous horizon.

The day after, many families not only kept their kids from school, but left town entirely, cars packed with essentials—computers, pets, clothing, whatever would fit. Everyone assumed that the dragons would retaliate again and that they'd come to Silver River first.

And the dragons did strike again, but not at Silver River.

The news channels reported that fires had broken out at Vancouver, Duluth, and St. Petersburg. Her mother, red-eyed and silent, had woken up and come to the living room. Kay sat with her on the sofa, wrapped in blankets and watching reports, images of burning buildings, panicked people running, and fleeting footage—like ghosts flitting across the sky—of dragons. They'd come from the territory in the Rockies and in Siberia, crossing the Arctic Circle to strike all over the world. Terrorist attacks, some of the news shows called them. Buildings burned, people were injured, and by some miracle no one was killed. The strikes were quick. The dragons appeared, flying low, and sprayed the outskirts of the cities with flame-thrower breaths. The attacks seemed designed to frighten rather than inflict damage. People had thought the dragons had restricted themselves to limited territories. But this proved they could go anywhere, at least in the northern hemisphere. They could still shock.

No one could tell if the military's bombing had any effect. The news channels interviewed lots of people in uniform, and they said things like "calculated risk" and "viable targets." But the bombing only seemed to make the dragons more angry.

Kay started to understand about people bringing food. After she woke up and emerged from the bedroom, Mom looked in the fridge at all the casserole dishes and Tupperware, and for a long moment, she just stared. She took a breath that sounded a little like a sob. Then she retrieved a tray of lasagna, spooned out a couple of servings, and heated them in the microwave. They had food without having to think about it. Otherwise, they may not have eaten at all. With all the food that Dad's coworkers, Mom's coworkers, the neighbors, and even a couple of Kay's teachers had brought over, they wouldn't have to think about what to eat for a while. There was something comforting about that.

It had only been a day. Kay had to keep reminding herself of that.

Mom spent time on the phone that evening, some of her friends stopped by—and brought more food—and they spoke in hushed voices in the living room. Kay retreated to her bedroom. Right before she did, her mother called to her, gestured her closer.

"If you need to talk, if you need anything, you'll tell me?" She squeezed Kay's hand, rubbed her arm, like she hadn't done since Kay was little.

"Okay," Kay said, her voice soft. Her mom was acting weird, which wasn't at all surprising, but Kay didn't know how to behave. She almost said, *What do I do? How do I act? I don't know how to act.* People kept looking at her with gazes of terrible pity, and Kay didn't know how to respond.

She fled to her room. There, she retrieved *Dracopolis* from its hiding place under her bed. Lying on her bed, she turned the pages, studying them, the pictures, the vines and flowers that wound around the text. She had an urge to run her fingers over the lines, over the stiff parchment, but didn't dare. She wished she could read it but didn't know how much further she could get on her haphazard translation. The pictures showed towns being burned. Did the words tell why the dragons did it? If she could pick that apart, maybe she could understand what was happening now. The pictures, which had seemed so beautiful, so benign, now seemed as cryptic as the words. *I should be angry*, she thought. *I should be angry at them.*

She studied the manuscript, searching for some kind of wisdom. This had happened before; people and dragons had been through this before. But she couldn't translate enough of it to learn what it said. She had only the pictures to study, and she couldn't tell what she needed to know from the ornate drawings. Why would dragons do this? She couldn't tell if they started burning towns before or after people started hunting them. It seemed important.

She should never have gone back to talk to Artegal. Then she could just be angry.

Kay knew she should call Jon and Tam, but she still didn't have anything to say. Nothing at all. They'd say they were sorry, they'd ask if there was anything they could do, and Kay would just shake her head. But while she didn't call them back, she left her phone on. They'd call again, maybe. She wouldn't ignore them next time.

Turned out, Jon stopped by with Tam and Carson.

A soft knock came at her door, and Kay shoved the book under her pillow before her mother came in. "Kay. Do you feel like coming out for a few minutes? Your friends are here."

She followed her mother back to the living room. There they stood, the three of them together, looking as round-eyed and lost as she felt.

They apparently didn't expect her to say anything. Jon took a step toward her; she took one toward him. Then they were hugging. Tam put a hand on her shoulder, and Carson, looking sheepish and sad, stood with his hands shoved in his pockets.

The funeral was at the end of the week. He was buried in the city cemetery outside town, a modern stretch of lawn with flat marble blocks for headstones. Crowds seemed to fill the place—the whole town was there, an honor guard of people in sheriff's department uniforms, along with state highway patrol and people from the air force base. There were news vans and swarms of reporters. Just another news item. Hero and victim of dragons Sheriff Jack Wyatt, laid to rest.

A pair of jets wailed overhead. They patrolled constantly now. The sky still smelled like smoke. A haze had settled in the air.

Kay and her mother clung to each other and stared at the casket and the mountain of flowers around it. She hardly listened as the governor read a graveside eulogy. *Tireless public servant. Devoted husband and father.* She felt everyone looking at them. She wanted to go home.

She had decided to believe that Jack Wyatt had gone on a trip. He was just away. He wasn't in that box. She'd pretend he was, to go along with what everyone else thought. But as far as she was concerned, he was simply parked somewhere waiting to set his radar gun on her and pull her over for speeding. She could live with that.

Afterward, fortunately, no one expected her to say anything. All she had to do was stand there and look sufficiently sad while people told her how sorry they were. An amazing array of people. The governor and his wife. The vice president of the United States. There'd be plenty of pictures for the newspapers. The deputies guarded them viciously, and when Mom turned to Deputy Kalbach and Deputy Olsen with a pleading look in her eyes, they formed a barrier around Kay and her mom, hustled them to a waiting car, and took them home, to microwaved lasagna and a too-quiet house.

They thought—or Kay hoped—that they were finished with the constant press of visitors and condolences. But the next morning, a knock came at the front door. They were sitting on the sofa and glanced up. Kay had never seen her mother look so tired as she hauled herself to her feet, then to the front door. She cracked it open, and Kay craned around to see who it was.

An unfamiliar voice said, "Ma'am, I'm very sorry to bother you, but I was hoping I could speak to your daughter."

Kay scrambled to her feet and went to join her mother in staring at the man outside their door. The current deputy on duty—Michaels—stood a little behind him, shrugging as if to ask whether he'd been right in letting the man through.

The newcomer wore a blue air force uniform and a round hat with a brim in front instead of the olive green jumpsuit this time, but she still recognized him as the pilot who had bailed out over the border. The one who had seen her riding Artegal. All she could do was stare.

Mom glanced at Kay, who didn't know what to say. All she could think was that her secret was done, finished. It was all over now.

The pilot gave her a thin smile, but spoke to her mother. "Ma'am, I'm Captain Will Conner, the pilot who went down a few weeks ago." He pointed a thumb over his shoulder to the forest. "I met your husband. Sheriff Wyatt's the one who found me after I hauled ass across the border. I just wanted to say I'm sorry. I'd have liked to have known him better. But I'm mostly here to talk to your daughter, if that's all right."

Why had he come? Why didn't he have the whole military there demanding that she tell everything she knew? He was being too nice; she didn't trust him.

Mom glanced at Kay, clearly confused. "Why?"

Captain Conner looked apologetic. "May I come in?"

Kay's mother opened the door a little wider. "I think I can make some coffee—I'm sorry, it's been a rough few days."

"I understand. I wouldn't be here if it wasn't important." He took off his hat as he stepped inside.

While Mom was in the kitchen, Captain Conner and Kay looked at each other.

"It really is you," he said wonderingly. "I thought I recognized you in the picture from the funeral yesterday. But I wasn't sure."

She tried to ask him, pleading with her gaze, *Why are you here, what are you doing, why are you finally blowing my cover?* In reply, he seemed to be saying, *We can do this the easy way or the hard way.* Who was he kidding? There was no easy way. There was nothing easy about this. According to him—the way everyone would see it—she was friends with an enemy, an enemy that had killed her father, and she'd kept it secret all this time.

"Why didn't you say anything earlier? Why didn't you tell anyone about me?" she asked.

He shrugged and gave a wry look over his shoulder, out the window to the sheriff's deputies and news vans. "I'm not sure. I almost didn't believe it when I saw you. Thought I must have been going crazy, and why report a delusion? Then again, maybe I admired your guts. That's test pilot guts, flying with that thing. Maybe I didn't want to get you in trouble, one pilot to another."

"His name is Artegal," she said. She'd never been able to tell anyone before. He nodded, conceding the point.

He'd kept her secret. Not that it mattered now, when there was probably going to be a war. Dragons burned towns, and then people went after them with swords. Or vice versa. That was the way it had always been.

"The thing is, Miss Wyatt, the situation has changed."

"So you're going to tell them now. Now that you know who I am," she said. She sounded angry, on the verge of tears. She focused on keeping control of herself.

"Right now, you're the only person who has any real contact with them. I wanted to make sure you understood that, if you hadn't already figured it out."

"Why does it even matter? It's not going to change anything."

"Don't be so sure, unless you want this to blow up into an all-out war."

"No, but—"

"I was under the impression the military wants an all-out war," Mom said, standing by the kitchen with two mugs of coffee in her hand. "That you crashed your plane across the border on purpose to see what the dragons would do. That people like Branigan wanted to go to war this whole time. 'Like poking a wasp nest' is what Jack said. And now you want to talk? And what does Kay have to do with this?"

When he didn't answer, when he didn't deny it, Kay grew frightened. Her gut turned cold, which shocked her because she thought she was numb. Mom stood there, the coffee mugs trembling slightly in her hands, a lost, accusing shadow in her eyes.

Conner ducked his gaze and actually looked sheepish. "Ma'am, I know you'll never believe me, but I wasn't privy to all the details of that mission. My plane was rigged to malfunction, and I wasn't told. I didn't know. I was the plausible deniability. And I can't say I'm at all happy about being used like that."

Mom's voice was quiet, but harsh, filled with bitterness.

"I have a feeling Branigan's going to get a little more out of his war than he bargained for."

"I think you're right." He turned to Kay. "Planes have nicknames. The B-17 was the Flying Fortress. The P-51 Mustang. The B-26 Marauder. This new one, the F-22. You know what the guys are calling it?"

She shook her head.

"The Dragonslayer," he said.

If the military had been preparing for a war, what could she do to change anything? Maybe it was inevitable. The two sides had been stalemated for decades. It was just her father's stupid luck to be the first person to get caught in the middle of it. Kay couldn't do anything to stop it. Telling someone sooner about her and Artegal wouldn't have stopped it. Talking to Artegal now wouldn't bring her father back. She didn't want to do *anything*.

"What's going to happen?" she asked.

"I don't know. I'm sorry to bother you all. I'll go," the pilot said. He pulled a business card from a front jacket pocket and handed it to Kay. "Let me know when you're ready to talk. I think you can help."

He let himself out the front door.

"What was he talking about?" Mom said, staring after him. "What does he think you've done?"

"Can we—can we sit down?" Kay said.

In a moment, they were both seated at the kitchen table. Mom kept one of the mugs of coffee, gripping it with both hands and breathing in the steam. Kay studied her worriedly, not knowing how to start.

"Are you angry at them?" Kay asked. "For doing it—for starting the fires?" She couldn't say exactly what, couldn't mention Dad. Didn't want to make it real.

"What? The dragons?" Mom thought for a moment, her gaze distant. "I don't know. Right now I think I'm angry at him. Why'd he have to . . . why'd he have to be so goddamn brave? He should have known better, he should have known—"

Her voice choked, and she looked away, her mussed hair falling in front of her face. Kay put her other hand over her mother's, and they sat like that, clutching their hands together. Mom was crying quietly. Kay's own eyes were stinging, and she gritted her teeth to keep from crying. They were both working so hard to keep from sobbing she wondered what would happen when they couldn't hold it in anymore.

After some time, seconds or minutes, Mom sat back, let go of Kay, scrubbed her face, and smiled like she was okay—a fake, stiff smile.

And Kay said, "Mom, I have to tell you something."

16

The Federal Bureau of Border Enforcement building had been part of the block that burned that night, almost as if the dragons had known their target. The bureau—along with the sheriff's department, which had also burned—had set up temporary offices in the Silver River Middle School gym. Kay and her mother stood in the open doorway, looking in at chaos. A dozen workers set up temporary office partitions; another group of technicians strung miles of wires between desks and set up telephones and computers. Various people in suits scurried through it all, from one computer to another. Outside, news vans swarming with reporters and cameras were parked. Phones were ringing, people were shouting.

Kay wondered that they had anything at all to do now.

People were crossing the border all the time now—at least the military was. She thought the bureau's job would have been practically over. But people kept calling. The military wouldn't tell anyone anything, so people called the bureau instead.

Her mother hadn't been back to work since the fire, just like Kay hadn't been back to school. In the doorway, Mom put her arm over Kay's shoulders. Kay didn't know if the gesture was meant to comfort her or her mother.

In the end, Mom had been less angry about her crossing the border and meeting the dragon at all than she had been about the flying. She'd ranted for long time about how dangerous it was, how Kay could have been killed, and what was she thinking, and on and on. Kay tried to explain how careful they'd been, using her climbing gear. "You could have been killed, and I'd never know," Mom said, and Kay didn't have a reply to that.

When they arrived at the offices, people stared and reporters took pictures. They were famous, Kay supposed. That picture of them at the funeral—the one Captain Conner had seen—appeared in most of the national newspapers, was posted on hundreds of websites, and aired on all the network news channels.

It didn't help that no one knew what to say to them. If it had been someone else, Kay wouldn't have known what to say.

A middle-aged man in a suit, with the tie missing and

the shirt collar unbuttoned, walked straight toward them. "Alice, you shouldn't be here. You should be resting. Take all the time you need—"

Kay's mother took the man—the regional bureau director, her boss—aside and spoke in a low voice. Kay waited, feeling like she was going to be sick. Maybe this situation—the jets, the news, the fire—wasn't inevitable after all; maybe she had caused it. After she and Artegal met, the world started falling apart. It was still falling. The more Kay thought about it, the dizzier she felt. She kept thinking that she should have told Dad about her and Artegal. She shouldn't have kept secrets from him. If she'd told, maybe none of this would have happened. Maybe, maybe, maybe . . .

The temporary bureau had commandeered a classroom and turned it into a conference room, pushing desks together in the middle and lining chairs around them. The director guided Kay and her mother there and told them to sit, which they did, side by side in the cold, silent room. He kept giving Kay odd, sideways glances, as if he were trying to believe the story her mother had told him. Trying to imagine her with a dragon.

None of these people knew anything about dragons.

"It's better this way," Mom was saying. She'd been talking for a while, but Kay hadn't been listening. The sound of her mother's voice startled her. "You'll only have to explain everything once. I'll be with you the whole time. Just tell them the truth. Don't leave anything out."

Now Kay understood. The director had sent them there to wait. He needed to contact others, a whole group of people who had a stake in this. Kay didn't know who else or how many. The police, probably. They'd lock her up, and she'd never see the outside of a jail again.

Somehow, she was as numb to this thought as she had been to everything since the fire. Nothing mattered. She'd done something amazing, done the impossible, and now she was paying for it. And none of it mattered. She imagined her father, remembered the look on his face when he'd pulled her over for speeding. That wry look. Why did she even think he'd be wearing that expression now, when this was so much worse? Because maybe he'd have understood. Quickly, she wiped her eyes to keep from crying.

Mom was studying her. Both of them had the same glassy stare, Kay thought. Surely no one would be mean to them, after what had happened. Her stomach clenched.

"Your dad was worried about you," Mom said softly. "We talked about it. You were spending so much time by yourself, going off to do who knew what. But he wouldn't let me search your room. He said, 'Give her a little more time. I bet she'll come clean about whatever it is. She's a good kid.' That's what he said."

Kay wanted to tell her mother to stop. Just stop talking. This was going to make her cry and she didn't want to cry, not when she was going to have to talk to the police.

Mom smiled a grieved, wincing smile. "He was right. He was always right. I'm just trying to figure out what he'd say about this." She wiped tears away with the heel of her hand.

Kay bit her lips and looked away. "I'm sorry." Her voice was a whisper.

Then they didn't say anything.

When the door to the classroom opened again, Kay flinched, startled. She didn't think she could get any more scared, but her heart raced. A half dozen people in air force and army uniforms filed in, along with another half dozen in suits. One of them brought in an armload of stuff, a stack of poster board, and a dozen file folders. Mom stood and put her hand on Kay's shoulder.

Kay recognized two of the military men: the air force general from TV, General Branigan, and Captain Conner.

One of the guys in a suit arranged the sheets of poster board on the table. They showed blown-up copies of the photos of Kay riding Artegal, the ones taken by the jet that had seen them. Maybe they won't believe me, Kay thought. She'd tell them it was her, and they wouldn't believe a kid could do that. Then she could go home.

Wearing a stern, serious expression, the general took his hat off and approached Kay's mother. He radiated authority and demanded respect. But Kay felt herself growing angry. He was probably the one who ordered those fighters over the border, and that was the reason the dragons attacked.

So was it the dragons' fault? Was it the general's?

Was it hers?

"Mrs. Wyatt, I'm extremely sorry for your loss." He spared Kay a quick glance.

"Thank you," Mom said. Kay marveled at how calm her mother was.

Between them, the general and Mom's boss introduced everyone, but the names went right past Kay. She couldn't process. They all nodded respectfully and murmured words of sympathy. But the blood was rushing in Kay's ears. They were going to ask why she did it, why she and Artegal were even friends. And she didn't have a good answer.

General Branigan started by saying, "Miss Wyatt, is this you in these photographs?"

Kay wanted to laugh because she didn't think of herself as Miss Wyatt. She didn't know how to be formal back at him. She was wearing jeans and a thick wool sweater, not a suit or skirt.

Her voice scratched when she answered, "Yes."

He stared at her for a long moment, and the other men— they were all men—followed his lead, letting the silence grow heavy, weighing on her.

Conner shifted then, clearing his throat and throwing a look at Branigan, who scowled. The spell broke. Conner was the only person there who didn't seem as if he were studying an insect when he looked at her.

"Would you like to tell us how this happened?" General

Branigan nodded at the picture.

"It was an accident," she said, her voice small. Mom squeezed her hand. "We weren't hurting anything."

The general put on a fake easygoing smile and spoke in a condescending voice. "Now, nobody says you were. We just want to understand what you've been doing."

Kay decided she hated the guy. That gave her confidence. She sat up a little straighter. "We just talked—"

"You *talked* to it? It *talks*?" Branigan said.

Mom spoke up. "General, we know from the Silver River Treaty negotiations sixty years ago that some of the dragons will talk to people."

The general settled back, but his expression was sour.

"Go on," Mom prompted her.

"We got this idea about flying." Kay was a little vague on that. She wasn't ready to give up the book. "I do a lot of rock climbing. I used some of the gear. It worked." She shrugged. Maybe if she played out the sullen teenager thing they'd leave her alone.

"But what was it doing that close to the border?" Branigan asked.

It took her a moment to realize he was talking about Artegal. "He was curious. He wanted to find someone to talk to." She made sure to emphasize the *he*.

"So it was spying?"

"No—" But she realized she didn't know that for sure. Maybe Artegal had been sent to spy. "If he was spying, I'm pretty sure he didn't find out a whole lot from me. I don't know anything."

Then they started talking as if she weren't there.

"Maybe it thought it could use her to gather information—"

"Or it misjudged how much access she had—"

"If it could trick her into flying away with it, they'd have a hostage—"

"So did they think she was a source of information or a hostage?"

"No," she said, shaking her head. She knew she was right; they were wrong. "He was just curious. He just wanted to *talk*. We're just friends."

The group of men stared, disbelieving and speechless.

If she told them about the book, would they believe her? Would they believe a girl and a dragon could be friends then? Or would they take it away and keep ignoring her? She thought of *Dracopolis* as hers, and she didn't want anyone to find it.

She especially didn't want them to find the page with the map and coordinates slipped inside it. They'd go looking for whatever was there, and she wanted to keep that secret safe. *She* wanted to be the one to find it. She and Artegal should be the ones to look for it.

Her mother squeezed her hand again. She hadn't let go all this time.

"We just talked. Really. He isn't a spy," Kay said.

Branigan smiled that awful fake smile again. "We know you'd like to think that. Tell me, Miss Wyatt—why did you cross the border in the first place?"

"I told you, it was an accident. I fell in the creek and he—the dragon—pulled me out. He saved my life."

"I hate to start making accusations," Branigan said, but Kay got the feeling he was all too happy to make them. "But it sounds like if you managed to get close enough to the border to fall over it, the local Federal Bureau of Border Enforcement may have gotten a little sloppy."

"Now wait just a minute," Mom said, straightening and glaring across the table.

"General, if I may," Captain Conner said, hand raised. "I've been in those woods, and if someone determined enough wanted to get across the border, they could. Especially someone who grew up around here and knew the area and FBBE procedures. Am I right?"

"Nothing bad happened," Kay said again, pleading. "We weren't hurting anything."

"Young lady, we're at war here," Branigan said.

"That's your fault," she replied. She continued, before he could yell at her. "What's going to happen to me? I broke the law by crossing the border, I know. I knew it then. I'm the one who crossed, not him. So what's going to happen to me?" Whatever it was, she just wanted to get it over with. She wanted it all to be over.

Mom's boss, the regional bureau director, should have

been the one to answer that question. There were no cops in the room. It was his jurisdiction. But he, her mother, everyone, in fact, looked at General Branigan. Kay didn't want him to decide what happened to her.

"None of us is out to get you, Miss Wyatt. The situation we're in right now is a little too unusual to be worrying about something like that. But I think what you've given us here is an opportunity. I think you may be able to help us, if you're willing. If not—well, you're right. You've broken the law. Pretty spectacularly."

Mom's hand clenched even more tightly around hers. Branigan's meaning was clear. She'd help, or she was screwed. Kay didn't see how that was any choice at all. She had to play their game. She had a bad feeling she knew what he wanted.

The general said, "If we asked you to, do you think you could get in touch with this dragon again? You see, Miss Wyatt, you probably know more about the dragons than anyone else in this room. And we need to find out as much as we can about them. I think you can help us do that. Miss Wyatt—Kay—think about your father. Think about what they did to him. This is your chance to do something about that. Do you understand?"

Except that her father worked to keep the peace, that was how he saw himself. He wouldn't have wanted her to take revenge. He'd wanted to keep the peace. He'd always said keeping the peace was easier when you made friends rather than made threats.

"Well?" Branigan said. "Will you help us?"

"It's just talking," Conner said. "We just want you to talk." Although the glare Branigan threw him said that maybe the general didn't quite agree.

That was it, then. Artegal may not have been a spy, but Branigan wanted to turn her into one. She didn't know more about dragons. She just knew Artegal.

Kay's head really started swimming, but her response was mechanical. It wasn't much of a choice at all. She nodded, agreeing, because she would have done nearly anything to get out of that room just then.

17

Kay and her mother drove home from the meeting in silence. Kay didn't know whether to be terrified or furious. The general's threat had been obvious—spying was the only way she'd stay out of jail. At seventeen, she could be tried as an adult and sent to prison. But they were using her. She hated that.

When her mother spoke, she did so softly. "It's almost funny. All that bombing isn't having an effect because they don't know what their targets are. Those bombing runs have been random. They have satellite and infrared photos that show where their dragons may live, but they also think the dragons may be making decoys, setting fires to make some areas look hotter. So they need information. They need you, Kay. I can't believe they're basing their strategy on what a teenager can tell them," she muttered.

"What if I don't do it?" Kay said. "I could just not do it."

"Besides the fact they'll send you to jail? Without specific targets, they'll start using more destructive weapons. Branigan's talking nukes, but he doesn't have that authority. At least not yet."

He would do that? Kay thought, disbelieving. Did he think it was okay to destroy that much land, to risk the radiation—to make such a large area unusable for everyone, just on the chance that it might harm the dragons? Did he hate the dragons that much? She didn't understand. Even before she'd met Artegal, she wouldn't have understood wanting to destroy the mountains and forest to get to the dragons, who just kept to themselves, after all.

Kay's mother continued as if speaking were difficult. "I know you think of the dragon as your friend. I know you think of this as betraying him. But, Kay, he doesn't need you to protect him. He can take care of himself. You have to think about *you*. And your family. I can't lose you, Kay. I can't lose you, too." She shook her head in a slow denial, staring straight ahead over the steering wheel with wide eyes.

Kay and her mother had only each other now. Kay loved her mother, of course, but this felt like a burden. Kay could barely keep her own head on straight; she couldn't keep her mother safe, too.

The next day, she dressed for winter hiking and packed

a backpack of supplies. She was vaguely relieved that she wouldn't have to worry about sneaking around this time. She had official military sanction for what she was doing now.

She found her mother in the living room, curled up with a blanket around her, clutching a mug of steaming coffee. The whole house smelled like fresh coffee. It was a sign of normality—but a little normality made things seem even more surreal. On a usual morning, Mom would have been at work before dawn. Kay would have been getting ready for school, but she hadn't been back since the fire. Her mother was watching TV, but not news. A shopping channel or an infomercial. Something completely neutral. Even more surreal.

Kay stood for a long time wondering what she should say. Maybe she should just leave her mother alone. But she couldn't do that. She wouldn't do that to her mother.

"I'm going," she said.

Mom looked at her like she hadn't understood.

"He probably won't even be there, so I'll be back in a couple of hours, I think," Kay continued. "I won't go far, I promise. Just to our usual spot across the border. I wouldn't know where else to go anyway."

Then Mom started to get up, setting aside coffee mug and blanket. "I should go with you. You shouldn't have to do this alone."

Kay held up a hand to stop her. "No, Mom. It's okay. I can do this."

The look of anguish on Mom's face was as bad as Kay

had ever seen it. Like the world was falling apart all over again.

"Mom, I'll be careful."

"At least let me drive you there." She went for her coat across the arm of the sofa and her purse on the dining room table.

Kay started to argue, then didn't, because it would be easier just to let her mother drive her. And if it made Mom feel better, well, it didn't cost Kay anything.

Kind of nice, Kay thought, not having to worry about hiding the Jeep.

During the drive, the silence between them was delicate, like handling well-packed explosives. As long as they took care, nothing would blow up.

They drove past the trailhead to the dirt service road, until the trees blocked them. Mom stopped the car, but kept her hands on the wheel and stared into the forest.

"I'm almost jealous," she said, donning a tight smile. "I've always wanted to meet one of them. Your grandfather was part of the delegation that negotiated the Silver River Treaty. Did you know that?"

Kay had, but didn't know much more than that. Rough details, an old black-and-white photo in the family album. It was a group photo taken outside Silver River, with the northern mountains as a backdrop. Her grandfather was one of the young men in a suit standing to the side, in the crowd surrounding the generals and ambassadors who'd made up the core of the delegation. He'd died when she was too young to really remember him.

"He was just a junior assistant secretary of some sort. But he was there. He met them. And then they were just . . . gone. I think he's part of why I got into this line of work, just to be close. As close as I could."

Maybe, if this all worked out, Kay could bring her mother to meet Artegal. Kay hoped she didn't ask for that now. Kay just wanted to get the car ride over with. She wanted to get out to the woods, to their spot, confirm that Artegal wasn't there, and then tell Branigan this wouldn't work.

"I'll try to hurry up so you won't have to wait long," Kay said.

Mom leaned toward her—fell, almost—and caught Kay up in a tight hug. "Leave your phone on. Call me if you need anything, if anything happens.Though they're probably listening in on our phones now," she said with a short laugh.

"What?" Kay said in a panic.

"Never mind, don't worry about it." But Kay couldn't not worry. She couldn't say anything now without thinking about Branigan listening in. Spying on *her*. Mom said, "If you're not back in an hour and you don't call, I'm coming after you."

Kay wanted to argue, but strangely, the idea comforted her. She couldn't just vanish. "Okay."

She slid out of the car and started into the woods without looking back. She could feel her mother watching her.

Branigan and the others assumed she'd be able to contact Artegal as easily as calling him. That wouldn't work, so she had to come up with another plan. Start a bonfire and send smoke signals? That would attract attention—but probably not Artegal. That was exactly what she needed, to explain herself to a horde of strange dragons.

Even the dragons who'd been coming to the border didn't come to this section, the tumbling stream, the climbing rocks, the narrow glen. So, she was going to leave him a note. She'd already written it out and would tack it to a tree in the place where they'd first met, setting a meeting date for the weekend. She assumed he would come here, if he could. Just to check. She was guessing—hoping— that his people hadn't drafted him for their war or had restricted him or started watching him so he couldn't travel. Any of a million things could happen that would keep him from coming here. Part of her hoped he did stay away.

When the news carried footage of dragons soaring over other cities, racing away like rockets after they'd started fires, she studied them, searching for the lithe, slate gray and silver form of Artegal. She hadn't seen him yet.

She came to the creek and followed it upstream to the place where Artegal had fished her out that first day. The creek was rimed with melting ice, and the log bridge was still there.

So was Artegal, a gray mound settled among the trees, wings tucked to his side, tail wrapped around him. He faced the creek, his neck raised, so he could watch the forest on the other side with those deep onyx eyes.

She stopped and stared for what seemed like a long time.

He lowered his head and blew a steaming breath.

"I've been waiting," he said.

18

She almost hated to cross the border again, now that they knew about her and were watching. But she did, running straight across the log before she could change her mind. Artegal lowered his head so she wouldn't have to crane her neck back to see him. It felt as if years had passed, and she didn't know what to say. She'd *wanted* just to leave the note, like calling someone specifically to leave a message rather than talk to them. But she was so relieved to see him. She had so much to tell him—so much to ask about what had happened, what the dragons were doing. Her throat closed; she could hardly breathe.

"Are you well?" he asked. The first thing he'd ever said to her, months ago. What a strange question now.

"No," she said, and started crying. Stumbling almost, she sat on the ground and buried her face in her arms. All this week, she hadn't cried. It came out now, all at once. Each time she tried to stop, to pull herself together, to talk to him, she choked, and the crying started all over again.

She felt a warm breeze, air smelling of iron and embers. Artegal hovered over her, a worried purr sounding deep in his throat.

"So much has happened," she said, blubbering the words.

"Yes."

She scrubbed her face. They had to talk, and they didn't have much time before her mother started worrying.

"They know about us," she said. "They—the military—got pictures, and they were looking, and I finally just came out and told them because, because . . ."

"Because of the attack. The fire," he said calmly. Not that he was ever anything but calm.

"Are you okay?" she said. She realized she couldn't do it. She couldn't keep secrets anymore, and she couldn't be a spy. The only way she could get the information was to come out and ask him what Branigan wanted to know, and then tell Artegal that the military wanted the information.

He didn't answer right away. Kay's heart sped up. She wondered if things would ever be the same after all this, if they would ever fly again. Already the few times they'd flown together seemed like a memory from another life.

"Some elders say this was inevitable. That people and dragons could never live together. That war is inevitable." The words sounded like an avalanche in his throat. "Some want to talk. But they are afraid."

"I can't imagine you ever being afraid of us," she said, looking up at him, as large as a bus, so powerful. "That's why the military's doing what it's doing, because it's afraid of *you*. They think they have to do this, before you do."

Artegal sighed. "I wish dragons had remained in hiding."

For a fierce, angry moment, so did she. Everything would be normal. She'd be talking with Jon and Tam about prom, college applications, and only one more year 'til graduation, and her father would still be here, and everything would be normal if the dragons hadn't come back. She wouldn't miss the flying because she wouldn't know that she should.

She started crying again.

"You're angry. At me," he said. This time, she couldn't read the curl on his lip, the arc to his brow. She'd been able to read curious, amused, confused, glad. But not this.

"The fire—my dad." *Don't say the words*, something in her cried. *Don't say it, don't make it true. Find a different way to tell him.* "I lost my dad."

He tilted his head—the confused look. After a long silence, though, he lowered his head nearly to the ground. Almost, she was looking down on him.

"Tragedy?" he said, as if confused, seeking confirmation

for the vague way she'd told him.

She hid her face again. He waited for her to collect herself and reemerge.

"It was a warning," he said. "To show that we are not afraid. The elders did not think your people would be so quick to reply."

"So you knew about it," she said. "You knew it was going to happen." *And you didn't stop it, you didn't warn me, you didn't say anything.*

"Not before. After. I almost told them about you. To persuade them not to do it again, if I could."

"Could you? Would they have listened?" The human military finding out about her and Artegal hadn't stopped the bombings. Branigan was driven; he had plans, or else he wouldn't have wanted to her to spy.

Artegal didn't say anything, so she knew the answer was no. "Now it's too big to stop," she said.

"And yet, you risked coming here. I hoped you might. I did not think you would." He tilted his head—glancing up, she realized. He'd been glancing up every minute or so, looking for aircraft or dragons.

She told him, "They want me to spy. They keep bombing, but they don't know where to go. They don't know exactly where you live, and they want me to find out. I'm supposed to spy."

"Surely they're watching now."

Scrambling, she stood and looked around, through all

the trees, upward to the crisp blue sky. The forest was very quiet. She only heard Artegal breathing, like a whisper of air through the trees.

They could be anywhere. Soldiers hiding in the trees, waiting to strike. They wouldn't kill him, she quickly thought. They wanted to talk, they wanted contact with them, that was what they'd told her. But they might try to capture him.

And what if they did? Wouldn't everyone say that she was supposed to want revenge? Shouldn't she be feeling angry?

Her father used to say that his job wasn't about catching the bad guys so much as keeping the peace, that he got further by being friends with people than by being a hard-ass, that if the people in his jurisdiction felt like he was their friend, they wouldn't want to break the law. They wouldn't want to disappoint him, not because he was the sheriff, but because he was their friend.

Her mind moved quickly, turning over everything her father had said, any advice he may have given her about this. Also, what her mother said, about taking care of herself rather than worrying about the rest of the world. And what the military said, about staying out of jail and doing her duty. But she kept going back to what her father said about keeping the peace.

And she realized that the military *wanted* to keep her a secret. They hadn't released the photos or news that Kay and

Artegal had flown together because they didn't want anyone to know that a person and a dragon could work together, could be friends. But if people knew, if they saw—

"What are you thinking?" Artegal watched her. She'd frozen, standing still, staring at nothing as she pondered.

"Can you come back tomorrow?" she asked.

"If I am careful, yes."

"We need to fly again," she said.

He snorted. His eyes widened, and he raised his head—a gesture of surprise. "It won't stay secret."

"We don't want it to. We want everyone to see. That means the military can't keep it secret, either. We want everyone to see it. Your people, my people, everyone."

He thought for a moment. A back claw scratched a furrow in the earth. "Dangerous for us."

It was. She couldn't pretend that it wouldn't be. She'd get in trouble with her people, he'd get in trouble with his. They may never see each other again. But it seemed worth it, just to show people what they could do.

She felt insane when she grinned and said, "Yeah, but if we don't, we'll always wonder if we could have made a difference."

He made the curl in his lip that meant he was smiling. "For all their long years, dragons are not so daring."

"Then you think we shouldn't—"

"I will be here tomorrow. Take care."

"You too." He was already backing up, turning his bulk

through the trees as he slipped away. She waited until she couldn't see him before she ran back.

When she reached the clearing where her mother had parked, Kay stopped at the edge of the trees and stared. Her mother was outside the car, leaning on the hood, a strained look in her eyes.

Two more cars—dark sedans with monochrome government plates—had pulled into the space behind her, and a group of men in uniform were milling around. General Branigan was there, leaning on one of the sedans, an echo of her mother. A couple of guys in olive green fatigues carried machine guns and seemed to be patrolling, moving around the fringes of the clearing and looking into the trees.

Artegal was right. They'd followed her. They were keeping track of her.

This was going to be hard. What she should have done was make herself look disappointed. She should have buried all her anticipation, excitement—and fear. She should have trudged back slowly and used the time to think of a story, either that she hadn't seen Artegal at all or that she had, but she couldn't convince him to tell her anything. But she hadn't thought of it, because her mind was racing with a plan. She considered lying to them, telling them that Artegal hadn't been there, she hadn't talked to him, and she would have to try again another time. But she didn't know how far they'd followed her or how much they'd seen and heard. She assumed they'd been too far away to hear, but she couldn't be sure. If they'd heard the conversation, they'd know they couldn't trust her.

Kay's mother straightened, and her face suddenly shone with relief. "Kay?"

Kay met her and let herself be embraced. But she looked over Mom's shoulder at the military people, who studied her warily.

"Are you okay? Is everything okay?" Mom said.

"It's fine."

A moment later, Branigan was standing next to them. "Well?"

Her mother stiffened, frowning with a spark of anger. Kay knew she'd protect her if she could. Kay didn't need anyone looking out for her; just the same, it made her feel stronger.

"'Well' what?" Kay said.

"What happened?" Branigan said, enunciating, clearly frustrated. *Good*, Kay thought.

After a moment, Kay said, "Nothing."

"Was it there? Did you talk to it?"

"Yeah."

"Well?" Branigan demanded again. Kay thought that he probably didn't have kids.

She shrugged. "It's going to take time. I can't come out and ask how many dragons there are and where they live. I have to be sneaky about it, right? That's what spying's all about, isn't it?"

He glared. "I thought you said it was your friend."

"*He*, not *it*," she said softly. "I just need more time."

"You don't have more time!" He was done being the nice, benevolent father-figure, which was okay, because Kay had been done with him a while ago. "I'm not going to sit by and let a kid like you play games when the fate of humanity is at stake."

Was that at stake? The whole fate of humanity? Branigan was wrong, it didn't all depend on her, but the general had lost control of the big picture. All he could do now was harass her. Like her mother's anger, that knowledge made her feel stronger.

"There wouldn't be a problem if you had just left things the way they were," Kay said.

"As long as those animals exist, humanity's in danger," he said.

So, he was a bigot. That made dealing with him easier.

"Sir," she said, because it would appease him, "I'll try again tomorrow. I'm coming back to talk to him then. I'll try again."

"You're not telling it anything, are you?"

"I don't know anything *to* tell him."

Branigan seemed satisfied at that. She thought, *What a small-minded man*. He thought he knew what she was thinking.

"I look forward to seeing some progress," the general said. Kay nodded.

Branigan and his soldiers waited until Kay and Mom had

climbed in the car and began driving away before following them. They were probably being watched all the time now, which meant she'd have to be very careful when she brought the gear out next time.

After a few minutes, Mom said, "You *are* hiding something. What aren't you telling him?"

The general may have been clueless, but not her mother. Kay started to talk, then swallowed and tried again. "Mom, do you think there should be a war? Even after what happened . . . do you think we should fight them?"

Mom didn't speak right away. The tires hummed in the silence, trees rolled past the window, and Kay thought her mother wasn't going to answer. "I don't know, Kay. They were wrong to go after the town like that. It never should have happened. But then our side was wrong, too. I just don't know. But a war is going to do a lot of damage and hurt a lot more people. I think that would have upset your father."

It wasn't the best answer Kay could have had. It wasn't a yes or no. This whole situation was muddy gray, and she felt as if she were being selfish, wanting to fly again and trying to justify it.

"I think we can stop it," Kay said softly. "We want to try."

"I don't like it," Mom said, shaking her head. "I don't like the idea of you going off by yourself. I don't like thinking of you with dragons."

"I'm sorry. I'm sorry I didn't tell you before, but I couldn't."

Her mother's eyes were red, like she'd been crying, the way they'd been for the last week, ever since the fire. "I'll tell you, though. I like Branigan even less."

"They're watching us, aren't they? They're going to be watching the house. They'll know every time we leave and wherever we go."

"That's what happens when you become interesting to them." After a few more miles of driving, Mom continued, "They don't want to hurt you, Kay. I know they're jerks, and I know you don't like them, but they're following you to protect you. Think about it: If we know who your dragon is, then the dragons know who you are. What's to stop them from coming and taking you? From using you? I don't want you to go to jail, but at least I'd know where you were. The dragons, they could hold you hostage, they could—" The words stopped, and she covered her mouth.

Kay just couldn't think of Artegal hurting her.

"What's to stop Branigan and them from doing the same thing to Artegal? I'd be leading them right to him."

"But, Kay, the dragons are so big and you're not."

Was that what it all came down to? That people were small next to the dragons, and it made them afraid, made them want to destroy the creatures? Or was the problem that dragons were also smart, like people?

Kay couldn't tell her mother the plan. Her mother would

try to stop her, for her own good, and Kay couldn't let that happen.

After they got home, she called Jon. "Let's go out," she told him.

"Are you sure?" he asked. "What about the curfew?" After the night of the fire, an eight P.M. curfew had been set. It was supposed to keep people safe.

"We'll just go to the Alpine or something. We'll be home before then."

He knew her well enough to catch the urgency in her voice.

"Kay, what's going on? I've been by your house, and there's cop cars and people watching—"

"I'll tell you later. Can I meet you at the Alpine at five?"

A pause. Then he said, "Yeah. I'll be there."

In the meantime, she had a ton of gear to get together.

19

The Alpine diner was more crowded than Kay thought it would be. Many people had left town entirely, other families were keeping their kids at home, and with the curfew and all the cops out, she wasn't sure anyone would be around. But it was the usual crowd; Kay recognized most of the faces. It wasn't like there were that many places to go in Silver River, and everyone was probably stir-crazy from worrying. From hearing the sirens, from watching for dragons, and from wondering when the rest of Silver River would burn.

She felt strange being around so many people after she'd been at home for so long. While it would have been nice to lose herself in the crowd, to be anonymous and not have anyone scrutinizing her, when she entered the diner, a momentary hush fell. Faces turned toward her, stared, and quickly looked away. A few people gave her tight-lipped, pitying smiles.

Scanning the booths, she found Jon when he raised his hand. Ignoring the lingering stares (*That's her, Sheriff Wyatt's kid*—she could almost hear the whispers), she rushed to join Jon, sliding in to the seat and falling against him for a heartfelt hug. He turned his face, searching for a kiss, and she gave him one, quick and fleeting. Like everyone else, he was walking on eggshells around her. He looked concerned.

"Are you okay?" He kept his hand on her arm, holding her.

No, of course she wasn't, on so many levels. But she couldn't explain it all right now. She glanced away and blinked to try to keep her eyes from watering. Jon rubbed her shoulder, awkwardly, as if he wasn't sure it was the right thing to do. She wasn't sure either. Part of her wanted to stay close to him, crying, letting him hold her. But she couldn't afford to do that right now.

"It's just been tough," she said finally.

She had considered her problem: Somehow, she had to get her gear to Artegal. But a government sedan was parked outside the house all the time, which meant as soon as she lugged out her climbing gear, Branigan's people would know she was planning something and try to stop her. But if she could get someone else to take the gear to their meeting place, she and Artegal could get the harness on before anyone could stop them. The hard part was that—it had to be someone she could trust, someone who wouldn't freak out when she explained what this was for.

She trusted Jon. But she wasn't sure he wouldn't freak out when she told him. Not that she could blame him. Anyone would freak out.

The waitress came and took their orders. Jon got a hamburger; Kay wasn't hungry. She couldn't remember the last time she'd been hungry or what that felt like. She ordered fries and a Coke just to be eating something and tried to think about how to tell Jon what she needed.

"How's your mom?" he asked, after the silence that followed the waitress's departure.

Upset, Kay thought. Upset about Dad, about the fact her only daughter had been consorting with dragons, about her life's work going down the tubes. Like everything else, it was too much to explain. She shrugged instead.

"Oh my God, you guys are here!" Tam raced over to their booth from the front door. Her eyes were wide. "Are you okay?" she demanded.

Kay was going to get sick of that question. Resigned, she nodded. "About as well as can be expected."

Tam slid into the seat across from her and gazed at Kay as if the world were ending.

"Where's Carson?" Jon asked. Tam's seat looked very empty without Carson squished in beside her. At that,

Tam's face scrunched up, and she started crying. Now it was Kay's turn to hold her hand.

"His family left," she said, sniffing around the words. "He didn't want to go, he was going to stay behind, but they wouldn't let him. They're going to stay with family in Colorado until this is all over, but who knows when that's going to be?"

Kay moved into the seat next to her and hugged her while she sobbed.

Tam went on, "I shouldn't be this upset. It's not like what you're going through with your dad. It's not like I'll never see him again, but I just can't stand that he's gone!"

Kay wouldn't miss Carson like Tam would. But looking at the empty booth, seeing Tam all by herself and not kissing her boyfriend—it was more evidence of just how far from normal everything had gotten. Kay wondered if things would ever feel normal again.

"My folks are waiting to see what happens," Jon said. "Until there's an official evacuation, we're staying."

Kay felt a lurch at the thought of Jon leaving. She wondered if he would stay, if she asked him to.

"Even if you did leave, I'm not sure anywhere's really safe," Kay said. Not that it would make anyone feel better.

"What does your mom say?" Tam asked, wiping her face and recovering. "Are you guys going to leave?"

"I don't think we'll ever leave," she said. Everything they had was here. Everything they had left. And Artegal—she should tell them. Right now, she should tell them. But she'd been keeping the secret so long, the habit was hard to break.

They fell quiet, and then their food came. Tam only got a soda. Kay shared her fries, but none of them was really enthusiastic about eating.

Tam glanced around, then leaned in to tell Kay, "That's so rude, how people are looking at you."

Kay shrugged it off. "I guess I'm kind of famous because of my dad."

Another moment of silence. Jon took her hand. "It's still rude."

Kay had too much on her mind to think about it. Let them stare. If her plan went off, she was going to be even more famous—even though that's not why she was doing it.

Tam's phone rang. It was her mother wanting her to come home. Kay couldn't remember Tam's mother ever calling her when they were out. Tam's mother seemed to operate on the benign neglect theory of parenting. But now she was worried.

Tam hugged them both tightly and left.

Kay didn't have much time left to tell Jon. It was already six. "You want to get out of here?" she asked.

Jon seemed willing to do whatever she wanted. They paid their check and left.

"What are we doing, Kay?"

She looked around, and sure enough, across the street

a dark sedan was parked. She could just make out a pair of men in the front seat. They weren't doing anything.

"You want to go for a hike somewhere? Maybe out by Red Hill?" That was a trailhead on the other side of the town from the border. If the military guys didn't think she was running off to sneak over the border, maybe they wouldn't follow her.

"It's a little late, isn't it?"

The sun was setting—they had another hour of twilight before the sky turned completely dark. She had a flashlight in her glove box.

"I just want to get out of town for a little while."

He shrugged. "Your car or mine?"

"Both. Can you follow me?"

She was grateful that he wasn't asking questions. He looked like he wanted to. As she pulled out of the Alpine parking lot, she kept an eye on the sedan. Jon followed her in his hand-me-down truck. They both turned the corner to head out of town to the highway and the Red Hill trailhead. She lost sight of the sedan, but it hadn't immediately followed them. She breathed a sigh.

Now, they had to hurry.

Fifteen minutes later, she reached the trailhead and pulled into the farthest corner, which was sheltered by trees and mostly dark. Flashlight in hand, she opened the back of the Jeep before Jon had fully parked.

She double-checked the coils of climbing rope, the

nylon straps and carabiners, her harness, and the duffel bag with her extra winter clothes and chemical hand warmers, making sure for the tenth time that everything was there.

"Kay, what's going on?" Jon said, coming to join her. He saw the gear, and his expression became even more confused. "What are you doing? You don't actually want to go climbing right now—"

Here it was. Moment of truth. How little could she tell without him guessing the rest? And if he guessed the rest, what would he do?

"I need a really big favor," she said, wincing, because that didn't even begin to cover what she was asking him to do.

"Sure. What?"

Suddenly, she didn't want to bring him into this. She didn't want to get him in trouble or put him in danger. This was asking too much. "You can say no. If you don't want to do it, that's okay. But you can't tell anyone. Okay? I'll find another way, but you can't tell anyone."

He frowned, worried. "Kay, just tell me what it is. You've been acting weird for weeks."

She supposed she had. She hadn't realized it showed. Grimly, she moved forward. "Tomorrow morning, as early as you can, I need you to take all this out and hide it in the woods, near the stream where it comes down along the border. I've got GPS coordinates marked on a map here." She dug the topographic map out of the bag, handed it to him. "Mark it with a ribbon in a tree or something."

"Why? What are you doing that you can't take it your-self?"

"I don't want anyone to see me with it. They'll know what I'm planning, and I want to surprise them. I have to surprise everyone." She was speaking quickly, with a desperate edge to her voice. She had never sounded like this before, not even after the fire.

"Surprise who? Who's going to see you?"

"The military's watching me. It's a long story. It's too long to explain. But can you please just do this?"

He hesitated, but he put his hands on the rope when she pushed the coils toward him. He studied the map. "So I hide the ropes out there. Kay, this is right next to the border, there's no way I can get out there. There's no way either of us can get out there."

She shook her head. "If you go early and you're careful, you'll be fine."

"What about you?"

"I just have to do this."

His eyes grew wide, and her stomach did a flip-flop, because he was too smart for her to fool him. It was one of the things she liked about him.

"You're going across the border? Kay, why? What's that going to accomplish? You think you can go talk to them? Yell at them for killing your dad or what?"

"I've been crossing the border for months," she said softly.

For a long moment, he stared. She felt awful, because

she'd been lying to him all this time. But she couldn't have told him the truth before now. The whole truth still caught in her throat—she couldn't tell him about Artegal. That secret wasn't only hers to tell.

"All those times you said you were off hiking by yourself, that's where you were," he said finally.

"Yeah."

He chuckled, a harsh sound. "I guess I'm relieved. I thought maybe you were hiding another boyfriend somewhere."

She huffed. "Who would that possibly be? There's nobody else. I'm still the only virgin at Silver River High."

"No, you're not," he said.

She felt a warm flush. Glancing at him, she put her hand over his, where it rested on the ropes.

"So," he said, looking at their hands together, but not moving. "Have you ever seen a dragon? Up close, I mean."

She didn't answer, which was answer enough.

"And why do you want to go back now? When the military is watching and jets could be bombing you any minute—"

"I have to do something. The military found out what I've been doing, and they want me to spy, but I can't because if there's even a chance I can stop this, I have to try."

"Kay, there's a reason we're bombing them. Those things killed your dad!"

Her eyes stung. She hadn't cried enough over this. But there was too much to do, she couldn't stop to cry. When she spoke again, her voice cracked. "And how is sitting around being angry about it while the whole world goes up in smoke going to change that?"

She wanted to think that her father would understand. That he'd want her to try to stop this. That he'd be proud of her.

"What does this have to do with going over to Dragon?" he said, indicating the ropes and harness.

If he knew, he wouldn't do it. He wouldn't help her. He'd be like her mother, horrified that she had put herself in so much danger, supposedly just for a thrill. Apparently, rock climbing was one thing. Dragon riding was completely different.

"I just need to," she said, and left it at that.

He frowned, but he loaded the gear into his truck. "I hope you know what you're doing."

So did she.

When they finished, she said, "I wasn't kidding. I'd still like to go for a walk, if you want. We can stay along the road, where we can see." The sky was a deep, dark blue, the light of day almost gone.

Jon glanced at his watch. "It's an hour 'til curfew. It'll have to be short."

"That's okay."

Side by side, they set off. Jon fumbled until he found her hand, then clasped it tight. They went a hundred yards in silence. Kay realized her hand was stiff in his, because she was nervous. More than nervous—scared. Terrified. She didn't have to do this; she could walk away. But she remembered what the pilot, Captain Conner, said about her and Artegal being the only ones who could talk to each other. If people and dragons were going to talk, it had to start with them.

She had to try, or she would have to watch this war get worse and wonder if she could have stopped it.

"If Tam knew we were out here, she'd start spreading all kinds of rumors about what we were up to," Jon said. "Your reputation would be ruined."

"Maybe that would be a good thing. She'd stop nagging me."

"She nags you?"

"She thinks everyone ought to sleep with somebody."

"What do you think?" He looked at her, his gaze searching.

"I don't know," she said after a moment. She was suddenly warm, and if she closed her eyes, she could feel Jon studying her. "I think I don't want to do it just because everyone else is."

After another long hesitation, Jon asked, "Do you ever think about it? Do you ever want to?"

She remembered something Tam had said about dying a virgin, thought about what she was going to be doing tomorrow, and wondered if she and Jon should run off into the woods and have sex right now. That wasn't how she imagined them sleeping together for the first time—not that she was sure how she'd ever imagined it. Like it was in the movies or in the romance novels her friends used to pass around with the corners turned down on the pages with sex scenes. Something full of passion, on a bed with big fluffy pillows and candles burning. Not out in the cold, scared, worried, distracted.

"Yeah," she admitted finally. "Sometimes. Then sometimes I just can't picture myself, you know, having sex."

Jon spoke softly, "I think about it a lot."

She watched her feet, scuffing the dirt, unable to look back at the intensity in his eyes. "Tam says it's the best thing in the world. Half the time I don't think she knows what she's talking about. She doesn't think it's normal for two people to go out and not sleep together."

"What about you?"

Her whole body felt flushed, being so close to Jon, having this conversation. Something in her, some loud voice—it didn't even sound like Tam—whispered, *Come on, just turn your face. Just look at him. Just kiss him. Just turn and kiss him. Think of how wonderful kissing him would be.*

She gripped his hand more firmly. "I keep waiting for something to tell me it's the right time. I keep thinking I'll get some sign telling me when I'm ready."

"And what if you don't? I mean, does it really work like that?"

She tried to figure out if he was trying to tell her that he wanted to sleep with her and that he wanted to do it now but couldn't find the words.

"Are you trying to tell me something, Jon?" she said, because she was too tired and confused to work it out on her own.

They walked a few more steps, arms brushing, closer than ever, even though it was awkward with them both wearing heavy coats and bundled against the cold. He said, "Just thinking out loud."

If she were waiting for a sign, she wondered if she'd notice it before it passed. And if she missed one chance, would she get another? This was too much to think about right now, when it should have been such a little thing next to dragons, war, and death.

She stopped, turned toward him, tipped her face up, started to stand on her toes—but she didn't have to move far, because he was right there, kissing her. As if he'd been waiting, holding back until she made the first move. After that, she could barely keep up with him. Their lips touched, moved together. A pleasant dizziness washed through her—far from cold now, she almost wanted to take her coat off, to be closer to him. His hand moved to her waist, found the edge of her jacket, and slipped under it. He'd taken his gloves off, and she shivered as his skin touched hers.

They could do it. They really could. No one was out here, no other cars around for miles—

Then a jet roared overhead. Far to the north, an orange glow burned on the horizon, the remnant fires of bombing raids. The air smelled of soot.

They broke apart. Jon glanced at his watch. "It's almost eight."

"Yeah. Okay." She had to catch her breath.

They almost jogged back to their cars, their breath smoking in the cool air. He was right—if she really was being followed by military agents, she should have paid more attention to the time. They'd love to catch her out after curfew.

Before leaving, they hugged one more time. "You'll take that stuff for me?" she reminded him.

He pressed his lips in a grim smile. "Yeah."

"Thanks."

Kay had the worst time trying to act normal around her mother that night and the following morning, although she wasn't sure Mom noticed. They'd been away from normal for a week now. She wasn't expected to act normal.

Mom wasn't acting normal. When Kay announced she was going to bed, her mother got up from the couch where she'd been watching TV and came over to give her a long, earnest hug. She didn't say anything, just held her as if she were afraid Kay would vanish in the night.

Kay almost gave up on her plan right there.

Over breakfast the next morning, Mom eyed her carefully.

Kay's hand kept shaking when she tried to eat her cereal.

"You're going to try to talk to it again today?" her mother asked.

"Yeah," Kay said, not meeting her gaze. "I have to be all patriotic, I guess."

"Kay, if you don't want to do it, I'll stand by you. General Branigan has *no* right to ask you to do this. Whatever he threatens you with, we'll deal with it. We'll take it to the press to generate support if we have to."

That was exactly what Kay was planning on doing. She shook her head and still couldn't look at her mother. "I want to help. I want to do it."

Pale, tight-lipped, Mom nodded.

Once again, Mom insisted on driving, and once again Kay didn't argue. Even though she waited, there was nothing her mother could do once the plan started. She couldn't interfere. But she hoped Jon got the gear out to where she could find it.

As they drove, Kay looked around and found one of the sedans behind them on the highway. Her mother's glance in the rearview mirror showed she saw it, too.

"They followed me last night," Kay said. "Just like they've been watching the house."

"Bastards," Mom muttered. "But that's okay. They can follow us all they want. We're only doing what they want us to. We're not doing anything wrong."

Kay's stomach had turned into butterflies.

They stopped in the same place and repeated the ritual, Kay's mother urging her to call. Kay wondered if she'd even get reception a thousand feet up. Or if it was anything like flying on an airline. *Please turn off all cell phones and pagers . . .*

She almost laughed.

Kay hugged her mother extra hard, then went off into the woods. She had to concentrate not to look back.

She'd given Jon a pretty detailed map, marking off an easy-to-find spot where the stream turned, but that still left a fairly wide area where he could have left the gear. Marking a spot or trail by tying something to a branch at eye level was a common practice. So, when she reached the general area, she started searching for something that stood out, for anything colorful and fluttering that would mark the spot.

She didn't have too much time for this. She'd have to meet Artegal, and then they'd have to move quickly.

"Kay! Over here!"

She spun, panicked, looking for the source of the call. Who had followed her? Her first instinct was to run.

Then she saw Jon, duffel bag over his shoulder, waving his hand.

20

He was right where she'd asked him to be, near the creek, downstream a ways from where she met Artegal. She stared for a moment then, angry, scrambled to him.

"Jon! What are you doing here?"

"I can't let you do this by yourself."

"You don't even know what I'm doing!"

He didn't say anything, because she was right. She was sort of disappointed, because she wanted to argue with him.

"It's better if you stay out of it," she said, grabbing the strap of the duffel bag and pulling it away from him. The coils of rope were lying at his feet, and she picked those up as well. She started hiking along the stream toward the clearing.

Jon followed. She thought of yelling at him, but that

wouldn't make him stop. She'd have to go back herself, not meet Artegal and not go through with the plan.

Tempting.

"Jon. Please." She turned on him and glared.

"I'm worried about you. I want to help."

She didn't have time for this. She didn't want to have to worry about him, too. Maybe she'd been wrong to ask for his help at all. She kept walking. "You can't help."

"Why not?"

"Because it's . . . it's too big. There's too much to explain. I'm sorry, Jon. I'm just . . . I'm sorry."

She hiked, he followed, and she didn't argue with him again. The whole point of this was to reveal the big secret, to go public. May as well start now. She had no idea how he'd react once he realized what she was doing. He may never speak to her again for keeping this from him. That almost made her stop; she didn't think she could handle it if Jon stopped talking to her. But he wouldn't do that; she wouldn't like him so much if he was the kind of guy who would do that.

Only a few minutes of hiking brought them to the creek. It glittered in the sunlight. Beyond, the forest looked no different than it did on this side of the border.

"That's the border, isn't it?" he said, stopping at the edge of the water, staring. "We can't go over there. They'll kill us." He pursed his lips. "*Somebody'll* kill us."

"It'll be okay," she said, wishing she sounded more

confident. She looked around; if anyone else had followed her, she couldn't see them. "Jon, no matter what happens, don't be angry with me. Please?"

"No, of course not. I just . . . I just want to understand with this is about."

He would, soon enough. She kissed Jon's cheek, squeezed his hand, then crossed the log bridge over the partly frozen creek.

He held back, looking at her with panic in his eyes. She hadn't realized how much she'd taken crossing the border for granted. How deeply ingrained the rules had been until she'd met Artegal by accident.

"Kay?" Jon called, not moving.

Kay had only just touched the opposite bank when a familiar noise grew louder—at first, it blended with the jangle of running water. It sounded like a breeze. But Kay knew what it was. Something large with heavy footfalls moved through the forest.

Artegal appeared, neck snaking forward, shadowy body moving into view.

Jon's eyes widened. "Oh my God—"

"No, Jon, wait."

He stumbled back, tripping over himself as he started to run away. At the same time, Artegal reared back, curling his neck, spreading his wings, making himself appear larger. A hot breath snorted from his nose and fogged in clouds.

Jon was beyond words, his face locked in terror.

"Jon! Artegal! Stop!" She called to Jon and looked over

her shoulder to Artegal, unsure who she should yell at first.

Jon fell, limbs splayed, gazing up at the monster that had stopped at the edge of the water, as if he might spring forward. Artegal had lowered himself to peer more closely at the strange human. Kay was standing next to his huge head, but he hardly seemed to notice her.

"This is my friend, Jon," Kay said to the dragon. "Jon, this is . . . this is Artegal."

Kay's two friends studied each other.

"Oh my God," Jon breathed, his voice shaking a little.

After a long moment, the dragon breathed, "Hello."

"Jesus, Kay!" Jon said. Kay tried to remember the terror she'd felt the first time the scaled face looked down on her. She couldn't remember it very well.

"It's okay, Jon! I swear to you it's okay."

Artegal turned to her, head shifting on snakelike neck. "Why is he here?"

Sadly, she said, "He wouldn't stay away."

"It talks!" Jon said.

"Of course he does," she said.

"You can't come with us," Artegal said.

Jon looked like he was having trouble breathing. Never taking his eyes off the dragon, he sat up. "C-come with you? Where?"

Artegal nodded, a tip of his narrow snout, and turned to Kay. "We should go."

"Go? Kay, what are you doing?" Jon demanded.

"Jon, please go home. If you see my mom—I don't know what to tell her. Make up some excuse. Just keep them from looking here." She put on her climbing harness and started laying out the ropes. Artegal crouched to where she could throw them over his back.

"Are you doing what I think you're doing?" Jon said. "Kay, that's *crazy*."

Kay secured the knots over Artegal's chest before turning on him. "Jon, please, we have to do this."

"But why—"

Artegal's head lifted, his neck straightening. He looked around, scanning the area, nostrils flaring.

They'd been arguing, not paying attention. Kay tensed, anxious to spot what had startled the dragon. She heard only one thing: the rapid beat of an approaching helicopter. Then she saw people, men in black fatigues, rifles pointed ahead of them, emerging through the trees. The first was visible a dozen yards behind Jon, but when Kay turned, she seemed to find them everywhere. She hadn't heard them at all.

Now, they surrounded the area.

Action erupted. A couple of the soldiers shouted cryptic one-word orders and replies. Something launched from the trees, and Kay choked on a scream because she thought it was a bullet or a rocket. She realized then that she'd believed no one would shoot at her, that even if the soldiers did follow her and find her with Artegal, they wouldn't shoot.

But the shot wasn't a weapon—it was some kind of net, weighted on the corners, that flattened as it sailed toward Artegal, too fast to dodge. The dragon turned, shouldering it away. Instinctively, he batted at it with a claw, and the net tangled around his arm and wing—as it was supposed to. Twisting his neck, he snapped at it, snarling, exhaling smoke.

Branigan hadn't really expected her to spy on Artegal. So he used her to trap him.

Shouting now, Kay ran forward to tug the net away.

"Artegal, stop a minute!" He did, looking at her, his black eyes wide.

She jumped up to reach the tangled length of the net, grabbed it, pulled. She couldn't find the ends, couldn't find where it had gotten caught; the more she tugged and twisted the net's ropes, the more snarled they became.

Artegal stretched his head high, his neck curving over her, which must have given him a view of the whole clearing, and of the soldiers swarming toward them. She was close to his chest and heard him inhale, his body expanding, and a sound like a growl rattling deep in his chest.

Then, he exhaled, an explosive burst of air—and fire.

The dragon turned, sweeping a line of fire in a long arc around them, clearing a space, keeping the soldiers at bay. It sounded like a forge, a blow torch, and Kay fell to the ground, arms over her head, choking at the soot-and-ash smell of it, her head ringing with the sound of trees catching fire. Heat washed over her. It was just like the fire in town, flames meant to kill. She was in the middle of it, and she couldn't move.

"No! Don't shoot! Don't shoot!"

Sheltered under Artegal's body, Kay looked. Jon dashed across the stream, splashing in the water, not bothering with the bridge. He was yelling at the soldiers, who now turned and leveled their weapons at him. Once again, Kay almost screamed in panic. But there came a shouted order to stand down. A few of the trees burned, orange flames climbing, sending up tendrils of smoke, and one of the soldiers yelled into a radio.

Artegal's fire had kept the soldiers back, had made them hesitate. He'd given her more time. She got back to work, and this time the net came free. With a shudder the dragon shed the rest of it.

"Kay, now," Artegal said with a snort. He crouched low, hunched protectively over her.

Kay grabbed the ropes and hauled herself onto Artegal's back. He launched, straight up.

"Stop! Hold it!" There must have been a half dozen gruff male voices yelling at her, commanding her.

A noise popped like a firecracker.

"Don't shoot!" she heard Jon yell again.

Then she didn't hear anything but wind in her ears.

She didn't have her harness clipped on. She looped the ropes around her arms and clung to them, keeping herself flat against the dragon's back because that made her more stable.

"I'm not hooked in!" she shouted to him, and thumped his shoulder. She felt the snort of acknowledgment echo through his lungs.

They didn't have to do any fancy flying. That wasn't the plan for this trip. They just needed to be seen.

Once clear of the trees, Artegal leveled off. His wings flapped hard, and she hadn't realized how much soaring he'd done on their other flights. Those had been almost leisurely, riding thermals, swooping in circles, his wings stretched like sails, sometimes not moving at all. Now, his muscles bunched, released, the wings scooping over and over as they flew faster and faster, wind whipping past her. She wasn't built for this. Artegal, on the other hand, was streamlined, cutting through the air like a missile. She couldn't see over his shoulder to judge their location, but he must have covered miles in the last few minutes.

She heard a strange, distant thumping—mechanical, sinister. Helicopter. She looked around and saw it past the shadow of Artegal's moving wing. There were several of them, coming from all directions; a couple were black, sleek and military, but a couple of others were white, with news channel markings on the sides. Artegal tipped up, spun, and banked out of the way. They couldn't follow. But there was no doubt that they'd seen her. He showed his back to them all.

The military had kept the pictures of their earlier flight

secret. This time, Kay and Artegal needed to be seen by the cameras.

When Artegal banked again, she saw that they were well over the border, just like they'd planned, sailing near the highway that ran toward Silver River. Someone had to see them. The news crews wouldn't be able to resist getting pictures.

She'd planned to have the harness clipped on. Then, she'd be able to straighten, lean back, wave her arms around, shout, and draw as much attention as possible. They may still see her, flattened and clinging to Artegal's back, but it wouldn't be as impressive. It wouldn't be as clear that they were partners in this. Hell, unless she moved around, she might look dead, strapped to his back in some morbid display.

After unlacing one hand from the rope, she found the carabiner at the front of her harness. Her heart was racing. She hoped Artegal didn't make any sudden lurches while she was dangling like this. *Don't look down*, she murmured to herself over and over. *Don't look down, don't look down.* She kept her gaze focused on the ropes and the gleaming scales of Artegal's back.

Her gloved hand couldn't work the carabiner on the harness, so she took the glove off with her teeth. Her hand started shaking in the freezing air. Or maybe she was just that scared.

This will be worth it, she told herself. Writhing, she

maneuvered up the rope to the loop in the middle of Artegal's back, clinging so tightly, her hands were going numb.

Then, finally, she snapped on to the loop of rope.

"I'm hooked in!" she yelled.

Artegal roared. Then he corkscrewed. Kay screeched with fright. And, if she was honest, excitement.

The land, snow-patched spring meadows and stretches of forest, rolled under her, then buildings from the town appeared. Artegal dipped, swooping close enough that she could see cars on the road, see them screeching to a halt, and see tiny people climbing out and looking up. The news vans, where were the news vans?

Outside the temporary FBBE headquarters, where they'd been parked all week. She found the knots in the rope of the harness and pressed the left-hand one into Artegal's shoulder. He veered in that direction. She wished she could explain to him exactly what they were looking for. Satellite dishes on top of vans. People with cameras and microphones.

If they circled long enough, though, someone would call in the cameras.

Unless Artegal banked, she couldn't see what they were flying over. She could, however, see what else was flying. Craning her head, she spotted two or three military helicopters. Rapid popping noises, like stuttering fireworks, rattled the air.

Machine guns. They were firing.

Artegal veered sharply, and for a heart-stopping moment Kay thought he'd been shot. She looked around for blood. But there'd been no flinch of pain; the dragon was simply altering his flight path to make himself less of a target. He rose, dived, and spun, and Kay started to feel a little airsick. She clamped her eyes shut, but that made it worse, so she concentrated on keeping her gaze on the ropes across the dragon's back.

He kept ahead of them—that was what had always maintained the balance, that dragons were as fast as anything flown by humans. But they kept firing. Artegal dropped in altitude, and dropped again. They weren't shooting at him, she realized. They were trying to force him to land.

In response, he dived sharply and twisted, and she gasped, clinging even harder to the ropes. She was sure she was locked in, but that didn't stop the panic. He was weaving, turning, swooping in circles, barely high enough to clear buildings, and he'd left the helicopters far behind. When he leveled off, he was skimming the ground. She looked across and saw trees at their level.

If this didn't work, nothing would.

Kneeling on his back, Kay let the harness take her weight. She raised her arms, stretching them straight up. The wind punched into her, and she laughed.

They would be seen. No doubt about it. A role model for the community, her father had said. *The sheriff's daughter—the hero's daughter*, the captions on the photos had read. Kay didn't know how real any of that was. She certainly didn't feel like a role model. But her father had been right, and people would pay particular attention to this, and treat it as more than a stunt, because of who she was.

Looking up, she saw news helicopters along with the military helicopters, and Kay wondered what kind of conversation was going on between their radios. The air was getting crowded. But she waved at them, hoping they could see her smile.

Artegal must have also felt they were getting hemmed in, because his wings started pumping again, and he climbed, ignoring gunfire and pursuing helicopters. She was so worried about him getting shot, she stopped worrying about falling.

This was only the first part of it. They'd been seen by the human side. Now, they needed to be seen by the dragons. He headed north and west, to the border, to the narrow valleys where they had practiced flying. Kay huddled on Artegal's back, wrapped in her coat for warmth, as he rocketed deeper into dragon territory.

This flight wasn't as exhilarating as the others had been. Before, they'd been playing. This flight had purpose. It was serious, more serious than anything she'd ever done. More serious even than her father's funeral, which had, in some ways, seemed like watching a movie about someone else.

But this—she felt her blood rushing in her ears.

She wanted to know she was going to be okay when this was all over. Artegal was taking her to see dragons. She wondered if this was what it felt like to go to war.

She wondered if she ought to be waving a white flag of truce.

The mountains grew closer. Artegal pointed toward them like an arrow. All the times she had looked north, watching the dragons, specks soaring in the distance, she never thought she'd be this close. Now, she wondered if she had secretly wanted to go to them all this time, like climbing a rock face that was off limits, an exotic spot on her map. She wanted to see, just for a moment.

When Artegal veered, she looked over, around the sail of his wing, and saw them. Dragons, three of them, like castles in the sky, growing larger as they approached.

It was far too late to change her mind, to turn back, and she grew afraid. She didn't want to do this; she didn't want to be here. She huddled on Artegal's back, but there was no way the blue and red ropes and her black parka would blend in with his scales.

A roar echoed toward them, then modulated, changing pitch, tone, rhythm. Artegal roared back in a clipped way she'd never heard before, different from his full-lunged shouts. Speech. This was how dragons talked to one another.

He climbed and spun so that his back faced them. This

was what they'd come here to do, just like showing off for the news cameras. She had to do her part now.

She crouched to her knees, braced against the harness, and waved, making sure the dragons could see her.

Two of the dragons were different shades of green; one was brilliant red, like a ruby. They split apart, arcing around Artegal, coming from both sides, and flanked him, penning him in.

They could force him down in a way the helicopters couldn't. They could match his speed, his maneuverability. They were bigger than he was. Artegal was a young dragon, after all. If they caught him, what would they do with her?

Take me home, Kay wanted to yell, but the wind would carry her words away.

Then she thought, maybe Branigan was right. He was a spy, and he'd been planning to carry her back to Dragon and keep her hostage all along. Everyone would know where she was because they'd flown over Silver River. They'd advertised the fact that he was kidnapping her. She was an idiot. She should have stayed home. This whole time, she should have stayed home. She never should have gone back to meet Artegal that second time. The dragons were soaring toward them now, gaining altitude, getting above Artegal so they could force him to the ground. And Artegal wasn't doing anything.

But that was a ruse. A moment later, he dropped a wing.

His whole body tipped sideways and fell, low enough that his wing cut into the treetops. Then he raced up, wings pumping hard. The pressure of the harness dug into her, and ropes dug into the scales of his shoulders, and she was almost floating, hanging against the harness.

He flew higher than they ever had, and she started to wonder how high he could go, and if it would be too high for her, because the air was thin even here, and she was having trouble drawing breath. But he wasn't flying straight up. He was making an arc. A high, narrow arc. At the apex of it, he seemed to hang for a moment, hovering, motionless, his wings swept back, his nose pointed down. The other dragons were far below them.

He dived. As they dropped, his speed increased. He fell like a bomb to the silver ribbon of water that was the border, and while the other dragons might reach him, they couldn't stop something going so fast.

The speed and cold tried to flay the skin from her face. She wanted to look, to watch the ground come up, to see what the other dragons did. But she had to bury her face in her sleeve and cling to the ropes while she tugged against the clip on the harness, seemingly weightless.

When Artegal spun, she tried to brace and ride with it as they'd practiced. But this was different, flailing, out of control—his wings stuck out, flapping loudly, caught against the air instead of using it. Kay jerked against the harness. And Artegal fell.

It shouldn't have been possible—he was made for flying, built for the sky. But he tumbled until, with a massive grunt and shudder through his whole body, he spread his wings, which filled with air. His body jerked, swung, yanked to a stop. Kay crashed into his back. Then she saw what had happened.

Jets rocketed overhead—Kay didn't hear them because they were moving too fast, leaving the roaring sound of their engines behind them. They went right overhead, maybe only a few hundred feet above them. Probably more, but it felt close, close enough to knock Artegal out of the air with their passage.

Artegal climbed again. As far as she could tell, he was trying to regain his bearings. She could almost feel his heart beating through his back, and she wished she could see his face, to tell if he was worried, scared, angry, or something else.

Now that the jets had passed on, she could hear them, a mechanical scream that didn't sound at all like the dragons calling to one anther. Two of them, flying side by side, the new, super-agile jets. The Dragonslayers. They arced around, tracing a vast circle around the area.

The other three dragons turned to pursue the jets. The jets broke apart, made sharp turns, and moved to face them. Artegal hovered, watching. He seemed poised between wanting to join in the fight and wanting to flee.

The three dragons engaged the jets.

If they'd been conventional jets, the dragons would have flown circles around them. But when the dragons spun and twisted, their long tails coiling and snapping behind them, wings dipping and flapping, these jets turned with them, pivoting on their specially designed engines. Two of the dragons worked together to keep one of the jets between them—for a moment, they looked as if they were trying to trap it, to grab it in their claws as they'd snatch at their prey. The jets and bodies of the dragons were almost the same size, but with their long necks and tails, the dragons were bigger and could envelop the aircraft. The jet's afterburners flared, and it rocketed ahead, out of reach.

At the same time, the other jet spun toward them, dodging out of the way of the third dragon, harassing it. It fired. Guns or missiles or something. Kay only saw something flare like a spark from the jet's underbelly, and trails of white smoke flew away from it. But nothing happened. Whatever it was, it didn't hit anything.

It was a real dogfight, like in an old war movie. They looked like crows fighting over a scrap of food. Kay couldn't follow the actions, couldn't guess what each player would do next. Artegal groaned. Kay felt it through his back, a rumble like thunder.

The first jet broke away from the two pursuers, and again the other jet fired. The dragons dodged—nothing would hit them. The second jet was intent on helping the other, on firing at the two dragons, which were leading it away, drawing it on—giving the third dragon, the scarlet one, a chance to act.

The red dragon pounced. That was what it looked like. It leaped up in the air, gaining extra altitude, somehow flying even higher than it had, as if launching from a solid base. Then it fell over the apex of its arc. But it didn't spread its wings, it didn't try to halt its descent, it didn't catch its fall. At the last moment, when it was right on top of the aircraft, it reached out with its hind legs and landed hard, claws digging into steel, scrabbling for purchase around wings, engines, canopy, rivets, and seams, whatever it could catch.

The jet fell. The dragon's weight slammed into it, and the pilot lost control. The plane flipped sideways and plummeted. Engines flamed to life as the pilot tried to regain control. Kay tried to imagine what he was saying over the radio. She wondered if it was Captain Conner.

Spinning now, the two tangled together, the dragon's tail coiled around the craft's body like a snake, his fanged jaws closed over the canopy. The jet straightened, wobbled— then the dragon lurched, stuck out a wing, tipping the plane off balance again, and they went back to tumbling.

If he had let go, if he had let the aircraft escape, they both could have survived. Maybe he couldn't let go. Maybe he was locked in, stuck, trapped—too dizzy to think. Or maybe he just wouldn't.

Artegal screamed his own fierce jet-engine roar and

plunged after them, wings flapping, reaching toward speed. But it was too late; he was too far behind. And he couldn't have done anything. Jet and dragon together plunged into the treetops of the forest, and a moment later a fireball exploded, rolling, cutting a path of flames through the trees. The sound was a different kind of roar, a rush of fire. A moment after that, a wave of heat passed over them. A thick, black tower of smoke, like the one they'd followed to Captain Conner's crash, rose high over the forest.

Kay was crying. Her nose was running. She couldn't think. She would never get that image out of her mind.

The other jet climbed, circled, then sped south, back toward its base.

Artegal lurched forward, flying fast, but without purpose or destination. He dipped, swooped, and finally fell into a pattern that made a wide circle around the place where the jet and dragon had crashed. She didn't look down toward the fire burning below. She didn't want to see what was there.

The other two dragons, the green ones who were left, circled with Artegal. They called to one another across the distance with roars and whistles. Kay wished she knew what they were saying. It may as well have been Latin. Were they older dragons? Could they remember a time when people and dragons worked together? If so, would they understand, or would seeing Artegal and Kay together only make them angry?

She almost thought she could understand them—the roars became deeper, the whistles more insistent, angrier, maybe. The green dragons loomed above Artegal. She could imagine them plunging down on her in the same way the red one had landed on the plane.

Artegal stretched his wings and wheeled away. South, back toward the border. He flapped his wings and stretched out, the way he flew when he wanted speed. Kay looked over her shoulder—the other dragons didn't follow. They looped, soared, dived, and watched them fly away, but continued marking the spot where the red dragon had fallen.

When they came within sight of the river, Artegal didn't dive, but slowly descended until he skimmed the treetops, the tips of the pines brushing and waving at his passage. Sailing on outstretched wings, he landed, touching his feet to the ground, leaning forward on his wings, and settling his body to earth.

They stayed there, still, a long time. Artegal rested, catching his breath, head hung low on a curved neck. She lay flat, trying to understand what had happened, trying to think of what to do next. It was easier simply to lie here.

Finally, because it probably annoyed Artegal having her hanging off him, she braced her weight to put slack in the harness and unclipped herself. She slid down Artegal's shoulder to the ground.

He turned slightly, only changing the angle of his head,

to look at her. His eyes were shining. His mouth was long, frowning. They gazed at each other for a long time. Kay didn't know what to say. She was still crying, softly this time, tears falling, freezing on her cheek.

"Now I've lost someone, too," Artegal said.

"Who—who was he?" she managed to stammer.

"Brother's mentor."

It wasn't quite an uncle. She wondered what the relationship meant to a dragon, how important someone like that would be. She didn't understand. How could she grieve with him if she didn't understand? How could they even talk?

"I'm sorry," she said.

With a sigh, he tipped his nose to the ground. He'd never done that before. He'd brought his head low; he'd looked her in the eye at her level. But she'd never seen him rest his head, as if it were too heavy to hold up.

She wondered if dragons cried.

Hesitating, she touched his face, the narrow ridge of his snout that ran between his eyes. He blinked, left his eyes half closed, and nudged himself closer. Then she was hugging him, wrapping her arms around the narrow part of his neck, behind his head.

"Was this our fault?" she said. "Did they fight because of us?"

His breaths were sighs, like he was tired. "Would have happened. If not now, then later."

"What are we going to do?"

He shuddered slightly—a shrug, almost. She stepped away so he could look at her more easily. "If we can, we should make something of this. Already too many sacrifices. This will make it worse. Before, it was two warriors shaking their claws at each other. Now, there will be armies. Not skirmishes, but battles."

She could see it, because the *Dracopolis* book had pictures of it: a swarm of dragons filling the sky, a tapestry of wings. Below them, a sea of human beings with siege engines. Now, when the humans had jets and bombs, how much worse would it be?

How did you stop such a thing? *Too many sacrifices*, he'd said.

Artegal looked up, studied the sky, as if he had heard something that she had not. "We should go. Quickly. They'll find us. Catch us. Can't let that happen."

It seemed inevitable at this point. Why fight it? She wanted to throw a tantrum. Stand up and just scream for them to stop it—why couldn't they all just stop it?

Maybe she ought to try it. What was there to lose? Herself and her mother. A friendship. She undid his harness, helped him pull it off his back, and began coiling it. She had a weird idea.

"Artegal?"

He'd been studying the sky again, but snorted and looked at her. They'd discussed the book. She'd brought translations to share, and he'd told her what he'd been able to translate. They'd studied the extra sheet of paper tucked in the back and tried to understand what it meant—a treasure map, Kay thought; a lost cave of dragons still in hiding, Artegal thought. *In Greenland?* she wondered. But they hadn't talked about everything in the book, and so she asked.

"The *Dracopolis* book talks about virgin sacrifices. About how, in the old days, villages would give virgins to the dragons to make them stop attacking. Did that actually work?"

He tilted his head—a sign of curiosity. "I think it did. It was a sign of what people were willing to give for peace."

She swallowed a lump in her throat. "Did the dragons actually eat the girls who were sacrificed?"

"I think it depended on the dragon. Some were kept, like pets. At least that's what our stories say."

This was grim. She could understand the knights coming after the dragons, willing to fight to stop such a thing. But she could also understand being desperate enough to sacrifice one person to save everyone, to stop a war.

One last question, one that should have occurred to Kay a long time ago. It was the big overriding question of her life, at least according to Tam.

"Why virgins?" she asked Artegal.

He snorted a foggy breath. "I don't know. That was the humans' idea. We can't tell the difference."

She clapped a hand over her mouth, but that didn't stop the bubble of laughter. It was sharp, too loud in their quiet clearing. Artegal jerked, startled, raised his head, and stared.

We can't tell the difference. That made the whole question wonderful, didn't it? It didn't matter. It didn't matter if she was or not.

She shook her head. "I can't explain it. It's just—you're right. It's not important. But here's the thing, Artegal. I am one. And if we could, do you think it would work?"

"A sacrifice?" he breathed.

"I mean, you wouldn't have to eat me. You wouldn't, would you?"

"Silly. No," he said.

"It wouldn't even have to be a real sacrifice. We pretend that it is. We make a big show of it—" And then what? Go back to the way they were? The whole point of a sacrifice was to change everything, to make sure things didn't stay the same.

"The elders wouldn't believe it. They trusted humans to keep the border. They were betrayed."

"That's why we don't leave it up to them. Not the elders, not the air force, not anybody. We do it ourselves."

He thought for a moment—still, unmoving. A great statue of a dragon. "We do this—then what? You can't return home, for it to be true."

You can't offer yourself as a sacrifice and expect to go back to school the next day. Was she willing to do that, to leave home? She'd never been sure about what she wanted to do with her life, except have adventures. Well, this was it.

"East," she said. "We go to the place on the secret map."

"May be nothing there."

"But I think there is," she said.

"Yes. Me too."

The rhythmic thumping of helicopters sounded nearby. The world intruded. Fallout from the battle was about to sweep over them.

"We must go," he said, ducking, his neck curving close.

How were they going to plan this thing, if they really were? She wished he had a cell phone. She wished a cell phone existed that was big enough for him to use.

"How will I talk to you?" she said, her heart pounding.

"The other place, where we met to fly. Your people don't know of it. Leave notes. I'll look. Every morning, if I can."

"Okay, yes."

"This thing. We should try." The ridges over his eyes were arced, giving him a fierce look. His eyes shone. It may have been her imagination, but the colors of his scales seemed to shimmer, taking on blacks and reds.

"We'll think of something. Hey, I need to hide the harness somewhere. It almost got me in trouble this time. They're watching me. They'll take it from me if they catch me. Can you hide it? Would you be able to take it?" She pulled off her own climbing harness and clipped it to the ropes, to keep all the gear together.

To answer, he stretched forward a hind foot and closed

the claws around the coils of rope. They looked like a tangle of thread in his grip.

"Kay," he said. "Take care."

"You too." She reached out her hand, and he nudged it with his nose. He turned and launched, and the trees around the clearing swayed and rustled at the sudden burst of wind his wings made.

She went south, toward the river.

21

Kay was able to run faster and farther without carrying all the gear.

She was now west of Silver River and a good ten miles from where her mother had parked. Ten miles from where she had left Jon behind with the army, wondering what had happened. They must have seen the smoke from the crash, if not the entire battle. Not to mention all the showing off beforehand.

Digging in her backpack, she found her cell phone and gave it a try. She didn't care if the military was listening in—she figured they'd find her sooner or later at this point. But she had to know if people were okay. She got reception, barely. She called Jon, but he didn't answer. He'd probably been arrested, and it was her fault. But she'd warned him, she'd told him to stay away. But she wouldn't blame him if he never spoke to her again. She left a message begging him to call back.

She called her mother. The phone rang and rang—

Her mother must have been talking as soon as she the saw the caller ID, before she even clicked talk.

"Oh my God! Kay, where are you? Are you all right? Kay!" The voice was scratchy, coming in and out of range.

"I'm okay, Mom. I'm fine. I'm heading south, I'm trying to figure out where I am." She wasn't sure she was getting through. She couldn't hear a response. "Mom—"

The connection cut out. Her mom must be hysterical. Kay quickly texted a follow-up message: IMOK.

She hiked another mile, maybe two, exhausted but still moving quickly, determined to get across the creek. She could hear running water. Just a little farther.

Her phone rang—she must have been back in range. Looking, she expected it to be her mother, but it wasn't. It was Tam.

Her friend didn't even say hello. "Kay, what's going on? What have you been doing? Was that even you? The news is saying it was you, but that couldn't possibly have been you. Could it?"

For a moment, Kay debated about what tell her, how little she could get away with saying. Then she realized that Tam would know she was holding back, and Kay didn't want to lie anymore.

"It was me," she said, and felt a flush of relief to be talking with her friend again.

"Oh my God, you're *crazy*. Are you out of your *mind*?"

"Yeah, maybe," Kay said with a sigh. "I tried talking to my mom, but the phone cut out, and I can't get ahold of Jon. What's been happening? What are people saying?"

"The army's everywhere. I mean everywhere. And the cops and the newspeople. The pictures of you and that thing are all over the TV, the internet—"

Artegal, Kay wanted to tell her. *That thing's name is Artegal.*

"—someone told somebody I'm your best friend, and they've been camping out on *my* lawn!"

"I'm sorry," Kay murmured.

"Kay, how long has this been going on? I saw the video—you've obviously been doing this a while. How long?" Kay didn't answer, but Tam barely gave her time to. "Why didn't you tell me? Why didn't you tell me what was going on?"

"I was scared," she said.

"Did you think you couldn't trust me?"

If they'd been face-to-face, they both would have been crying. But right now, Tam sounded too **angry** for it, and Kay was too tired. Her shoulders and arms ached, the blisters on her hands had come back, and she still had a long way to hike.

"That's not it," Kay said with a sigh. "I just didn't know how to tell you."

"Where are you now?" Tam said. "Do you need a ride? I'll come get you."

"I can't really say, I'm afraid they're listening to my calls."

"Oh my *God*!" Tam said, outraged.

"Hey, I think I figured out where I am. You know that picnic area where we had my birthday party a couple of years ago?" Maybe that was cryptic enough to confuse any eavesdroppers. "Can you meet me there? Tam, they may try to follow you."

"What is this, some kind of spy movie?"

"Never mind, I don't want to get you in trouble. You should stay out of it."

"Hell no, I'm coming to get you."

"Tam—"

"No arguing. I'm walking out of the house right now."

"Okay. Thank you, Tam. Just—thanks."

"You sound awful, Kay."

"I'll be okay. Have you heard from Jon?"

"No. But the news says the military has a 'person of interest' in custody. That couldn't be him, could it?"

"Probably. Crap."

"Hang in there. I'm on my way, okay?"

"Okay. Tam—thanks."

"Just be careful, Kay."

They clicked off, and Kay kept hiking.

She finally reached the stream—it was wider here, farther downstream than where she usually crossed. Without a bridge or even stepping stones within sight, she plunged into the freezing water and waded across, slogging against the current, gritting her teeth as her hiking boots soaked through and her legs grew cold. She just wanted to get to safety. Once she got to the main road, she could follow it the picnic area where she'd told Tam to meet her. She guessed it was just a mile or so away, and hoped she was right.

Her feet and legs were numb, and she was shivering, but she kept moving and it wasn't so bad. She'd stay warm if she kept moving. Helicopters—news and military—passed overhead, but she pressed herself to a tree for cover, stayed still, and they didn't see her.

She hoped Artegal was okay.

Kay heard sirens in the distance, coming closer.

She stayed in the trees, away from the road and trails, as she slogged on, as fast as she could. She was cold, wet, shivering; the faster she moved, the warmer she'd be, and that kept her going. The sooner she met Tam, the better.

After the sirens faded, the voices started. Men, shouting at one another in the woods. "This way. . . . She's been here. . . . We're getting close. . . ." The voices seemed to surround her.

In a panic, she almost sat down and gave up. But no,

if she were quick, if she kept to the trees, they wouldn't find her. She'd been running around these woods her whole life, climbing, hiking, kayaking on the river, camping in all kinds of weather. But these guys were trained military. They probably had guns—and she couldn't trust anymore that they wouldn't shoot at anything that moved.

Now she knew what it felt like to be hunted.

She tried to remember the rules of climbing: She had to keep breathing. She had to breathe, slow and steady, because that would keep her from getting even more scared. So she concentrated on breathing and on where she was putting her feet. One foot in front of the other, quick and careful. She kept an eye on the forest floor ahead of her, all the protruding branches, stones, and detritus waiting to trip her up, every place she could slip.

The cops or army guys or whoever they were made a lot of noise. They crashed through the trees, skidded on the ground, their heavy boots pounding, shouting at one another. Maybe there were just a lot of them.

They seemed to be moving along the river, downstream. They figured she had to cross somewhere, so that was where they concentrated their search. She never caught a glimpse of them, which she figured was a good thing—if she never saw them, maybe they never saw her. When the noises came close, she crouched low, close to a tree trunk, and didn't move until they'd faded again. She wasn't camouflaged, wearing jeans and her black parka.

But she wasn't brightly colored, and if she stayed still, she blended into shadows.

That was how she got past them.

She waited until the forest around her was quiet. Not even a breeze rattled the trees, although she could hear aircraft in the distance. For a long moment, she didn't believe she was really safe—they were waiting to pounce as soon as she started moving again. But no one was there.

Carefully, she moved from the trees to an open meadow. She still had to work to keep from breathing in panicked gasps. Looking around, she recognized landmarks—the big hill that the highway curved around, a rocky crag that looked kind of like a hunched bear. The picnic area was a half mile south. Her parents had a pocket GPS tracker—it usually lived in the glove box of her mother's car. She mostly used it for work, but sometimes they used it hiking. Kay wished she had it now—she'd have to think about taking it for next time. She felt a twinge at that—was there even going to be a next time?

Fifteen minutes later, she stumbled into the clearing of the picturesque picnic area, a few tables arranged around an iron fire pit half buried in the ground.

The gravel parking lot beyond the tables was empty.

Kay leaned against a tree and slid to the ground. Tam wasn't there, but on the plus side the cops and military weren't there, either. But she worried that Tam had been caught. She pulled out her phone again, willing to risk another call—and jumped at the sound of tires crunching on gravel as a car pulled up. Kay was ready to run back to the woods. Then she recognized Tam's blue hatchback.

Kay ran toward her, and Tam tumbled out of the driver's seat. They crashed into each other for an epic hug.

"Are you okay?" Tam said. "God, I'm so glad to see you!"

"We gotta get out of here." Tam nodded, and they climbed in the car. She'd left the motor running and peeled out of the parking area way too fast, but Kay didn't complain.

Tam said, "I had to take back roads. People are everywhere. There's a whole traffic jam of people trying to get out of town. That's the only reason they haven't caught me yet."

"Thank you," Kay said yet again. "I'm sorry, I didn't want to drag you into this—"

"Stop apologizing. I'll do whatever I have to. But, Kay, are you all right? Really all right?" Her eyes were wide, as if she were in shock, and her face was taut, serious.

Kay nodded quickly. "Yeah, I think I am." She couldn't wait to see the news, to see what they were saying about her and Artegal, to see if all this had gotten them the publicity she'd hoped for.

Tam crossed the highway and stuck to county roads, mostly narrow dirt trails that had connected neighborhoods and ranches before Silver River was even a real town. Maybe that would keep them out of sight as they returned to town.

"What are we doing? Where are we going?" Tam said. She looked scared—her white-knuckled hands gripped the wheel, and she chewed her lower lip. But she drove like a pro.

"I don't know," Kay said, shaking her head. "If they grab me, they'll lock me up and I'll never see the light of day again."

"We'll go to the store," Tam said. Tam's mom had a souvenir shop in town, selling T-shirts and stuff to tourists. Tam worked there during the summer. "Maybe no one will be looking there. It hasn't been open since the fire."

"Okay."

They'd driven a couple of miles in silence before Tam looked at Kay, anguished. "Oh my God, Kay! What have you been doing? What the hell's going on that you were with—that you were *riding* that thing?" She sounded like she'd been betrayed, and maybe she had. Maybe Kay should have told her about this all along.

She told Tam the whole story, start to finish, from that day she fell in the creek to the book to flying to today. When she got to the part about Branigan and spying, she trailed off, not sure yet how the story was going to end and not knowing what else to say.

They continued a little farther in silence before Tam laughed. The laughter was tense, her jaw clenched like she was trying to stop it. Kay looked at her, questioning.

"It's like *Romeo and Juliet*," she said. "Like trying to be friends when your families hate each other. Like that, but bigger."

"I guess it is," Kay said wonderingly. This was another story of two people running around behind the backs of their families because their families were unreasonable. There were people dying on both sides and everything.

"I mean this dragon, Artegal. You aren't, like, in love with it or anything. Are you?" Tam sounded incredulous.

Kay didn't even know what it meant to be in love. She thought most of what she felt for Artegal was awe. She was glad she'd met him, even if they never saw each other again. But that wasn't love, was it? Wasn't love supposed to be more about feeling safe, wanted, and beautiful? More like what she felt when she was with Jon.

"I think maybe we both thought it was so amazing we could be friends at all that we didn't want to give it up."

"Get down," Tam said. She stared intently out the windshield.

"What?"

"Down, out of sight."

Police cars with flashing lights were parked ahead. Kay unbuckled the seat belt and slid onto the floorboards, curling up as much as she could and keeping her head down, covered. All that was visible was her back, the dark surface of her coat. As the car slowed, she wanted to look. Keeping her head down was almost impossible, she wanted so badly to see what was going on. But she didn't. She could hear Tam's fingers tapping on the steering wheel.

They drove slowly, but they didn't stop. Then, Tam increased speed, and they were back to driving normally. Another ten minutes passed before Tam said, "I thought maybe it was a roadblock, like they were checking cars, but they just seemed to be watching. I think maybe you should just stay down there until we get to the store, okay?"

"Yeah." Kay shifted to keep her legs from falling asleep and settled into the pocket under the dash.

When they slowed and started making turns, Kay guessed they'd entered the town. After another minute, the car stopped.

"Can I get up?"

"Wait a minute. Let me get the store unlocked first."

Tam climbed out of the car and a few minutes later returned to call back to Kay, "Come on. Hurry."

Grateful to be out of the uncomfortable position, Kay sat up and tumbled out of the car to follow Tam inside.

When the door closed behind them and they were safe in the store's backroom, Kay finally relaxed. She sank onto a bench by the door and realized she was shaking. From fear, stress, exhaustion—she didn't know what. From everything.

Tam sat next to her and put her arm around her shoulders. "It's going to be okay. It's going to be okay, isn't it?"

Kay shook her head. "I don't know anymore. I don't

know what's going to happen."

"Maybe there'll be a war, but it can't last forever, right? There'll be another treaty, and it'll all settle down. Maybe they won't be looking for you, then. You can stay here for a while. I'll go get some food, and there's a bathroom, so you can wash up. You'll feel better."

Kay leaned against her friend, and they hugged. Tam was trying to make her feel better, but none of it was going to happen like that. This could go on for years. Forever. She couldn't live in the backroom here for years.

"What are we going to do, Kay?"

She and Artegal had a plan. Maybe it wouldn't work, but no one would be able to ignore it. *Something* would happen because of it.

Tam wouldn't like it. No one would like it. But that was what made it a sacrifice, wasn't it?

22

Kay stripped off her coat, used paper towels to wash her face and hands, and shook out her ponytail, trying to pick apart some of the tangles in her hair. If she didn't feel clean, she at least felt a little more awake. The water was hot. She finally felt warm for the first time all day, for the first time in forever. She'd forgotten what warm felt like.

Then she called her mother, rehearsing what she could say without giving too much away, in case anyone was listening.

Tam watched intently as Kay tapped her feet nervously, waiting for the ringing to stop.

"Kay, where the hell are you?!"

"Mom, I'm okay. I'm fine."

"But where are you?"

"Mom, are General Branigan and them looking for me? What's going on?"

"It's a real mess. Just tell me you're south of the river. Are you?"

"Yes, I'm fine." She and Tam exchanged a glance.

"Thank God." Mom sighed. "Kay, the dragons are striking everywhere, a dozen cities all over the world. They're not avoiding fatalities anymore. People are dying, Kay, and the air force doesn't have enough jets to counter them. It's not just Branigan talking about using nuclear bombs in Dragon now; it's the defense secretary, the national security advisor—I'm sorry, you probably don't want to hear all this."

Kay stared at nothing, trying to picture it. Wanting to see a TV and not wanting to at the same time. "So it didn't do any good. We wanted people to see us to try to stop the fighting, but it didn't do any good."

"Oh, but it did. Everyone saw you. The news people are having a field day with this. They all got footage of you on that thing, and nobody knows what to make of it. Everybody, *everybody's* looking for you."

That didn't surprise her, but Kay had a sinking feeling that the rest of the plan wasn't going to be easy because of it.

"But, Mom, what are people saying? What's going to happen if I show up?"

"I think all hell will break loose. Half the commentators are saying you're a traitor. Half of them are calling you some kind of ambassador. This is riling up both sides."

This had been so much simpler when all she was doing was breaking the law, sneaking over a little tiny river. Then she hadn't been thinking about becoming a celebrity. She hadn't meant this all to get out of hand.

"But, Kay, here's the thing," Mom continued. "I don't think Branigan can hide you away, not when every reporter in the country wants to interview you. Maybe he can get the police to arrest you, but it'll all be in the open now." She paused, then said, "That's why you did it, isn't it?"

"Yeah, kind of."

"I think it worked." Her mother actually sounded pleased, or relieved, maybe even proud. "Now we just have to figure out what to do next. I wish . . ." But she didn't finish, and Kay knew what she wanted to say. Her father would have known what to do. She wished Jack Wyatt were here.

Kay didn't want to think about that. And she didn't want to tell her mother what she wanted to do next, what she thought needed to happen next.

"We'll talk to the press," her mother said, not noticing how quiet Kay was. "Let me talk to my boss. We'll set up a press conference. I don't like putting you out there like that, but it may protect you from General Branigan. We can get a voice in there for the other side, to show everyone you're okay and haven't been brainwashed by dragons."

Was that what people were saying, that she'd been brain-washed?

"Are you okay with that, honey?" her mother said.

If Kay told anyone what she was planning, no one would let her do it. They really would lock her up.

"Mom, can you find out what happened to Jon? He was with me this morning. There were soldiers out in the woods, and I think they may have arrested him or something."

"I'll find out. Kay, can you come home?"

She wouldn't be able to avoid it. She needed to get ready, she needed to plan, and she needed the book. "I think so. We can try."

"Wait until dark," Mom said. "I'll call Deputy Kalbach and have him help you. Okay?"

The plan would have to do. "Okay."

At least her mother was feeling better.

"So what's the plan?" Tam asked after she'd put her phone away.

"I guess I'm going home. Mom says to wait until after dark. Can you drive me?"

"Yeah, of course. More dodging cops. It'll be fun, right?" Her smile was forced.

Kay had to give her credit for looking on the bright side.

Tam went to get some food—instant soup from home, because everything nearby was closed, even the Alpine. They waited in the shop's backroom until dusk, eating soup and drinking sodas, when Kay's mother called her and said that Deputy Kalbach was waiting in his car at the end of the street to make sure she got home okay. Mom said the news vans and swarm of reporters were worse than they'd been after her father's funeral.

Kay braced herself. Tam had her hand on the door.

"We ready?" she said.

Kay nodded, and Tam opened the door. She half expected the back parking lot to be swarming with army cars and news vans. But it wasn't. No one had found them. No one was looking for Tam's car.

As they drove, Kay resisted an urge to crouch under the dash again.

Silver River wasn't a huge town and definitely wasn't that busy except during the height of tourist season. But along Main Street, there were usually cars and people around, enough to make the place look interesting, inhabited. Now, it seemed like a ghost town. Most of the storefronts had CLOSED signs in the windows. No cars were parked on the curb. The empty Alpine parking lot seemed wrong. Several blocks in the center of town were roped off with yellow caution tape. The street was still barricaded, to keep people from driving that way. Around the corner, Kay could see bands of black soot on a brick wall, the only hint that the group of buildings had burned.

Kay wanted it all to go back to the way it had been. She wanted to see her father, in his uniform and cowboy hat, walking up the street. But nothing she could do would make that happen. She could only try to make things a little better than they were right now.

Finally—Tam was driving extra slowly and carefully—

they reached Kay's neighborhood, then her street. It was like a circus had camped out there. A dozen news vans lined up, blocking driveways, and they all had huge antennae sticking out the tops and people with cameras and microphones milling out front. The neighbors must have loved it.

Kay slipped down to crouch on the floor before Tam told her to. "Park here," Kay said, whispering, as if the people on the street could hear her. "Find Deputy Kalbach and ask him what to do."

Tam parked, and as she left the car, she looked over both shoulders and all around, as if searching for signs of an ambush, as if they were in some kind of spy movie. Kay waited, hugging her knees to her chest, for Tam to return. Hoped no one happened to walk by and look in the window at the girl huddled on the floor.

More quickly than she would have expected, Tam returned, climbed back in the driver's seat, and started the engine. "He said to park the next street over and sneak in the back. He's going to go tell your mom."

A few minutes later, she and Tam were running from the next street, past a neighbor's house and across the back lawn to the door of the garage at Kay's house. The door was unlocked, and they made it inside safely.

Kay was coming from the garage to the kitchen when her mother met her and engulfed her in a hug. She was almost crying, murmuring meaningless phrases, pressing Kay to her as if she'd believed they'd never see each other again.

"I'm okay," Kay kept saying, but her mother didn't seem to hear. When Mom finally pulled away, sure enough, she was crying, quiet tears streaming from red eyes.

Maybe this was a mistake, Kay thought. Her mother would never let her leave the house again.

Mom made her and Tam sit down to dinner, and she explained the situation over more lasagna brought by well-wishers.

"Did you find out about Jon?" Kay asked.

Mom nodded. "They let him go. They wanted to charge him with some kind of aiding and abetting, but I managed to pull some strings. Nice to know I still *have* a few strings." She looked at Kay with a raised brow. Kay couldn't even remember back to this morning. "The bureau asked him to stay at home and be available for questioning." So he was home. She could call him.

Her mother continued, "Branigan issued an order to stand down. He's not following you anymore; he's not sending anyone to arrest you, at least until after the press conference. You'll get a chance to have your say, answer questions. Then I'm afraid it'll go to the higher ups."

"Who's higher up than Branigan?" Kay said.

Mom gave her a look. "All the way to the top. Congress, the president. They can't ignore this. You should see the polls, Kay. As soon as the pictures of you flying went out, the numbers in favor of negotiating went way up. Just showing people that cooperation is possible completely undermined the military's argument."

But guys like Branigan wouldn't stop fighting, because they were like bullies on the playground. Neither side could back down without losing face.

Her mother and the FBBE director set up the press conference at the temporary headquarters in the morning, and Kay went along with it, unable to argue. And maybe it would work. But she didn't think so; it wasn't just a matter of convincing the military to stop bombing. She had to convince the dragons to stop attacking as well, and a press conference wouldn't do it.

She and Artegal could get their attention. They'd proven that. She needed help, though: She needed someone to leave a note for Artegal.

Her mother was on the phone, still talking about the press conference. Without a word, she and Tam cleaned up after supper and went to the living room to watch news on TV. As soon as she saw the images—of cities burning, landmarks in Washington, D.C., forests in Florida, buildings in Japan, like an old postwar dragon movie come to life—she wasn't sure she wanted to see the news after all. The footage of her and Artegal soaring over Silver River was just a footnote to the destruction.

She tugged on Tam's sleeve. "I have to show you something." She went to her room, and Tam followed.

All afternoon and even now, Tam had been looking at her strangely, as if something were wrong with Kay, like Tam expected her to do something weird or crazy. She looked like the best friend of the drug addict trying to tell her to get help in those public service videos.

This wasn't going to make things any better.

In her bedroom, Kay pulled the book from her dresser. Sitting by Tam on the bed, she held it open on her lap.

"What's this?"

Kay said, "I think it's kind of a history book. Artegal—the dragon—gave it to me."

"The *dragon* gave it to you?"

"They have books too. And libraries."

"Nobody ever said that—why wouldn't they teach us that in school?"

"I don't think anyone knows." And would it change anything if they did? If people knew dragons wrote and read, would people like Branigan still want to destroy them?

Tam turned the pages carefully, using only her fingertips, and after a few moments murmured, "It's beautiful. But—do you think it was really like this?"

She was looking at a picture showing a dragon blowing fire into a blacksmith's forge. The blacksmith was making something curved, unidentifiable—a tool, not a weapon, Kay thought. The weapons came later.

"I think it was. I think it must have been. Tam—I need your help." Kay swallowed. "I want to do something kind of crazy."

"Crazier than usual?"

Kay turned pages until she reached the one showing the sacrifice.

Tam stared at it for a long time before shaking her head.

"You're joking. This is a joke."

"They used to do this as a pledge. We talked about it—it was supposed to show what people were willing to give up to have peace. And it'll be okay because Artegal and I have a plan, but I need your help."

Tam shook her head. Horror furrowed her brow. "I can't do this. You can't ask me to do this! How can you even think like that? How can you even look at this after what they've done? You saw what they did to the town!"

"That wasn't Artegal's fault."

"Kay, dragons killed your father."

"I know." She hadn't meant to, but her face screwed up, and the tears fell. She hadn't meant to admit it at all. Tam was at her side, moving the book away and hugging her. Face pressed against her shoulder, Kay choked back sobs. She didn't want any of this to be happening. But she was the only person who had any chance of talking to the dragons. She could imagine her father saying that, which meant she had to try. The sacrifice was something, a symbol that the dragons would understand.

She said, "I think he would understand. I think Dad would understand about this."

Tam was still shaking her head, not so much in denial but in disbelief. "What can I do?"

"I need to get a message to Artegal. If I try to do it, they'll know I'm up to something and stop me. But you can go. I'll show you where."

"Kay, no, I can't go talk to that thing!"

"Artegal. His name is Artegal, and he's my friend." Kay held Tam's hands, trying to get her to be quieter. "You won't even see him. Just leave a note for him. Tomorrow morning, before the press conference."

"I can't cross the border!"

"Just for a minute. Everyone else is looking up, looking for dragons—they won't even see it."

"Kay—" Tam had tears in her eyes. Strangely, Kay was worried about her makeup smearing.

She touched Tam's cheeks. "Don't do that. It's going to be okay."

"Kay, why are you doing this?"

She had to think about it, because she hadn't tried to put it in words. "Because I have to try."

"It's not up to you to . . . to save the world!"

"Hey, maybe there's a reason I'm the only virgin at Silver River High. You ever think of that?"

As she had hoped, Tam laughed, at least a little.

Kay hugged her. They held each other tightly for a long time.

Tam said, "What's going to happen?"

"I'm not sure."

Kay wrote the note on a huge piece of sketch paper, the biggest paper she could find. She described what would happen as briefly as possible, large, so it would be easier for him to read. She folded it up, found a map, and showed Tam where to take it.

"I can't read this. I'm not the big mountain chick like

you are," Tam said, staring at the topographic map as if it were in a different language.

"Take it to Jon. He'll show you exactly where it is."

"Kay, I'm scared."

"I know. Call me if you can. It'll be okay." If they just kept saying it, maybe it would be true.

After that, they came out to the kitchen, Tam said good-bye to Kay's mother, and they had to act like nothing was wrong, even though their eyes were red. They hugged once more before she left to go home. Tam looked at her like she was convinced they'd never see each other again.

Kay went back to her room, found her phone, and dialed Jon's number. He picked up halfway through the first ring, as if he'd been waiting with the phone in his hand. "Kay!"

"Hi."

"Are you okay?"

"Yeah, I'm fine," she said tiredly, before he finished asking. "Are you okay? What happened? What did they do to you?"

"They put me in a room and asked me a lot of questions. But I couldn't tell them too much because you haven't told me anything." He sounded accusing.

Her impulse was to say she was sorry, but she was tired of feeling sorry. She wasn't the one who made the world this way and put the military in charge. "What was I supposed to do? I couldn't tell anyone."

"Until you decided to tell the whole damn world. If you wanted attention, you've got it."

"I didn't. Not really," she said. She said it after all. "I'm sorry."

"No, Kay." He sighed. "It's . . . it's amazing, what you've done. You've shocked the whole world."

"It was an accident, Jon. The whole thing started as an accident. It's just that since then . . ."

"You're glad it happened," he said.

"Yeah."

"So what happens now?"

"Tam's probably going to be calling you soon," Kay said. "I asked her to help me with something. She doesn't like it—"

"Is it anything like you asked me to help you with?"

She hesitated—but maybe Jon was right, maybe he'd been right all along. She couldn't keep all these secrets to herself anymore. "I need to get a message to Artegal."

"What are you planning?" he asked after a pause. He knew her too well. The thought startled her.

"It's big, Jon. It's dangerous. But if it works—" What was she saying? This wasn't going to work. She was being naïve. "It'll at least make everyone think about this, about what's happening." That, she decided, was the best she could hope for, and it would still be worth it.

"Kay—"

"There's a press conference tomorrow at noon. Mom set it all up. It's going to be at the middle school. Outside, in the parking lot. Can you be there? I'm going to need help."

"Are you trying to kill yourself?" he asked.

It was going to look like it, wasn't it? The trouble was, none of them trusted Artegal. And none of them knew about the secret map. That was one secret she couldn't reveal. People like Branigan could never find out about it. She'd taken it out of the book and kept it with her.

"No," she said finally. "But I may have to go away for a little while."

"What about school? What about your mom?" She could hear him swallow over the phone. "What about us?"

Her eyes stung with tears. She was trying not to think about the really hard parts of all this. "Jon, if you had a chance to stop a war, would you?"

The logical thing for him to do would be the reality check. To tell her that nothing she could do would stop a war. Not this one, not any. But he didn't do that.

He said, "Yes, I would."

"If it weren't for me and Artegal accidentally meeting, we wouldn't have this chance. We have to try."

"Okay," he said, his voice steady now. "Just tell me what you need me to do."

23

Kay made one more call that evening. After digging out the business card he'd given her, she dialed Captain Will Conner's number without really knowing what she was going to say. She had only a vague hope that he would listen to her, maybe even help her. After all, he hadn't ratted out her and Artegal.

The connection clicked on. "Yes?"

She recognized the voice. "Captain Conner? This is Kay Wyatt." Her mouth dry, she waited for a reaction.

When he did speak, he sounded angry. "That was some stunt you pulled. Just what exactly were you trying to prove?"

"It's like you said," she answered, defiant. "I can talk to him. I had to show people—"

"That's not what I said—I didn't tell you to start a fight. That was a friend of mine in that plane that went down. He *died*."

Kay's eyes stung and her tears slid free. "Like my dad," she said, her voice thick.

Conner let out a heavy sigh. "Kay, why are you calling?"

"I need a favor. I don't know if you can do it, but if you can, I had to try. I just had to see."

"What favor?"

"Can you make sure there aren't any jets over Silver River tomorrow at noon?"

He hesitated. "What are you planning? What's going on?"

"I can't tell you," she said, trying to stay coherent. Trying to stay strong so she could get through the next day. "It's . . . it'll be fine. Everything'll be fine." She had to believe in the mantra.

"Kay, how dangerous is this? Maybe you should let the adults handle this one. Stay safe and help out your mother."

She hadn't expected Conner to be able to help, but she had to try. Let the adults handle it. And wasn't that what they always said? The adults had started this whole mess. She didn't like the way adults like Branigan handled things.

"But you were right. I may be the only one who can talk to them."

"Maybe that's what I said, but that was before—"

Kay said, "I'm sorry. I'm sorry about your friend."

"Kay, whatever you're planning, it's not worth it—"

She hung up.

Kay didn't sleep. She tried. She didn't know when she'd have a chance to get a good sleep again. Maybe never, but she tried not to think of that. She'd packed a bag of supplies—warm clothes, hand warmers, granola bars, beef jerky, and bottled water. She found the GPS tracker in her mom's glove box—she was going to make sure she knew where she was this time. She had coordinates to follow. She didn't think her mother would mind, when all was said and done. She tried to think of what else she'd need, but her mind couldn't focus. She put the gear in the car that night, so she wouldn't have to explain it to her mother in the morning.

Breakfast with her mother was strained. Kay wanted to have breakfast with her, wanted to spend this time with her. This was the worst part of the whole plan, knowing what it would do to Mom. But Kay couldn't tell her. She couldn't even really say good-bye without revealing everything, and if Mom knew, she would stop her. Even with all the good this could do, Mom would stop her.

But it wasn't forever, she reassured herself. This wasn't like Dad at all.

Her mother kept glancing at her, her expression worried, searching. Kay couldn't eat. She'd have a bite of cereal, and it would take forever to chew it. Swallowing it was like swallowing sawdust.

"You look nervous," Mom said, and Kay flinched. Of course she was; she just didn't think it would be so obvious. She nodded. "It'll be okay. You don't have to answer any of the questions if you don't want to. Just look at this as a chance to tell your side of the story. You can stick it to Branigan." She was trying to be funny, but her smile was strained.

"All right," Kay said, but she thought about what she could tell the world if she had a chance.

She was cleaning up her dishes when the phone in her pocket rang. Tam's voice over the connection was panicked, which made Kay's gut turn with worry, sure that something had gone wrong, until she made out the words.

"I saw him," Tam gasped. "He was there. I saw him. Neither of us crossed the river, but he was there and we talked. Kay, he talked to me—"

Kay rushed back to her bedroom and closed to the door, cupping her hands around the phone as if the sound would leak out and her mother would hear.

She wished she'd been there to see the look on Tam's face. "I told you you'd be okay."

"He said he couldn't stay, he was being watched, but that he understood. Kay, he said he understood. Does that mean what I think it means?"

"It means everything's going to be okay."

They had a plan. It was going to work.

"Jon came with me, he showed me where to go, but he's being watched, too, so he went the other direction to throw them off. I don't know if it worked. Kay, does Jon know? Does he know what you're planning?"

"Yeah." Her heart was racing. Scared, but excited—there was something amazing about having a plan come together. "The press conference is at noon. Can you be there?"

"I wouldn't miss it. Kay—I talked to him. I trust him. I don't know why, but I do."

"I told you."

Kay had a few more things to get together. She found the book *Dracopolis* and the notebook with the translations. Most recently she'd worked on the final page, because she wanted to know what happened, how it all finally turned out—not that it was a story and not that it had an ending. But, obviously, the dragons leaving the world, going into their secret caverns and into hiding, hadn't been the end or the book wouldn't have been written, and the dragons wouldn't have returned.

The last page, or what she could make out of it, didn't explain it all. But it explained a little.

There is a haven for those tired of this war. There is a haven, out of view, where dragons and people still keep peace. It will always be a haven, and we pray that those who need it will find it in time.

Kay tore the sheet out of her notebook, folded it up, and put it in her pocket, along with the extra, hand-drawn map that had been slipped between the pages. She didn't want anyone to find it. She didn't know what keeping it secret was protecting, but she was going to find out.

She left the book on her bed, open to the page depicting the virgin sacrifice, so people would understand.

In her closet she found her homecoming dress, wrapped in plastic, destined never to be worn again. It sparkled white, shimmering even in the closet's shadows.

This part of it was probably just like the virgin part—it didn't really matter; the tradition had just built up over the centuries: The virgin always wore a white gown, a bridal gown, when she went to the sacrifice. She took it anyway, folded it as carefully as she could, and put it in her back-pack. The weather outside had turned warm. Maybe she wouldn't be too cold.

"Kay, we should get going," her mother called from the living room.

So this was it. It was time. She had everything she needed—she hoped. Her cell phone was fully charged. "Just a minute!"

She looked around her room one more time, then the hallway, then the living room. She looked over the house where she'd lived her whole life and tried to remember. On one of the bookshelves in the living room sat the family picture from last Christmas: her, Mom, and Dad. All smiling, laughing almost. Dad had cracked a joke right before the camera clicked. Something about this maybe being their last formal Christmas picture together because Kay would be going away soon, to college and the ends of the earth to climb foreign mountains.

His image seemed to be looking at her. "Dad, I hope this is okay," she whispered.

Her mother drove them both to the press conference. Kay watched the house slip away.

She turned to her mother, who in her pantsuit and pinned-up hair, looked more put together than she had since the funeral. She even wore makeup for the cameras. "I don't want to just answer questions. I want to say something. I have a statement. Can I do that?"

"Yes, of course. Do you want me to check it over for you?"

"No, no—that's okay." She was kneading her hands in her lap. Mom glanced at them and smiled another tight-lipped smile.

"Maybe they'll make you an ambassador," Mom said, full of false cheer. "I've talked about it with the director. I've given him all the arguments why we shouldn't prosecute."

"You're biased—they'll never buy it coming from you."

"But what sounds better, putting a cute seventeen-year-old girl on trial or making her into an ambassador? This is all about PR. It's all about public opinion. I know which option will make the bureau look better." She quirked a smile. PR indeed.

They drove a little while longer. Then Kay said, "What would that involve, being an ambassador?"

"Nothing, if we can't get the dragons to talk to us."

They were about an hour early. Mom wanted to be early. She said it would give them the high ground. Let them control the situation better. Maybe she was even right. Kay let her go on her PR kick. Kay had one of her own.

Jon and Tam were already there, waiting in Tam's car, lost among all the news vans. Kay spotted them on the drive to the middle school gym.

"Mom, stop! There's Tam. I want to go talk to her."

Mom looked hesitant, but Kay pleaded with a longing expression she hadn't used since she was thirteen.

"Okay, but just for a minute. I want you out of sight of all those cameras until the press conference. I'll wait by the doors there." She gestured to the gym doors, where two men in army camouflage stood guard. Just seeing them made Kay's stomach knot.

Kay ran out, and her mother went to park. She went straight to Tam's car, and Tam saw her just before she pounded on the window. Jon, sitting in back, opened the door for her and slid over to give her space. Almost the whole gang—they were missing Carson.

Longing and anxiety furrowed Jon's thin face. If anything was going to make her change her mind, that would be it. She leaned toward him and threw her arms around him, holding tight.

"I can't believe it," he murmured. "I can't believe this is all happening."

None of it should have happened. From Kay falling into the stream, all the way back to the atom bombs dropping, to before that to when the first battles between dragons and humans took place. A cascade of terrible events.

And she was continuing the cascade. But the alternative was ending up in jail and watching the world burn.

"Are you really going to go through with this?" Jon asked.

"I don't know. I guess I could still chicken out," Kay said.

Jon stared at her. "I'm right on the verge of telling Tam to drive away. We could kidnap you. For your own good."

Tam shook her head. "I couldn't do that." Kay met her gaze in the rearview mirror. She should have kept them out of this—how much trouble were they going to get in because of her? But she was glad they were here.

"Jon, I need you to hold some stuff for me. Wait out by the football field, that's where he'll land. And can you look out for my mom?"

"Okay."

Kay swallowed. "Tam, can you drive out toward the border? Keep a watch out for him. Call me when you see him, so I know when he's on his way."

"This isn't actually going to work, is it?" Tam said.

"I don't know."

"You're bringing your phone on this adventure, right? I expect you to call me."

Kay got out of the car, and Jon followed. "Totally."

"Be careful!" Tam said out the window.

"You too."

Tam pulled out of the parking lot and drove away. Kay and Jon watched her. He grabbed Kay's hand and squeezed; she squeezed back.

"Where's this stuff?" Jon said.

Kay went back to her mother's car and found the backpack. Before giving it to Jon, she pulled out the dress. The gesture was starting to seem overly dramatic. But she didn't want there to be any misunderstanding.

Jon touched her hand, holding the gown. "Is that your homecoming dress?"

She was kind of thrilled that he recognized it. She doubted Carson remembered what Tam's gowns looked like. "Yeah."

"You're not the only virgin around here. I should do this. *I'll* do this. Why does it have to be a girl in a white dress?"

"Tradition?" Kay said.

"That's sexist bullshit and you know it. I'll do it."

"Jon. You don't know how to ride. Artegal doesn't know you. I don't want to you get hurt."

293

"I don't want *you* to get hurt."

"I won't. That's why I have to do this. I'm not afraid." And she realized she wasn't.

"Kay. When are you coming back?"

She looked at him, the worry in his eyes, a tightness in his jaw. He looked at her so intently, and she wondered if it was love. She said, "I don't know."

They kissed. None of their kisses had ever felt like this, long, intense, rough almost, as if they were making up for lost time. She gripped his shirt in her hands, and he held her close. When she had to catch her breath, she turned away and rested her head on his shoulder. She was crying.

It was almost noon. She was running out of time. She pressed the backpack and her heavy coat into his hands. "Wait for me, okay?"

He nodded, and she pulled away. As she slipped through the door to the school, she glanced over her shoulder to see Jon looking back.

Mom came toward her, as if on her way to meet her. Kay scrunched up the dress and hid it behind her back.

"Where are Tam and Jon? Did they come with you?"

"They wanted to watch from outside."

"Are you ready?" she asked.

"Can I hit the bathroom first?"

As she'd hoped, her mother gave her a look of sympathy. "Come out the gym doors when you're ready." She walked off in that direction herself, toward the hubbub and chatter of the temporary offices.

Kay ducked around the next corner, into the bathroom, and into the gown.

She was going to *freeze* in this thing.

Temporary, she told herself. It was only temporary. As a compromise, she kept long underwear on and wore her hiking boots. It wouldn't look great, but she had limits she'd go to in the name of fashion.

Squaring her shoulders, she looked in the mirror. Her hair was in a quick ponytail, coming undone, brown strands loose around her face. The dress looked lumpy rather than sleek, with thermal underwear and without heels. With all those cameras out there, she was going to end up on every TV channel and a million websites looking like this.

But it didn't matter if she looked glamorous. It was the symbolism that mattered; she looked like the image in the book. People wouldn't need to be able to read to understand what was going on. They'd look at her and *know*, from that deep tribal memory of the stories.

She pulled the elastic out of her hair, shook her head, and smoothed her hair out anyway. It looked a little better.

A knock came at the door, and Kay's mother asked, "Honey? Are you okay? We can still call this off if you don't want to go through with it."

"No, Mom. I'm fine. I'll be out in a couple more minutes." Pacing now, avoiding the mirrors so she wouldn't keep messing with her hair, she waited for the call. She wouldn't be able to stall for much longer. What was taking Artegal so long?

Even though she was expecting it, when her phone rang, she still jumped and fumbled when she answered it. "Hello? Tam?"

It was Tam, in a panic. "He's on his way! Oh my God, Kay, he's flying so fast."

Which meant she didn't have much time. "Okay. Thanks."

"Kay?" Tam said, when she was about to hang up. "Be careful, okay? Whatever happens, be careful. I want to hear the whole story when this is all over so you have to be there to tell me, okay?"

Kay couldn't help but smile. "Okay, I promise."

Head up, chin out, copping all the attitude she could muster, she marched to the gym and to the press conference outside. She hadn't figured out how she was going to explain why she was wearing her homecoming dress for this, so she just wouldn't explain.

When she entered the gym, where the temporary FBBE offices still resided, the bustle fell still. It wasn't an immediate thing. Instead, one person noticed her and stared, then another, then a few more who looked up to see what the others were looking at, until the whole room was quiet.

Kay's mother was waiting by the outside door, where Kay could just make out another waiting crowd.

"Kay?" Mom said, confused. "Kay, what is this? Why are you dressed like that?"

"I wanted to look nice," she said.

Her mother looked quizzical but didn't say anything else. As much as Kay tried to act as if this were all normal and nothing were wrong, this was too weird. She wasn't fooling her mother. She wasn't fooling herself.

Mom glanced out the door and pressed her lips together in an expression of satisfaction. "Are you ready?"

"I'm ready," she said, breathing too fast, then marched past her mother and through the door.

On the pavement outside the gym, a podium, microphones sprouting up from it like a spiky mechanical flower, had been set up in front of several rows of folding chairs. Reporters sat in many of them, while many others stood, gathered in clumps, talking.

She went to the podium and tapped on one of the microphones. An echoey thumping noise came from somewhere. She couldn't see where the speakers were. Reporters looked up, looked at her, and made their way to their seats, murmuring.

"Hi," Kay said, and winced because it sounded stupid.

Everyone sitting in the two dozen chairs must have raised their hands and shouted at the same time, asking questions before she had a chance to collect herself. Kay stepped back, assaulted by the aggression of it. Mom came up beside her and took charge.

"My daughter has a statement she'd like to read," Mom said, and the crowd settled.

Her hands shaking, Kay unfolded the paper on which she'd written her statement. Her throat was dry; she had to swallow before she could speak. She glanced at the sky; Artegal wasn't in view yet, but he would be any minute now. She wanted to do this carefully. She wanted to make sure people heard every word.

"I'm not going to stand here and tell you war is bad or wrong, we shouldn't do it, and we should work for peace instead, because it would be too easy for people like General Branigan to say I'm naïve, I'm just a kid. To blow me off and act like nothing I say could be important. But if you think about it, I have more right than anyone to talk about what's going on here, to have an opinion about it. I think if I'm allowed to stand up here and talk at all, then I'm allowed to have an opinion that matters.

"My father died because of a misunderstanding. Because of laws and a border that exist because we couldn't be bothered to try and get along. I've spent the last several months crossing the border and talking to a dragon. I know that dragons and humans can talk to each other.

"I've thought, I've wondered, if maybe it was my fault." Here, her mouth grew dry again, and she paused to wet her lips before continuing. "If what happened to my father was my fault. If this whole war was my fault because of what I've been doing. If me crossing the border and talking to my friend somehow started this or made it worse, then maybe the same thing can maybe make it better.

"The history of people and dragons goes back thousands of years. There used to be a tradition where human settlements would show they were serious about negotiating for peace by offering a symbol. A sacrifice. A virgin in a white dress."

"Kay, no," her mother whispered in a harsh voice. Kay couldn't look at her, not even a glance.

Somebody screamed and pointed up. Artegal had arrived.

He moved like one of the jets, soundlessly, almost too fast to track. His wings tilted like oars, and he banked into a circle over the school. Half the crowd ducked; the other half ran. More people screamed. A couple of guns fired, then stopped, because there were too many people around.

Kay shouted into the microphone, "Stop it! He isn't doing anything wrong!"

People looked at her, then looked back at the dragon, as if they were trying to keep both in view at the same time. But Kay was right, and Artegal wasn't doing anything but circling, dipping a lazy wing to bank his silvery-gray body, keeping one dark eye on the proceedings below. Maybe people would pause to notice that he was beautiful.

Three more dragons approached, flying fast and hard, their wings swept back, their necks stretched forward, heading for Artegal. They'd followed him, or chased him rather.

People scattered, leaving news crews with their cameras pointed to the sky and soldiers aiming their rifles.

The dragons weren't heading for the now-fleeing crowd, the news vans, or the buildings. They were heading for Artegal. Artegal responded, banking sharply, swooping, altering his flight. But they followed his erratic path, made their own swoops and maneuvers to surround him. Artegal was smaller than the others, younger, less experienced. No matter how much he dodged, veered, and changed his course, the others stayed with him. He might have escaped by flying high, straight, fast—away, in any direction. But he wouldn't leave the area. He was waiting for her.

His pursuers stretched their hind claws forward, bared their razor teeth, and prepared to pounce on him. Then the familiar sounds of jet engines roared overhead: A pair of the F-22s, flying close, swung in a wide arc overhead, as if preparing to attack the dragons. The trio of dragon warriors veered and scattered. The jets looped around them in a circle that seemed to encompass the entire town.

"No!" Kay shouted. This gave her and Artegal even less time. She tried not to be angry at Captain Conner for this; it wasn't his fault. But she wanted to be angry at someone.

She doubted that the dragons could hear her—the pilots in the jets certainly couldn't hear her—or that they would even glance at what must have sounded to them like an insect buzzing. But she knew from Artegal that their eyesight was good, and that they had to see her in her blazing white dress. She ran.

Kay's mother grabbed her arm and yanked her back, like an anchor. Kay nearly fell over.

"What are you doing?" Mom yelled.

Kay turned on her, pleading. "Mom, I have to do this. I have to try."

"Try what? Kill yourself? Is that what you're trying to do?"

"No, Mom. I wouldn't do that. I wouldn't. We've got a plan. We can do this."

"You want them to take you." Her mother glared, intense, hard. Her hand bit into Kay's arm.

"Me and Artegal. We want to stop the fighting. No one can ignore this." She wondered if she should have told her mother. She should have asked for her help—she could make sure no one ignored this. She *had* to make sure no one ignored this.

"Kay, I don't want to lose you, too. I can't lose you both!" She was crying, as anguished as she'd been the night at the hospital.

"Mom, I'll be okay."

Her mother studied her, her eyes shining. Then, she let go.

Kay wrapped her arms around her mom and squeezed. For the first time, she realized they were the same size. She and her mother looked alike. She'd never noticed that before. "I love you," she whispered. "You and Dad both."

"Kay—"

She ran. Straight across the pavement of the parking lot to the football field, which was dried winter brown and spotted with patches of snow.

Jon waited in the middle, holding her pack. He caught her as she slid to a stop.

"This isn't working, Kay. This isn't going to work—"

"Wait, just wait." She slung the pack over one shoulder, looked up, and waved. She must have glowed against the backdrop of the field.

The dragons, all of them, hesitated.

The three attackers hovered, their wings scooping the air to keep them aloft, and looked down at her, their necks stretched forward and their heads tilted with what Kay thought must be amazement. They must have known what they were seeing. They must have thought they'd never see such a thing again. She could hear the jets, but it took her a moment to catch sight of them. Their path hadn't changed, their circle bringing them back over the school—maybe they wouldn't attack this near the town. Or maybe they were waiting to see why the dragons were waiting. Maybe the pilots were watching her, too.

"What's happening?" Jon asked, his voice low.

"I don't know." But she was smiling.

The three dragons surrounded the field now, circling, hovering—keeping their distance, but watching carefully.

They growled and grumbled at one another. Meanwhile, Artegal dived, straight toward her.

She stood her ground.

"Kay!" she heard her mother scream from the edge of the field.

Kay looked at Jon one more time. His face was stone, and his hands were clenched into fists. On an impulse, she ran forward, hugged him one more time, remembering how his arms felt around her. She thought that maybe Tam was right and they should have slept together. As Artegal said, no one could tell she was a virgin unless she told them. But there was no sense regretting anything now. Besides, she would see him again. She would. She had to believe that.

"Go," she murmured. He nodded and ran toward Mom. Quickly, she put on her coat and put the backpack over both shoulders.

Artegal landed beside her. She felt his weight tremble through the ground, he was so close. But so precise, so careful. Despite his size, he would never damage anything by accident. Surely her mother would see that.

She looked up the scaled slope of his body, the sails of his wings that blocked out the sky, his graceful neck and the monstrous head, his shining dark eyes.

"Ready?" he said, his voice rumbling.

"Yes." Her own voice was fearful.

He reached one hind foot forward, and she grabbed hold

of it. His clawed toes wrapped around her, and she hugged his leg.

He launched. She looked down once to see her mother clinging to Jon. She was crying. Jon was just staring at her. Kay dared to let go and wave at them.

Mom waved back. Pulling away from Jon, she waved with both arms.

Then Artegal flew fast, straight up, ahead, and away.

She was throwing off his balance, she could tell. His wing beats felt harder than usual, and he dipped to the left, where he was holding her. She tried to curl up as small and streamlined as she could. She found she was more sheltered here than on his back. She was in a pocket of still air while the wind swept around her. His toes were rigid, holding her as tightly as he could without crushing her. They were both afraid of her falling.

Turning her head, she could look between his toes, past his scaled belly to see what was happening, to see if the two of them were going to be knocked out of the sky for this, either by the dragons or the fighters.

The trio of dragons followed, but only briefly. They circled without turning their gazes from the sight of the girl and dragon racing away. Then, after about a mile, they arced their backs, spread their wings, and went away. Back toward Dragon.

The two jets followed a little longer. Artegal struggled to keep up his speed, despite the awkwardness of holding her.

His lack of speed meant the jets could come close, though they stayed behind and to the side. Kay couldn't see much detail on them, just their silver wings and bright sunlight glaring off the canopies. But after a few minutes the lead jet wagged, rocking back and forth a couple of times, before both planes tipped to their sides and peeled away, roaring back south. She imagined that was Captain Conner flying the lead plane.

They had seen. They'd all seen. They'd understood.

She and Artegal flew north.

24

As soon as Artegal flew across the border, the requirements of the sacrifice were fulfilled and the dragons would call a truce. Or so she and Artegal hoped. Artegal was confident—he said the dragons had the greatest respect for this ritual. Kay hoped that the human side of the conflict would also respect what she had done and abide by a truce. As her mother had said, what they needed was a chance—a reason—to talk.

Neither could be sure what their people would do.

After entering Dragon, they turned east and landed an hour later so Kay could get warm again. She broke open a pack of hand warmers and put on her winter clothes, then secured their climbing ropes and harness, which Artegal had hidden yesterday. Flying with her clipped into his harness would be more comfortable for both of them. They didn't stop for long; they didn't want to be found.

Artegal wanted to avoid dragons entirely. He couldn't be sure that either of them was safe. So he flew, straight and fast as he could, stopping only for a few minutes at a time, just a few times a day. The rest of the time, he went on, tireless, determined. She stayed strapped in, nibbling on beef jerky and granola bars from her pack, sipping water, watching the sky swirl past above her. She slept on his back, heat radiating from him, helping keep her warm. His heartbeat pounded in her dreams.

Many times, she heard aircraft, but could never be sure where they were. Sometimes she saw specks in the distance or running lights at night. Other times, Artegal would see something that caused him to veer and increase his speed. Dragons, in distant pursuit. But they weren't caught. Their pursuers almost seemed like escorts.

On the third day, they reached the Atlantic Ocean. They stopped briefly, touching down on the coast, flying a few miles along the shore. Then they touched down again, closer to a town on the horizon, where Kay's cell phone found reception. Kay sent a text message to her mother: I'M ALL RIGHT. I LOVE YOU. She texted the same message to Jon and Tam.

After that, they left land behind. Then they couldn't stop at all.

He startled her once by diving. She choked back a scream

as she felt him hit the water and saw waves splashing on either side of his body, but a heartbeat later he was beating his wings hard and pulling up. She saw the tail of a huge fish dangling from his mouth before he sucked it in.

Artegal was already tired, flying lower and lower, closer to the waves, and the beats of his wings slowed. But his neck was still straight, his head still pointed forward toward their destination. They were both coated in salt from ocean mist.

On the fourth day, they saw land again: Greenland, if they'd set their course correctly. The shore was rocky, and the landscape beyond it was white, endlessly white, inhospitable with ice.

Relieved, she sighed. Her muscles were stiff from staying crouched in the same position, and her body was sore from jerking against the harness. If nothing else, even if they didn't find what they were looking for, here was land, and they could rest awhile before deciding what to do next.

Artegal dipped his left wing, and they turned in an arc until they were heading up the coast. They were able to rest for a few hours on the shore. The wind blew harshly here. Artegal tucked his neck in, pulled his tail close, and napped. Kay sat in the shelter of his body and watched the slate gray waves tumble and break on the rocky beach. She didn't think she'd ever be warm again. But she also had a feeling, deep in her gut, that they were heading toward something, that they would find something, and the thought warmed her. She consulted the treasure map and its coordinates, comparing them to the numbers on her GPS tracker, and planned the next part of their journey.

It felt as if she and the dragon hadn't spoken in days. They would look at each other, ask a question with their gazes, and answer with nods. It was peaceful.

On the fifth day, they saw a thin column of steam rising from a far northern, ice-locked shore. Artegal steered toward it.

A moment later, they spotted another dragon, with scarlet scales that flamed yellow and orange in the morning sun, flying to meet them. Kay squinted and saw a leather harness around its chest and a person riding on its back.

ACKNOWLEDGMENTS

As recently as a couple of years ago, I didn't think I'd be writing a book like this. I had the idea of Kay riding a dragon and dodging cops, but back then the story was different and she had a different name. And it didn't work. Then I changed her name to Kay and made her a teenager, and the pieces of the story all came together.

Around that same time, Anne Hoppe emailed me to ask if I'd ever thought of writing a young-adult novel. "Why, funny you should ask," I replied. So, first off, I'd like to thank Anne for that email, which was sort of like the universe telling me I was on the right track.

I'd also like to thank all the usual suspects: Mike Bateman, for reading an earlier draft; Rob and Deb for doing the same; Ashley and Carolyn Grayson; Mom and Dad; and the local gang for getting me out of the house.

Read on for a sneak peek at Carrie Vaughn's

$\mathcal{S}teel,$

a swashbuckling tale of magic, romance, and pirates.

Gray streaks from cloud to ocean showed rain. The tour boat had traveled farther out to sea—the island was a rough smudge behind them, a crowd of foliage, no details visible. The laughter turned nervous—but they couldn't be heading into a storm, because a tour boat would never do that. Right?

Now this was exciting.

"Everyone take a seat," the guide said. "We'll be through this in a moment. And if you feel like heaving ho, do it over the side, okay?"

Most of passengers chuckled, but a few of them sat quickly on cushions around the sides, just in case.

"Jill? Jill, where are you?" Jill's mother called from the other side of the cabin. Mom was herding the kids; Jill recognized

1

the tone of voice. She stood and turned toward the front of the boat to answer.

A large wave surged under them then, sending the boat rocking steeply. Jill, the world-class athlete who'd never yet lost her balance in a fencing bout, fell. Stumbling back, she hit the side of the boat and went over. Grabbing uselessly for the edge, she rolled into the ocean. Her father shouted, scrambling to his feet. She saw his arms reaching for her as she went under.

From dry land, the ocean looked so calm, peaceful. Serene blue waters. All that great scenery the adults talked about. From underwater, it was chaos. Waves pitched her, her sunglasses were torn away, the water was cold, shocking after the tropical air. She couldn't catch her breath—swallowed water instead. Flailing, she searched for up, groped for the surface—couldn't find it. Her lungs were tightening. It had been sunny a moment ago—where was the sun?

Someone grabbed her. Hands twisted into her clothing and pulled her into the air. She clutched at her rescuers, gasped for air, heaving deep breaths that tasted of brine, slimy and salty. But she was out of the water. She was safe. She wasn't going to die.

She landed hard on an unsteady wooden surface. The hands let her go, and she grabbed for some kind of hold to steady herself against the rocking of the waves.

Scrubbing water from her face, she opened her eyes and looked.

She expected to see the tour boat. But this boat was too small, almost a rowboat, with two sets of oars. Bottom and sides of plain wood, not polished fiberglass. No motor grumbled. And what should have been a clear stretch of ocean was filled with debris—broken wood, barrels bobbing along the waves, tangles of rope and canvas floating on the water. Something had been smashed to pieces here. A faint scent of burning touched the air.

Then there were the people.

Inside the rowboat, five men surrounded her, one bald, the others with long, greasy hair tied back. The ones without full beards still looked like they hadn't shaved in days. A couple had gold rings in their ears. One had a ring in his nose, through the middle. They wore rough shirts and loose trousers, and went barefoot.

They'd started rowing the little boat to a ship a few hundred feet away. A long, two-masted sailing ship, sails furled, riding the waves, up and down.

Jill had seen some of the other party boats that advertised as pirate ships, with their tall masts, rippling canvas sails, and skull-and-crossbones flags. This must have been one of those, with a particularly enthusiastic crew. Maybe it was a theme party with costumes. She'd fallen out of the tour boat, and these guys came along and picked her up. Maybe they'd let her have some of the rum punch. But that didn't explain the wreckage in the water. She didn't think she'd been in the water that long. Maybe a minute. On the other hand, maybe it had been longer—she felt like she had almost drowned. Could she have drifted that far from the tour boat in that time?

When she leaned on the edge of the rowboat to look for the tour boat her family was on, she couldn't see anything. No other vessel was in sight. The shore of the island was even farther away—a gray haze, that was all. Maybe the tour boat was behind the pirate party ship. The sky over them was scattered with clouds, thin, dissipating in a brisk wind, as if the threatening storm had ended.

The men on the rowboat weren't smiling, and didn't look like they'd come from any party.

Jill stayed alone in the middle of the boat, gripping the sides, while four of the men rowed. The fifth, the bald one, glared at her but didn't say a word. None of them even looked at her, just a piece of flotsam they'd picked out of the water.

"What's happening?" she asked, her voice shaking. She tried to sound braver. "Who are you guys?"

They didn't answer.

The boat was coming alongside the larger vessel, with its wide, sloping hull, two tall masts, and collection of triangular sails. Maybe she could ask someone there what this was all about, and they could take her back to the island.

The bald man shouted orders, a few monosyllabic calls that Jill didn't understand, and ropes came down from the deck of the ship. She expected to see some kind of ladder, some easy way for them to climb on board—then there'd be a radio or something the captain could use to call the tour bout.

The men in the rowboat got to work tying ropes to cleats. The ropes looped over struts attached perpendicularly to the masts. Men on deck started pulling, ropes started creaking, and the rowboat lifted out of the water.

The rest of the men were climbing up the hull of the larger ship as lengths of rope were passed down to them. Instead of a ladder there were thin wooden slats nailed into the hull to use as toe holds. Not very helpful, Jill thought.

The bald man handed the end of a rope to her. "Climb," he ordered.

Was he kidding? She didn't know if she could, but she thought she'd better try. She watched the others expertly pull themselves up, hand over hand, using their feet to balance against the hull. Under other circumstances—like if this really was a party boat and she was supposed to be here—she might have had fun with it. But everything about the situation was wrong. Nobody checked to see if she was okay, and nobody was smiling.

She gripped the rope and started climbing.

The climb took forever, it seemed. She was shaking from the shock of falling in the water, and her muscles felt like rubber—too soft, too stretchy, like they did after a full day of fencing. And she didn't know what was going to happen when she reached the deck of the ship. But she climbed, slowly, one step at a time, remembering to breathe.

The bald man rode in the rowboat as it was hauled up the side.

Finally, she reached the side—made of plain, weathered wood, like the rowboat. She hooked her arms over it, managed to swing one leg up, then rolled onto the new ship. She sprawled out on the deck.

The boards under her smelled like mildew, rotten with salt and damp that was never going to go away. There were cannons on wheels lined up along the side and lashed into place. The ship creaked—wood bending, ropes twisting, waves lapping against the hull. She heard this because all else was silent. The deck was filled with people, all shapes, sizes, colors. All men. And all of them looked angry. Or hungry. They were all staring at her. They'd left a space open around her, but in a second they could close that space, they could close in on *her*. When they pressed forward, she could feel their steps under her hands, where she crouched on the deck. She stood clumsily.

"Guess the salvage wasn't a waste after all," one of them said.

"Not at all, we found ourselves a nice bit of cargo," said the bald man, and the rest laughed. They leered with rotten and gap-toothed grins.

"She's a bit skinny, in't she?" This one poked at her, pinching the flesh of her forearm. She slapped at his hand and lurched away, but another set of hands were there, grabbing at her. This only made them laugh more.

This wasn't a party boat. This was something else.

Whoever these people were, whatever was happening, they held their bodies like predators ready to strike, and their gazes showed wicked, murderous desire. She felt light-headed.

Thinking she'd be better off jumping right back into the water, she glanced behind her. A couple of the men had moved along the side, blocking her escape that way. So she was stuck. Trapped. *Screwed.*

Except that she recognized something else in the situation: Several of the men carried swords with long, slender blades. Rapiers. Besides the cannons on deck she didn't see any more serious weapons. Nothing like handguns. Only long knives. She understood rapiers. Jill could make a feint. Show them she wasn't easy pickings. It might even work.

Swinging back, she made toward the side, as if she planned to shove past the men and dive over in a spectacular and stupid bid to escape. A shout went up, and as she hoped, the men behind her reached out, grabbing at her to hold her back and keep her from jumping. She'd noted which one of them had a rapier—he kept it down, out of the way so as not to impale anyone while they hauled her from the side. Having misdirected them, she dug her shoulder into this one's chest, ripping herself from the others' grips in her sudden change of direction. With both hands, she grabbed the rapier's solid steel guard and yanked. The yelling around her was louder than the ocean's waves.

She took hold of the rapier and swung it point out,

sweeping an arc around her. The shouts turned to surprise and panic, and a space cleared around her. Holding the sword level, point out, her grip on the handle steady, she stared at her enemies over the edge of the blade. Now she could handle herself. *Now* she felt a little bit safe and in control.

The men backed away, keeping a good distance around her, as if not sure what to make of her. Some were still chuckling, like this was a game. Several of them had raised their own swords, but made no move toward her. Maybe waiting to see what their bedraggled refugee would do next.

Then things got even stranger.

Across the deck came a shout and the sound of heavy footsteps, hollow on the wood. The men looked suddenly alert—maybe even nervous, and the crowd parted.

The figure who approached, who the rest of the mob respectfully made way for, wasn't tall and didn't seem powerful like most of the men. She was a woman, sturdy, wearing a long coat belted around her waist, her curly cinnamon hair left loose over her shoulders. She wore a black three-cornered hat and polished boots. Her scowl was hard, angry.

"What have you louts fished up then, eh?" the woman said. When she saw Jill, she frowned, glancing at the bald man from the rowboat. "You found her in the wreckage?"

"Yessir."

Back to Jill now, she said, "What happened, then? How'd you survive the *Newark's* sinking? Or maybe you were on *Heart's Revenge?*"

Jill couldn't open her mouth to speak, but she shook her head, wondering when she was going to wake up, wondering if she was still underwater, hallucinating or unconscious. So much for feeling safe.

"Speak up, then," said the woman—she must have been the captain here. "Who are you and where'd you come from? Say something, wench, or I'll throw you to these bloody dogs."

At that, the men laughed and growled, like the dogs she'd called them. Jill swept the rapier again, trying to keep that clear space around her. Trying to give herself space to think.

The woman's scowl turned into a half smile and she said, "You think you can use that, then?"

The sword was much heavier than Jill's épée at home. Her arm trembled with the weight of it, and her breaths came in gasps. She didn't know how long she'd be able to fight. But she would fight. She nodded. "Yes."

"Very good. Henry!" the captain called. "You feel like a bit of a game?"

"I do at that, sir." A young man stepped forward, and Jill's heart jumped a little. He was *cute*. Athletic, skin the color of a rich brown wood, short black hair, and a wry smile. Like all the rest, he wore a loose white shirt, loose pants, and went barefoot. And he held a rapier.

He swung the weapon through a few circles like it didn't weigh anything. The crowd, including the captain, pressed back, leaving a wide circle of open deck for them to fight in.

A duel. A freaking duel. She'd lost her last bout—why did she think she had a chance now? She almost dropped the rapier and begged them to have mercy, to not hurt her. But this Henry didn't stop smiling. He even looked like he was laughing at her. That goaded her. The burning, competitive anger that rose up in her was the only familiar thing about the situation.

Henry stood, right foot pointed forward, arm lowered so the rapier's point rested on the deck, and waited for her.

She took a deep breath and steadied herself. Easier said than done when she could feel the floor shifting under her, rocking back and forth unpredictably with the movement of the waves. She reminded herself of her pre-bout mantra: stay calm, keep breathing, don't panic, don't let her opponent fluster her. But she didn't know how she could be more flustered. Which made it all the more important that she keep breathing and stay calm.

She stood *en garde*, right foot forward, left foot back, knees bent. Warily, she saluted him with the rapier she'd stolen and settled her arm into position.

Still seeming amused, Henry saluted her back, flourishing with his off hand and bowing his head besides. Then he stood ready. And why should he be any good, this scruffy-looking kid on a weird sailing ship? No reason she shouldn't be able to take him.

The edge of her rapier gleamed, sharp and dangerous. A real blade, meant for causing harm. For all her bluster, she had never held a sharpened rapier before. She almost stopped the fight right there, but the way the men around her looked at her hadn't changed. They were as dangerous as a real rapier; she had to defend herself. And she would.

He made the first move, reaching out with his blade to tap the end of hers. Nerves and panic made her overreact; she struck his weapon back with a hard beat and jumped back, retreating sloppily. The crowd laughed, and she blushed. That was an amateur move and they all knew it. The captain crossed her arms and frowned.

Before she'd completely settled back into her stance, he struck again, another lazy hit against her blade. But she was ready for it this time and disengaged—dropped her sword slightly so that when he expected to hit it, it wasn't there—and immediately lunged. She caught him off guard that time, and he swung his sword up in a hasty parry and stumbled back. His wide eyes showed surprise. He'd thought he was toying with her. Playing games with a weak opponent. Thought maybe that she was just a girl and no good at this.

Realizing she couldn't rest for a moment in this fight— she had to keep him constantly off guard—she pressed. Lunged again, was blocked again, but moved to attack on a different line.

He crossed to his left, moving in a circle around her, startling her. She shifted to keep up, to keep him in front of her. They were fighting in a circle, not on a strip, like in fencing competition. The change disoriented her. *Just keep him in front of you.*

They exchanged more passes, steel slapping against steel. He drew her thrusts and parried them, that smile still on his face. He was guiding the fight, not her. She tried not to let it make her angry. He never got past her defenses; all her parries were strong, even though her arm burned, and every time their swords met a tingling numbness traveled through her muscles. Her guard fell lower and lower. In a few moments, she wouldn't be able to hold up the sword at all.

When he struck again, she parried like before, but the move brought his blade down and the tip snagged on her pants, just above the knee. The fabric sliced through with a quick ripping sound. Everyone heard it, and Henry jumped back, startled.

She realized then that all of his blows had been at her arms and legs. Because anything else, any stab to her body with a real rapier, would kill her. He wasn't trying to kill her. Her stomach felt sick and roiling at the thought that a slip—any stab that got past her defenses—would really kill her. And she'd been trying to kill him, because she hadn't thought of anything but scoring the touch.

A four-inch slice cut through her pants, a gaping oval exposing skin. No blood; he hadn't broken skin. Suddenly, she couldn't catch her breath. She let her arm drop like a weight, rapier dangling from her hand. Henry looked at her, challenging, gripping his rapier hard like he was ready to go on. He wasn't smiling anymore.

"Knock off there, both of you," the captain called. They'd already halted the duel, but her order kept them from rushing into another attack—or from expecting an attack from the other. Henry relaxed, lowering his weapon and looking at his captain.

Jill was still trying to slow her breathing, which came in gasps. Her heart was racing. *She would have died, a wrong thrust and she would have died. . . .* And she had been so worried and frustrated about simply losing.

The captain's voice was kind when she spoke to Jill this time. "You know the forms well enough and stand pretty with a sword, but you've never fought for blood, have you, lass?"

Jill could only shake her head—no, she'd never fought for blood. Not real blood. Only ranks, medals, and maybe a college scholarship. She bowed her head, embarrassed, when tears fell. She wiped them away quickly. Her still-wet hair stuck to her cheeks. Salt water crusted her clothing. However much she wanted to sit down, pass out—or drop the rapier, which she wouldn't have been able to raise again even if Henry came at her in another attack—she remained standing before the captain, as straight as she could, which wasn't very at the moment.

"What's your name, lass?"

"Jill. Jill Archer," she said, her voice scratching. She only just noticed that she was thirsty.

"And, Jill, how do you come to be adrift in the wide sea so far from home?"

The tears almost broke then, and she took a moment to answer. "I don't know."